ISBN 978-0-9949873-0-3

Beyond The Red Carpet

Copyright @ 2015 by Debbra Lynn

Cover art by Matt Harris of Sky Events Agency

Editing by Audra Tettenborn

Website photos by Jaclyn Miller Photography

Author photo and website photos by Karla Muzyka of Lipstick and Lace

Acknowledgments

To my husband, Robin. I know my dream of writing a novel was not something I shared with you, simply because I was afraid it was a dream nearly too impossible to achieve. But as my story began to unfold on the pages in front of me, I couldn't wait to introduce you to the characters that were so quickly becoming an important part of my life. I am grateful for your continued support and encouragement to help me realize that no dream is too impossible to achieve.

To Christine, I am thankful for the words you spoke when I shared with you that I had always wanted to write a book: "Just start writing. It will come to you. Just do it." Simple advice, yet effective, because on that very day I began to type, I let the words flow, I did what you told me to do. Although you may not realize it, you are the person that gave me the shove to begin this journey and again I am thankful.

To my mother, Linda, your feedback on this was so important, as I know your love for reading. I am appreciative of your taking the time to read it not once but twice, and I am thrilled to have written a story captivating enough to leave you wanting more.

For the reassurance, and the motivation to keep going, from the closest people to me in my life: Rhonda, Tamara, and Val-Marie. It made this whole experience easier, knowing I had your support even when I convinced myself I could not finish.

To my editor, Audra Tettenborn, you were instrumental in making this story as amazing as it is, and I am so very thankful I found you. To Matt Harris, your hard work, and creativity on the book cover, will be sure to draw the readers' attention. To Jaclyn Miller, you're not only a very close friend, but your skills as a photographer helped me capture the perfect pictures to use on my website. And finally I would also like to thank Karla Muzyka of Lipstick and Lace, you helped capture my sexy side and fun side with the picture both on my book cover as well as on my website.

Finally, to all the readers who are about to take this journey with me. Because of each and everyone one of you, my dreams are finally about to come true.

Wherever you may sleep

Or wherever you may roam,

I'd give my all, my everything,

Just to bring you home.

In Loving Memory of Kenneth Ramsey

November 20, 1945 – September 27, 2003

You always said you hoped I would do something with my writing. This is for you, Dad.

July 20, 2015 – And So It Begins

As she sat and stared out the window of her immaculately kept bedroom, Sophia Donovan studied each raindrop sliding down the glass against a dark sky. The silence around her was overwhelming, but at the same time it was a sound she welcomed more now, more today, than ever in her life. Vivid memories of the last eleven years were etched wildly in every corner of her mind as if a movie projector was going through reels of the story unfolding on a screen. Every flash of desire, happiness, sadness, anger, fear, hope, doubt and realization resurfaced, and she replayed every decision she'd ever made, every motive she'd had for her choices, and she wondered: Am I doing the right thing?

"It's really quite strange," she thought silently to herself. "Should I be scared? Or should I feel guilty?" She thought the answers should be obvious, but, oddly, she felt neither of these emotions. What she did feel, looking around the room at the perfectly made bed, the impeccable closet filled with designer shoes, clothes and jewelry, and the beautifully hung art clinging to the walls, was calm. Relieved, even. None of it made sense, but all she could think was: there's no turning back now. What's done is done. Sophia wondered suddenly if something was wrong with her. Perhaps she was in shock?

The once-silence that surrounded her suddenly seemed to become loud voices echoing in the darkness, and the giant walls of the luxurious Master seemed to be all of a sudden closing in around her, making it somewhat hard to catch her breath. Sophia stood up quickly from the bench seat overlooking the garden. As she paced back and forth, still gasping for breath, Sophia wondered if she was, in fact, having a nightmare.

She ran to the bathroom and leaned over the sink and started splashing her now-sweaty face with ice-cold water, in hopes that it would somehow wake her. To no avail. She stepped back into the bedroom and frantically circled, like a dog trying to find a comfortable position to sleep. "I'm doing the right thing, I'm doing the right thing," she repeated over and over. Her pacing brought her to her husband's side of the bed. As quickly as the panic had come, it was gone again. Calmly, she softly kissed her fingers and placed them on the cold, blood-splattered forehead of the man who, only a half hour earlier, laid peacefully sleeping, unaware that his wife was standing over him, pointing a gun directly at his face.

"I am so sorry, my love, "she whispered softly. "I had no choice."

May 15, 2004 – There He Stood

Nestled in the Hollywood hills, the mansion was bustling with famous faces, fancy cars, and scantily-clad women who were practically tripping over themselves just to touch the celebrities attending Alex Preston's party.

A sought-after film director, Alex Preston was hosting one of his many fabulous parties in celebration of a new action flick scheduled to be released that summer. Every fresh-faced idol and every celebrated alumni of Hollywood was in attendance. And then there she was, Sophia Vaughn, a simple yet undeniably beautiful woman her long chestnut hair was piled high on her head, with soft wisps falling and framing her caramel skin. Dressed in her stark white button up shirt and her black skirt, which was covered over with a freshly ironed apron with the words "Fresh Catering" on the pocket, she stood wide-eyed at the sight of the enormous house before her. She walked towards the front entrance, fumbling her trays and bags containing the supplies for the event, and as she approached the door it suddenly swung wide open. A shirtless man, with a cigarette hanging out of the corner of his mouth, came bounding out of the house, whiskey spilling out of the half-empty bottle in his hand and down the front of his chest.

He jumped out in front of Sophia, yelling as he ran, "Come and get me you sexy little bitch!"

Just as Sophia quickly stepped out of his way, a twenty-something vixen came playfully following after him, laughing and giggling, loudly screeching, "Oh Charlie, you're such a bad boy".

Sophia leaned her back against the wall, shaking her head, blowing a loose strand of hair which had fallen in her eyes before mumbling to herself, "God, how did I end up here?

Sophia then cautiously snuck in through the front door and looked around the main foyer. She instantly noticed a gorgeous chandelier, which hung from what had to be at least thirty-foot ceilings, and off the main entrance to the right was an impressive library that housed hundreds and hundreds of books. To the left was a living room with plenty of big, plush furniture, expensively-framed movie posters, and a baby grand piano tucked in the far corner. As Sophia continued through the main entrance into the kitchen, she was welcomed by an amazing view of the infinity pool looking out over the Pacific Ocean. The kitchen itself was easily bigger than her tiny little apartment in Cypress Park. She set her bags and trays down on the Island in the center of the room and quickly began to get herself organized. Just as she was about to get started with cooking her hors d'oeuvres, she was suddenly startled by an unfamiliar voice.

"Slap my ass and call me Nancy, look at this bloody house".

Sophia turned to see Catarina Warner walk into the kitchen. Catarina was tall, blond and astoundingly attractive. She was also incredibly loud and boisterous. Her blonde hair was pulled back in a ponytail of wild curls, she was clearly trying to show off as much of her long legs as possible, in a too-tiny black skirt that was almost shorter than her apron. She was dressed in the same white button-up blouse as Sophia, but she chose to show a lot more cleavage than Sophia cared to.

"Um…. May I help you?" Sophia asked, annoyed by the woman's brash entrance.

"Oh, hey, you must be Sophia. I'm Cat. I'm the lucky one filling in for what's-her-name. I guess she called in sick, you know, one too many shots of 'Te-kill-ya', if you catch my drift."

"You mean Mags?"

"Yup, that's her name. Sorry, I just started this gig – don't know who's who yet. So, did you see how big this fucking house is?" Cat changed the subject as she gazed around the massive kitchen.

"Yes, I have," Sophia mumbled to herself as she walked to the back patio doors and gazed out over a sea of tanned, perfectly toned bodies lounging in the pool and at the bar. Couples were making out all over the lounge chairs like it was some kind of high school dance while people were doing cannonballs into the deep end of the impressive pool, splashing the other party-goers who danced wildly near the bar. She didn't recognize any of the faces – but then, she wasn't really up on the who's-who in Hollywood. Sophia led a somewhat quiet life and rarely got out, especially to see movies.

"So, let's get crackin' " Cat interrupted, as Sophia observed the party outside.

"Yes, okay. Cat you said was your name? Well, how about you start by getting the stuffed mushrooms ready and I will work on getting the meatballs out. Then we will get the shrimp and rest of the seafood going," Sophia ordered as she started running around the kitchen.

"Aye, aye, Captain," Cat mocked as she saluted, her hand to her forehead.

Moments later, as the two women began bustling around the kitchen, a short, stocky man walked in through the back patio doors.

"Well about Goddamn time you girls are here, my guests are drunk and hungry. Hurry up and move your tight little asses and get out there and serve them some food. I did not hire you two twits to sit around and gossip in my kitchen all day. Now hurry up, or you both can go find another fucking job!" Alex shouted drunkenly before heading back out to the party, slamming the door behind him. Sophia and Cat, who were both stunned, turned to look at each other.

"Well, ain't he just a cute little bundle of shit," giggled Cat as she nonchalantly gave the finger to the still-vibrating door that Alex had slammed. "This is the jackass that hired us for this party?"

"I guess so, but listen, it doesn't matter. Come on, we got to get this food out there before he comes back in here and does actually fire us!" Sophia exclaimed as she gathered her trays of meatballs.

Sophia and Cat entered the back yard to the feel of the heat of the sun and the sound of Jay-Z blaring over the speakers just to the right of the pool. A DJ stood grooving and moving to his own beats as he hollered over the speakers, "Come on all you fine looking ladies, let's get those booties on the dance floor".

Sophia and Cat began making their rounds from guest to guest, offering them food. Many of them declined because they had obviously been filling up on top shelf tequila and Dom Perignon. Sophia was certain many of the guests who did take their food would probably just dispose of it in the toilet in a few hours anyway. As they maneuvered their way in and out of the guests, Cat tapped Sophia on the shoulder and pointed. "Ha! Check that out."

Sophia glanced over her shoulder and saw Alex Preston taking a line of cocaine off the bare ass of some obvious groupie, as she bent over the table to take another man in her mouth.

"Now this is what I call a party," Cat remarked sarcastically.

Slightly appalled, and shaking her head in silence, Sophia noticed her tray was now near empty. She signaled to Cat that she was going to restock and would be back out. As she was heading away from the pool, towards the house, she glanced up from the ground and was suddenly taken aback: there was the most beautiful man she had ever seen in her life, leaning up against one of the large columns.

From the first moment she laid eyes on him, this man she knew nothing about, not even his name, Sophia knew this was the man she was going to marry one day.

July 20, 2015 – A Friend in Need

Sophia knew she couldn't waste too much more time and she needed to act fast. This wasn't something she ever thought she would do, but after the events over the last several months she knew this was the only way she wanted to protect herself. She was as prepared for this as she possibly could be, however, Sophia began to feel an uneasiness creep over her.

"Okay, Sophia, you're fine, and you know this was something that had to happen," she muttered to herself as she paced back and forth across the bedroom floor, but as the panic began to overwhelm her, she started to run the scenarios back and forth in her head, wondering if there was any other way possible for her to cover this up. She fought desperately with her own conscience, and wondered if there was a possible alternative to this? She sat on the edge of her side of the bed and placed her head in her hands.

Would anyone believe it was suicide? Sophia shook her head. She was smart enough to know that the angle he was lying at, and the way he was positioned on the bed, just wouldn't make sense. Besides, wouldn't she have to write some forlorn suicide note, explaining why he'd decided to do what he did, and how devastating it had been for him to come to this conclusion? "No," she thought, "that won't work." Anyone who knew Marcus Donovan would know he would never rid this world of such a God-given gift. Marcus Donovan was a highly sophisticated, wealthy, handsome, and desired man. He had it all, he really did. He was one of his time's most successful directors in Hollywood, he was People Magazine's 2010 Sexiest Man Alive. He had people falling all over him, and, of course, he had Sophia, his ever-loving, beautiful, doting wife of eleven years. No, suicide would most definitely not work. Nobody would ever buy it.

She struggled to think whether there was anyone else that could have hated him enough to break in and kill him with his own gun. But if there was, how would they have gotten in the house? Did anyone else even know where he kept the gun?

"Damn it," she muttered quietly.

She needed a little more time to determine if she could actually go through with this, however, the undeniable realization of the situation that she was in was clear and she knew she would not be truly safe and at peace until this was finished. Sophia knew it was time to reach out to the one person she needed to help her complete her plan. She reached for her phone, dialed the number and silently waited.

The line rang twice and finally on the third ring a raspy, sleep-laden voice answered.

"Hello?" Cat said groggily.

"Cat," Sophia whispered on the other end.

Cat sat up quickly in her bed, shocked to hear the sound of Sophia's voice. This was not a call that she was expecting at two in the morning. In fact, this was not a call she was expecting at all. Cat then replied, hysterically, "Sophia? What in the hell is going on?"

"Cat," Sophia repeated softly, "Cat, I really need your help. Something has happened, and I need you to come, quickly."

Cat could hear the desperation in Sophia's voice, and knew that something had gone horrifically wrong, so she frantically scrambled to release herself from the throws of blankets that entangled her long legs.

"Sophia where in the hell are you? You are supposed to be out in Malibu. What the hell is happening?" Cat could barely contain the panic that filled her chest.

"I am at home. Please, just hurry up and get here. I really need your help, Cat. I will explain later, just please hurry." Sophia began to sob into the phone.

"I'm on my way, just stay there," Cat ordered, then hung up her phone, tossing it on the bed. She scrambled wildly to find whatever pieces of clothing she could, and tried her best to remain as calm as possible. Her head was reeling with what the hell could have possibly gone wrong, but she knew she had to go find out fast. She ran out of her bedroom directly into the kitchen, searching for her car keys, and knocking over an opened bottle of the wine in her frenzy. She had to pull it together, she thought to herself as she grabbed her purse off the kitchen table. She hurried out the front door and hopped into her car. She reached up, pulled down the rearview mirror, and glanced at her own bloodshot eyes staring widely back at her. She turned away from her own gaze and started the engine. Before she pulled away, she glanced up into the mirror one more time and studied her pale reflection as she muttered softly, "Pull yourself together Cat. Just calm the fuck down and pull yourself together." She then threw the engine in reverse, backed out onto the street and headed into the dark.

May 15, 2004 – Hypnotize Me

He stood roughly 6′4″ in height and he had strong, broad shoulders, sculpted abs and powerful-looking hands, which Sophia instantly noticed did not bear a wedding band. He wore only a pair of white cargo shorts, Ray Bans propped on the top of his head, and a Scotch in one hand. His tanned, dark skin was almost glistening under the rays of the hot sun, and his thick dark hair was wet from the swimming pool he must have just stepped out of. Every angle of his face was masculine: his jaw, his forehead, and his mouth, a mouth she was sure would taste like the sweetest drop of sugar.

Sophia stood gazing at him as if in a trance, and her feet seemed to be cemented to the ground beneath her. She could not explain the impact this man, whom she had never even seen before, was having on her. She was not one to get caught up in looks. Living in LA had made her especially unlikely to have her head turned by an attractive person, but he was mesmerizing, and she could feel every fiber of herself drawn to him with a desire she had never felt before. Then, just as she realized she must look like a fool gawking at him, Marcus Donovan glanced in her direction. His eyes were dark and deep and they penetrated her soul like a knife and every hair rose to attention on Sophia's body. They stood in that moment with their eyes locked tightly on one another, and finally Sophia snapped back to the reality of where she was and immediately found the strength to tear her attention away from his stare. She fumbled with her tray and hurried to find her way back into the kitchen, passing Marcus as she did so.

Sophia walked to the back of the kitchen, where the ovens stood, and placed her tray on the counter before she braced herself on the counter and hung her head down low, shaking it. "What in the hell is wrong with you, Sophia?" she muttered softly. "Pull yourself together. He is just a man, just another LA man."

She took a few deep breaths to clear her head and regain her composure, and then reached into the oven and removed some more meatballs and placed them carefully on top of the stove. She half-heartedly dusted her hands off on her apron before she grabbed her tray and loaded it with some more meatballs. She took one more quick breath and then turned to head back into the yard. As she turned around, she saw him again, only now he was standing, alone, in the same room as her.

"Can I help you with anything in here?" he asked with a grin on his face.

"Um, no, no, don't be silly," Sophia replied waving her hand in the air.

"My name is Marcus," he said as he began walking towards her with his hand extended.

"Oh. Nice to meet you, um, my name is, um, Sophia," she stuttered as she wiped her hand off on the side of her skirt, before reaching to place her hand into his. The second their hands met she felt a shock spread through her like a lightning bolt. He squeezed her palm tight and smiled at her, revealing a row of perfectly straight, white teeth.

"I am sorry," he began, "but I could not help but notice you outside, and I really just needed to come in here and find out your name."

"Oh, I see. Um, my name is Sophia," she stated shyly.

"I know, you told me that already," he joked. "And that is a beautiful name by the way. Here, let me help you," he continued as he reached for her tray.

"Oh, please, no, thank you. I just really need to get back out to the guests. I have already been threatened to be fired once today by the host. I don't need him to see me mingling with you now."

Marcus responded with a big, hearty laugh. "Alex threatened to fire you?" He continued, chuckling, "Oh, trust me: he is drunk, stoned, and all talk. Don't worry about him at all. I can guarantee he does not even remember who you are by now." He left the tray with Sophia, but walked over to the patio doors and held them open for her so she could pass through. "Well, if you are not going to let me help you out, then it is only fair if you let me take you out for a drink after you are done here," he offered as she walked past him.

Sophia stopped and turned back to him at his sudden invitation, and again got trapped in his gaze. Almost hypnotized, at this moment she felt she would do nearly anything he asked of her, but all he was asking, for now, was a drink.

"A drink? Tonight?" she questioned him.

"Yes. I mean, that is if you are not busy, or unless you have to get home to meet someone?" He looked at her with his head tilted to the side, awaiting her answer.

"No plans, no meet – no one." Realizing how stupid she just sounded, she closed her eyes and shook her head. "I'm sorry. I am just a bit overtired, I think".

"Well, there is no better reason to join me in a drink tonight then. Looks like you need to relax and let somebody else wait on you for a change."

She stood thinking for a second, trying to come up with a reason to give him as to why she could not join him, but she just couldn't seem to think of any excuses. She knew she didn't want to think of any excuses, but she also wondered to herself, "Why would he be asking me out for a drink when this place is crawling with beautiful woman who would not even blink at the chance to join him. Why is he asking me out?"

Ignoring all the questions she was asking herself, she answered him, "Sure, you are right. Maybe I do need a drink, especially after this evening."

"Perfect, I will wait for you until you are done. I know a great little place we can go, they make the best margaritas in LA," Marcus replied happily.

"Okay, then," Sophia said as she turned around. As she walked away from him, she could sense his eyes on her, and even then she could feel an intensity running through her body that was unlike anything she'd experienced before. She wanted so badly to look back over her shoulder, but she kept her eyes straight ahead and kept walking.

"Who in the hell is that?" Cat came bounding up to Sophia, with an empty tray in her hand.

"I'm not really sure. I only know his name is Marcus," Sophia answered casually.

"Well, Marcus is hot as hell. Wow." Cat fanned herself with her hand. "What did he say to you? Oh, Jesus, was he threatening to fire us, too? He must have been, right? What the hell did we do wrong now?"

"No, no, he did not threaten to fire us. He actually laughed when I told him that we did have that little worm threaten us, and told us not to worry about him. No, he just asked me out for a drink after work, that's all."

"'*That's all*'? You get to go home with that fine piece of ass tonight and 'that's all'?"

"Go home with? Nobody said anything about going home with anybody, Cat. He asked me for a drink, that is it, and honestly I could probably use a drink after tonight, so I couldn't think of a reason to say no. I will not be going home with anyone tonight, for your information. I am not that kind of girl, thank-you very much," Sophia insisted.

"Okay, sure, sweetie, how about I just hear about it all on Monday at work then?" Cat teased as she headed back to the house. "I betcha he has a real big... house," Cat jokingly added over her shoulder, with her hand cupped over her mouth, and then turned to continue walking.

Unable to help herself from smirking at Cat's off-colour remark, Sophia continued through the crowd of excessively drunk people, handing out the food. As she glanced over near the bar she saw Marcus again, watching her seductively, giving her an uncomfortable, but at the same time an oddly arousing, feeling. Again, she could feel the hairs on her arms start to rise, her heart began to race, and her mouth starting to get dry.

"Who is this man, and what is he doing to me?" Sophia whispered in her head. The way that he was making her feel right now, with just one look, made her question what she told Cat, not five minutes ago. Turning her back to Marcus, and continuing her rounds, Sophia softly mumbled to herself, "Well, maybe I am that type of girl."

July **20, 2015 – And the Story Goes**

The Donovan home was tucked up high in the Hollywood hills and a long, winding road led up to the private property, which was sheltered by beautiful trees and shrubbery. Cat sped up the circular drive of her best friend's large and impressive home and, barely even allowing enough time for her BMW to come to a rest, she threw the car in park, turned off the engine, undid her seatbelt, and jumped out. She ran up to the entrance and began banging on the large oak door.

"Soph, open up, it's me!" she hollered through the door. Then she reached for the doorbell and began pushing incessantly on the big round button. "Sophia, come on, open the door, let me in!" She continued to bang on the door and ring the bell simultaneously.

Finally, she could hear footsteps running towards her and then the door slowly cracked open and Sophia's wide eyes peered through the opening. Sophia stood still for a brief second, almost as if convincing herself not to let Cat in, but then she moved aside and opened the door wider.

"Come in quick," Sophia said as she pulled roughly on Cat's arm, yanking her inside the house. After slamming the door behind them, Sophia turned to face her and Cat was instantly alarmed at the paleness in Sophia's face.

"OMG Soph, what is it? What is wrong?" Cat cried as she pulled Sophia in for a hug and held her tightly. Cat could feel the tenseness of every muscle in Sophia's body, and the moments slowly drifted by as they stood holding on to one another. Sophia began to sob hysterically and Cat reached for her and again held her as they both slowly fell to the floor. Cat sat and cradled Sophia in her lap as she cooed, "It's okay, Babe, it's okay. Just tell me what happened? Please, just tell me."

After what felt like an eternity, Sophia was finally able to calm herself and she slowly released herself from Cat's embrace. She cautiously stood up and looked down upon Cat, who was still sitting on the floor. Cat had a look of pure fear and confusion sweeping over her face as she peered up at Sophia. Sophia reached

14

out, offering her hand to Cat, to help her up off the floor. As she did so, she softly uttered, "Come, let's go upstairs."

The climb up the stairs felt as if she were trying to climb a mountain of quicksand, and when Sophia glanced back over her shoulder, Cat seemed to be struggling in the same manner, even though she had no idea what she was about to discover. As they reached the top of the stairs, Sophia reached for Cat's arm and slowly led her through the double doors into the large master bedroom.

As Cat entered the room, she saw Marcus lying on the bed, his limp head dropping to one side as it rested on a blood-soaked pillow case. Silently, she observed the splatters of blood against the plush cream headboard and the trail that continued up the walls behind the bed and onto the carpet surrounding it. Cat studied the scene before her and the images were slowly being branded into her mind, every vivid and gory detail that was laid out in front of her. Her heart began to race and her legs began to tremble beneath her. She was certain they would soon fail her. The bile rose into her throat and the color drained quickly from her skin as she turned to face Sophia in search of an answer. Sophia's dark, tear-stained eyes met with Cat's, and the only thing that she could seem to say was, "I had no choice, Cat, I just had no choice."

Sophia knew that Cat was struggling with what she should do next, and for a few brief moments she was not sure herself, but Sophia knew that she needed Cat here with her, that she needed her to help Sophia finish what she started.

"What in the hell happened Sophia? Jesus Christ, how in the hell did this happen?" Cat's confusion and desperation was clearly spread across her face as she swallowed deeply, trying to force the remnants of her stomach back down into her throat.

"Cat, please listen to me, I had no choice. I had to do this." Sophia began to sob again. "I had to. Please, you have to help me. I don't know what to do now, what do I do, Cat? Please, what do I do?"

Cat could see the sheer desperation and fear that had taken control of Sophia and, although almost paralyzed by her own dismay, she knew that she had to take control of the emotions coursing through her and quickly pull herself together. She glanced at Sophia, who was now sobbing hysterically, and then she grabbed Sophia gently by the shoulders, shaking her firmly so she could regain some sort of composure.

"Sophia, listen to me, I really just need you to calm down and tell me what happened. Who did this?"

Sophia continued crying for several more minutes while Cat held her at arm's length, waiting for an answer, trying her best not to allow the desperation to overcome her. Suddenly Sophia was jolted back to reality. She closed her eyes tightly and slowly inhaled a long, deep breath. Removing herself from Cat's grasp, she pulled the doors to the bedroom closed, leaving them both standing in the dark hallway. She then walked somberly past Cat and headed back down the stairs, directly into the kitchen, through to the Butler's pantry. After a moment, she returned with a bottle of Grey Goose Vodka in her hand. Cat, who had immediately followed Sophia, now stood watching her silently, as Sophia retrieved two glasses from the cupboard and poured a healthy offering of the liquor into each glass.

Sophia finally spoke, with a barely-audible and croaky voice. "Marcus was going to kill me. If I didn't do this tonight, he would have killed me, Cat."

She sat down on one of the stools at the Island and motioned for Cat to join her. Cat sat down and eagerly accepted the glass of Vodka Sophia was handing her, and listened as Sophia began to explain the events that had taken place in the Donovan home in the wee hours of that morning.

May 15, 2004 – A Kiss So Dangerous

Marcus and Sophia pulled up to a small but lively Mexican restaurant around ten that night. The outside was festively decorated in bright, vibrant lights hanging from the roof, and catchy Mexican music filled the speakers both inside and outside of the building. The smells wafting into the air were tantalizing, and after such a long day they made Sophia's mouth water. Marcus left the top down on his Mercedes convertible when he got out of the driver's side and went around to open Sophia's door.

"Thank you very much," she stated politely as she got out of the car.

"You are very welcome, Sophia," Marcus responded with a wink.

They walked up to the door and were greeted by a short, plump Mexican woman. She had a huge smile on her face and waved them both in through the front doors.

"Hola, hola!" she happily exclaimed as they approached closer.

"Hola!" Marcus and Sophia responded at the same time.

"What is this beautiful couple up to this fine night?"

"We have come to have some of your world-famous margaritas. If you could show us to a table on your patio, that would be fantastic."

The woman beamed widely at the compliment. "Follow me, Señor, I have the perfect table for you and la Señora" the woman stated, and she had them follow her through the bustling restaurant and outside onto the patio. "Here you go, Señor, the best table you can ask for," she proudly exclaimed as she set the menus on the table.

"Muchas gracias, and can we, please, get two of your finest margaritas?" Marcus requested politely.

"Sì, two margaritas coming right up," she answered, before she rushed away to get the drinks.

Sophia and Marcus sat across from each other at the small but comfortable round table, just off to the side of the little makeshift dance floor. She was feeling nervous all of a sudden for some reason, now that they were face-to-face once again. Generally, Sophia Vaughn was not one to feel shy or at a loss for words to begin a conversation, but this man sitting across from her made her feel like a school girl again after all these years.

Just as she was hoping he would say something to break the tension she was feeling, Marcus spoke. "Sophia, please, why don't you tell me about yourself? I really feel like I need to know everything about you."

Acting awkwardly coy, she replied, "Well, where do I start, then? I was born and raised just outside of San Diego, I am an only child, my father passed away when I was twenty-four, and my mother still lives in Imperial Beach, where I grew up. I moved to LA about two years ago, and I started working for the catering company shortly after that. I really came here to be a writer, and at this point it doesn't matter what I write: novels, screenplays, reviews, and hell, at this point, I will even write an advice column." She gave an uneasy chuckle and continued, "I have a small apartment, which I share with my cat Gracie in Cypress Park, and – let's see, what else?" She paused for a second. "I am allergic to peanuts." She gave a cute little shrug. "That is me, in a very small nutshell. And what about you, Marcus, what are the contents of your shell?"

Marcus gave her another one of his heart-stopping smiles and answered her, "Well, my nutshell is a little bit bigger than yours, I think, but to give you the CliffsNotes, I grew up in Seattle with my mother, father, and my little sister Olivia, until I was about thirteen. My father got a job that shuffled us all over the country, until I finally got accepted to Berkeley for their film program when I was eighteen. After that, I was pretty much on my own, and now I am the assistant director to Alex Preston, and…. Hmm, let me see." Marcus paused. "I am allergic to mushrooms." He gave Sophia a sly grin.

Just as he finished his brief synopsis of his life, the short little Mexican woman returned, with two heavily-salted margaritas. She placed them down and smiled at them and exclaimed, happily, "Buen provecho!" before turning to walk away to help the other guests.

"That means enjoy," Marcus explained after he noticed the confused look on Sophia's face. "I have picked up a bit of Spanish here and there in the industry, plus this place is amazing and I probably come here a tad too often. But once you taste that drink you will know why."

Sophia put her lips to the salty rim of the glass and took a healthy sip of the sweet margarita. The saltiness and the bitterness of the drink were a delicious combination, and she could taste just a hint of the tequila, but she knew more than one of these and she would be missing work like Mags had that day. She glanced up over the rim of her glass and noticed Marcus was watching her closely, almost too closely.

"You are a beautiful woman, Sophia, and this is a town full of beautiful women, but you – you are something else." He took a sip of his drink, and continued, "All I know is I need to see you again after tonight."

Sophia cocked her head subtly to one side and smiled at Marcus. "Well, I'm not sure if I should be flattered, or perhaps worried that maybe you talk like this to all your dates. Something tells me, Marcus, that you have no issues getting beautiful women."

He slowly shook his head in response to her remark and answered, honestly, "In this town it is really not difficult to get a date. You must know that, you have lived here for most of your life, but it is just not about getting dates with beautiful women anymore. You have something magnetic about you, Sophia, and you just have something about you, I barely know you at all, but I want nothing more than to know all of you."

Sophia felt the same intense heat that she'd felt earlier, at the party, creep over her body as she looked directly at Marcus across the table. As she tried to internally compose herself and hide the redness sinking into her cheeks, Marcus raised his glass. "A toast," he exclaimed. "A toast to assholes with way too much money throwing over-the-top parties, because without him I would have never met you, and that can be the second thing I can be thankful to that prick for," he said with a deep chuckle.

They clinked their glasses together, and before she could even put her glass back down, Marcus stood, grabbed her by the hand, and dragged her to the dance floor. The mariachi music was playing loudly over the patio speakers and many couples were swinging each other around in circles. He took Sophia in his arms and began moving her quickly around the floor. Neither of them really had a clue what they were doing, but they laughed and continued swaying to the music. They circled around the dance floor, bumping into the other dancers, apologizing every time.

As the song was coming to an end, Marcus spun Sophia under his uplifted hand and she came to an abrupt stop in his arms, her chest to his and his nose to hers. Her breath caught in her throat as he bore into her with his eyes, and before she could remember her own name, his lips were on hers. Never had she felt the heat that travelled through every limb of her body from a kiss, but every single cell in her body awoke. The way she'd imagined his lips would taste, the first moment she'd laid eyes on him, was massively underrated. He tasted like she never wanted to release her lips from his again, and she wanted to know how the rest of him tasted. They stood bound together for several moments, and then he pulled away and looked her in the eyes.

"Who are you?" he said, so quietly it was almost a whisper. After the song came to a complete stop, Marcus unwillingly pulled himself out of Sophia's arms and led her back to the table, where he threw down a twenty dollar bill and thanked the plump little Mexican waitress as they walked out the door, back to the parking lot. As they got to the passenger-side door, Marcus grabbed Sophia by the waist, pushed her up against his car and pressed his body against hers, and kissed her again. He drew his hands up the sides of her thighs, lightly up over her stomach and breasts, and they found the side of her face as he held her in place and continued to kiss her hungrily. She reached both arms around his broad, muscular back and pulled him so close he was almost a part of her. Putting his fingers in her long dark hair, he lightly pulled her head back to expose her neck and kissed every arch and every curve. Sophia let out a soft cry of pleasure and then, all too suddenly, she pulled away.

"Marcus, I can't do this. I barely know you."

Marcus allowed her to pull away, and replied, "I am so sorry, Sophia. I cannot help myself. You are taking control of every part of me, but please, just tell me to stop and I will."

Unable to allow her good intentions to win the battle, she pulled at him once more. He pressed tightly against her for a few moments, but she again pulled away. "I'm sorry, we have to stop."

Marcus respected her request and put his nose to hers and whispered, "I am sorry. Come, let me take you home. I will have someone from the studio bring your car from Alex's tomorrow."

He reluctantly let go of Sophia and opened the door for her. As she stepped in, he gave her another seductive wink. He walked around to his side of the car, got in and started the engine. They pulled out of the parking lot and drove down the road toward Sophia's apartment.

July 20, 2015 – In the Shadow of Doubt

The clock's ticking sound filled the room with every move of its hands, and as it reached 3:15, the two women sat silent and still at the Island. Cat's mind was trying to grasp what Sophia had just shared with her, and was certain this was some kind of sick prank. Sophia stared down into her now-empty glass of vodka. She knew she could trust Cat with this truth – she trusted her more than anyone in her life – but Sophia was still struggling with the silence as she waited for Cat to say something, anything.

"Sophia, Jesus, I am so sorry you had to go through all of this, but you should have come to me sooner. We could have tried to figure something out!" Cat exclaimed through her tears. Cat's head was swarming in every direction, and she knew that she was left with no choice but to help. That was the only way Sophia was going to get out of the situation she was in. "Listen to me, Soph, we are going to have to call the cops at some point tonight, but right now I need you to go upstairs and get dressed up. Like, throw on some party clothes. We are going out." As the words floated in the air, Cat realized how insane the idea must have sounded, but in her frantic state, it was the best that she could do.

"Going out? Cat, what are you talking about?" Sophia asked, slightly confused. She knew she needed Cat's help, but she hadn't thought this would be her answer, to go out.

"Sophia, listen to me, we need to go out. First, we need to figure out what in the hell our story is going to be, but we need to do that away from this house. I cannot think here. And second, we need to get our faces out anywhere we can tonight. We need to try and place you anywhere but here tonight. I don't know if you are seriously okay with calling this in right now, and explaining to the police that you walked up to your husband, who was asleep, and put a gun to his head and pulled the trigger. Sophia, there was no fight, there was no struggle, you have no marks, no bruises, and we cannot trust the police will believe what you told me tonight. We have to come up with something, and I cannot do that here, so let's go upstairs and get dressed, because we are going out."

Sophia was caught off-guard at Cat's response to the whole situation, but it was important to trust her right now. They both stood up from the island stools and started up the stairs. Soon they were again standing outside of the bedroom, and even though Sophia knew what was in there, she was almost afraid to open the doors, just in case. Maybe he wasn't on the bed anymore, and he was waiting for her to enter the room so she could "get what was coming to her," as he so often told her when she did something wrong. She pushed the doors open and, as her heart skipped a quick beat, she finally saw him, still lying on the bed, cold and lifeless.

Even though she was the one who created this scene in front of her, she still felt a slight trepidation in crossing the threshold from the hallway into their bedroom. The two women stood, speechless, afraid to enter the room. Cat could barely stand to look at the ghastly reality in front of her, and she could feel her throat beginning to restrict as the tears came rushing to the surface. Quickly wiping her eyes, she regained her composure and beckoned the last remaining ounce of strength she could muster.

"Come on, Soph," she ordered as she dragged Sophia across the room, making sure to not look at Marcus lying on the bed. They walked directly into Sophia's extravagant walk-in closet and closed the door behind them to escape the scene on the other side. Cat fell with her back against the door and she closed her eyes, taking a moment to allow her trembling legs to find their bearings. Cat was terrified, and she didn't know if this was the right thing to do, but she knew she had to do something, and this was the only thing that came to her.

Sophia sat down on the chaise in the middle of the closet and watched as Cat pulled down a simple but beautiful Dolce and Gabanna dress. She then walked over to the wall of shoes that lined the closet and pulled down a simple black pair of Louboutin's. Sophia continued to silently try to rationalize the choice that she had made, when Cat suddenly gasped, startling Sophia out of her thoughts.

"Shit, Sophia," she began, "where in the hell is the gun? Where did you put the gun, Sophia?"

Sophia paused, and fought to come up with the answer. "I think I put it back in the safe," Sophia replied, almost questioning her own response. "I didn't know what I was supposed to do with it. This all happened so fast. What was I supposed to do with it, Cat? I couldn't just leave it lying there beside him."

Cat turned and opened the doors to the walk-in closet, and then she walked over to a beautiful portrait hanging on the wall just above the dresser. She carefully removed the painting from the wall, revealing a subtle built-in wall safe. She laid the painting on the floor beside her and began punching in the code to the safe, which she had stored in the back corner of her memory. Sophia had shared everything with her during their long friendship, including the code to the safe, just in case – well, in case of emergencies, and this certainly qualified. As the door to the safe opened, Cat could see his gun case tucked in the back corner. She gently reached in and pulled the case out of the vault, and carefully propped open the lid. The gun was not in its resting place.

"Sophia, it's not in here. Where is it?" Cat asked with panic in her voice. "Where in the hell did you put the gun?"

"I don't know, Cat, I just don't know," Sophia replied.

Cat immediately recognized a change in the tone of Sophia's voice, as it was now eerily calm and soothing. Cat could sense something was horribly wrong, even before turning around to face Sophia. She came face-to-face with the barrel of the handgun that she was in search of just seconds ago. Cat became almost paralyzed with the gripping fear that was overcoming her as she tried to comprehend what was happening in this moment.

"Soph, honey, what are you doing?" Cat softly cried.

Sophia began guiding Cat to the foot of the king size bed. As she walked, Cat kept her hands up near her chest, hoping to prevent Sophia from any sudden reactions.

"Sophia, it's me, Cat. I am here to help you, you know that right? Why are you doing this? Please, you know you don't have to do this." Cat's body began to tremble as she was overwhelmed with uncontrollable sobs. "Why are you doing this?" she yelled out, in desperation.

As she watched Cat slowly losing control, Sophia kept her eyes locked onto her once-dear friend, and she could see the terror in Cat's eyes as tears streamed down her face. Once again, for a brief instant, Sophia's conscience wanted to step in, and she almost second-guessed her choice. Only after reliving her last eleven years, and especially the events of the last couple months, did she come to her final conclusion, that she was, in fact, doing the right thing. Sophia slowly tilted her head to one side and gave Cat a faint smile.

"Because you gave me no choice." And with her last words to her friend of eleven years, she pulled her finger back on the trigger for the second time that night.

May 16, 2004 - Awaken

Sophia's eyes slowly fluttered open as the sun crept through the curtains early Sunday morning. As her body unwillingly began to wake from her deep sleep, it took a moment for her to orient herself. She could still feel herself reeling from the events of last night. She was trying very hard to determine whether it was all just a vivid dream, or whether it really happened. She rolled over onto her back and stared up at the ceiling, reliving every moment that she and Marcus had shared only a few short hours ago. She could still taste the saltiness from the margaritas on her lips as she placed her fingers on her mouth.

Sophia continued to lie in bed for several more minutes, almost afraid that if she were to get up the memories may start to fade, and she would come to realize that it was all just a crazy dream. Finally, she threw her duvet to the side and sat up on the edge of her bed. As she stood up, she reached her arms high over her head and gave her tense body a long stretch. She walked over to the window, pulled back the curtains and instantly noticed her black Honda Civic parked on the curb in front of her apartment building.

"He already had someone bring my car back," she thought to herself, pleased. Almost immediately, though, she felt a sense of worry that she may not hear from him again. He could have just had her car dropped off, and that was the end of it. He had a bit of fun with her last night and that was it, move on to the next lucky lady. She did not like this sudden feeling of insecurity, but there was something about him that had her desperately hoping that it was not just some night of random fun. She really hoped that he would call her soon.

As she was about to head out of her room, to go to the kitchen to make herself a cup of coffee, her cell phone started ringing on her nightstand. Looking at the caller ID, she saw that it was work calling. "Ugh," she sighed. "Why are they calling me on my day off?" she asked herself before taking the call.

"Hello?" she answered.

"Hey Sophia, it's Trish. I am sorry, I really hope I did not wake you, I know it is a bit early and it is your day off, but honey, I need a favour," her boss asked, with a pretty-please tone of voice.

"What's going on?" Sophia asked.

"Well, normally I wouldn't ask this of you, but everyone is fully booked up for this evening and we just had a last minute dinner party request. Normally, I would have turned it down, but it is a very simple, intimate dinner, and they are willing to pay quite a bit above our rates if we can fit it in. If you cannot do it, I totally understand. I can figure something out. Just wanted to see if you maybe wanted to pick up some extra cash?" Trish asked Sophia, sounding almost desperate.

"Hmm, well I don't think I have too much going on tonight, and yes, I can definitely use the extra cash. Where 'bouts is it? Do you know how many people will be attending the dinner?"

"It's a small back yard dinner of just four, they said they would be providing the food, just want someone there to help serve it. Sounds like a very quick and easy event, if you are feeling up to it," Trish answered.

"Yeah, sure, just email me the details and I will swing by the shop today to grab some supplies."

"You, Sophia, are a life saver. I am going to owe you for this, my dear. I will send you the details right away, and again, thank you. If I don't see you at the shop later, I will see you tomorrow." Trish thanked Sophia again then hung up the phone.

Well, Sophia thought, maybe this would help her clear her head and stop thinking about Marcus for a while, at least, and she really did need all the extra money she could get her hands on.

Shortly after hanging up with her boss, her Blackberry vibrated, alerting her that she had an email. Sophia opened it up and quickly glanced at all the information for the dinner party. She threw her phone on the bed and headed out to the kitchen to make that cup of coffee before getting ready for the day.

Later that afternoon, Sophia pulled up outside of Fresh Catering and turned off her engine. She stepped out of her car, dressed impeccably, the same way she was the day before, same white blouse, same black skirt, and a newly-pressed apron. She walked into the building and went right into the back to gather some supplies she may need for the dinner.

"Well, well, well, look who it is," Cat teased as soon as she saw Sophia. "So, tell me all about it. Ooh, did he?"

Sophia chuckled under her breath, afraid to respond to Cat's question. "Did he what?" she bravely asked.

"You know... did he have a big... house? I bet it was huge, wasn't it? You can tell me."

"Geez, Cat, what is wrong with you?" Sophia chuckled again. "You are crazy you know that? Seriously, though, it was nice. We just went to this amazing little Mexican restaurant and had a drink and did some dancing. That is about it. Honestly, Cat, I didn't get to see his house."

"Well, that's no fun. I guess next time then, right?"

"I don't know if there is going to be a next time. I don't know that I will hear from him again, honestly. It was probably just another night for him, you know? What did I expect, really? That he was just going to fall madly in love with me after one night. This isn't the movies. I am a bit more realistic than that," Sophia stated, trying to sound somewhat confident. "I gave him my number and that is it, if he calls, he calls. If not, so be it. Chalk it up to a fun evening."

Cat looked at Sophia with a childlike pout. "Well that sucks, but fuck him, right? Oh, but wait, you didn't do that either." Cat slapped Sophia on the butt as she walked by, and headed out to the front doors while yelling back over her shoulder, "You know I am just kidding. He will call, I know it."

Sophia found herself oddly fond of this Cat girl she just met yesterday. She made her laugh. They were very different people, but she liked her nonetheless.

She gathered the rest of her supplies and headed back out to her car. She threw everything in the trunk and hopped in and started her engine and pulled out the address and began heading to her dinner party.

The sun was slowly starting to set as she drove along Mulholland Drive, cautiously checking her map for the address Trish had given her. The area was pretty, the homes were modern and lovely, and not nearly as large or intimidating as the home she was at yesterday. She quite preferred the smaller events over the big outrageous parties. The tips were generally not as gracious, but it was a lot simpler, and the guests were much easier to tolerate. As she realized she was near her destination, she found a spot to park on the street in front of the house. She pulled out her Blackberry once more and read the details one last time before heading in. Trish had told her that it was a small dinner party, taking place in the back yard, and she was to go around the back to set up at the outdoor kitchen. Thankfully, it was a gorgeous evening and did not look like there was any chance of rain. She gathered all of her things and walked to the side of the house, where she came to a beautiful wrought-iron gate. She pulled it open and continued walking to the back of the house. As she rounded the corner, she could see the yard was set up with beautiful twinkly lights, and tons of votive candles were shining over the ripples of the swimming pool near the seating area. She continued walking through to the outdoor kitchen, and was hoping she would see the host soon as it did not look like any guests had arrived yet. Just as she was about to put her bags down on the cement counter-top, she glanced over to the perfectly set table and was startled to see him standing there.

"Marcus?" she said, surprised. "What? What are you doing here?"

"Hello, Sophia" he replied. "You have no idea how happy I am that I was able to get you here tonight, but you can put your things down and come and join me. You will not be working this evening I am sorry to tell you."

Sophia looked at him, with many questions in her mind. "Is this your house?" She was pretty certain of his answer, but had to ask. "You called to book a dinner tonight?"

"I am just happy I was able to convince your boss that I only wanted your services. I raved about how fantastic you were at the party yesterday, and told her I just had to get you for my dinner tonight. Come, sit, I have dinner already prepared, you don't have to do anything tonight, Sophia." He pulled out her chair as he motioned for her to sit.

Sophia walked to the table and slid into the chair he had held out for her and as she sat he slowly pushed her into the table.

On the plates was a perfectly presented arugula salad, glazed salmon and vegetables. Marcus opened a bottle of red wine and poured each of them a glass then took his own seat.

"Why this, Marcus? Why did you go through the trouble of setting up a dinner to get me here? I gave you my number, you could have just called me. It would have been much simpler, don't you think?" she asked him with a sly grin on her face.

"Because, Sophia, you are far from a simple woman, and you do not deserve simple. You deserve grand gestures and surprises, and I knew that from the moment I saw you. After last night, I could not stop thinking about you, and a part of me was afraid that maybe you woke up realizing you made a mistake with me. So instead of calling you, I did this, and I hope you are not upset with me, but you are worth more than just a simple phone call."

They sat looking at each other and Sophia grabbed her glass of wine and took a drink to moisten the dryness she could feel taking over her mouth again. Marcus slid his chair closer to hers and put his hands on either side of her face. Without saying another word, he pressed his mouth on hers and kissed her deeply. Sophia knew any remaining inhibitions were going to be lost tonight, because the second she'd seen him she'd known, right then and there, that she was going to give into every desire she felt. The familiar taste of his lips quickly shot an intense sensation of desire through her entire body. Marcus stood up, holding his hand out to her. Completely forgetting about the delicious meal that sat on the table, she reached for his hand and he led her to one of the daybeds that sat near the pool. They sat down on the daybed, again looking into each other's eyes.

"Marcus, I don't know where you came from..." She paused to kiss him softly. "...But now that I have found you, I don't ever want to let you go."

They fell back onto the bed, and she could feel the sheer strength of his body on top of hers. His tongue found every trace of her neck, down to her collarbone. As he kissed her neck, his hands drifted up to her breasts and he let his fingers slowly caress them as he found the top button of her blouse. He slowly and carefully unbuttoned the first couple buttons, and as he did so her desire for him intensified, and she pulled him into her with a sense of urgency. He lost his patience and pulled at her blouse, and tore it open the rest of the way as buttons flew out onto the ground. Sophia pulled at his shirt and tugged it over his head, and tossed it to the side. He kissed her down her chest, and after he pulled her bra aside, exposing one of her nipples, he lightly put it between his teeth and gently let his tongue draw little circles around it until it grew hard in the air. He continued down her stomach, kissing until he reached the waist of her skirt. He reached behind her and suddenly undid her apron, and threw it away, almost tossing it in the pool. With one quick jerk, he pushed her skirt up around her waist, and before she could even react she could feel his hot breath through her lace panties. As quickly as he had her skirt up around her waist, he had her panties taken off, dangling on her ankle. Immediately, his tongue sent a shock through her spine, and her breath caught in her throat as she felt him between her legs, devouring her in his mouth. She could feel her whole body tremble, and within minutes, she released herself to him.

"Marcus." She was now panting his name. "I need you now," she almost begged.

He stood, and she quickly undid his belt and slid off his pants. As he stood in front of her, now fully naked, she took all of him into her mouth, and she was pleased that he tasted even better than she'd imagined he would. He could not contain himself much longer if he allowed her to continue, so he pushed her back on the bed and grabbed her hands, pinning them above her head. Slowly, at first, he slid into her and, while still holding her hands, he could not help but to go deeper inside her. Sophia groaned loudly in ecstasy and she wrapped her legs tightly around his back. He then released her arms, and she wrapped them around his neck, clinging to him as Marcus, using the sheer strength of his muscular body, stood up from the bed while Sophia's legs remained circled around him.

He turned around and sat on the edge of the bed, and Sophia unwrapped her legs from around his back and straddled his thighs. She began to slide slowly up and down, welcoming him deeper with every movement she made. Marcus reached his hand slowly up her back, and tugged firmly on her hair. As she exposed her neck to him, Marcus could not help but bite her roughly with desire. Sophia's hunger for him immediately intensified, and she let out an animal-like groan, and Marcus could feel her start to tighten around him. Sophia could feel herself getting closer and her pace increased. Their bodies moved together as they held each other tightly.

Sophia was no longer able to deny her body, and as she felt Marcus release himself into her, they both let out a cry of pleasure. Marcus fell backward onto the bed. Sophia could feel her legs losing strength, so she carefully stood before collapsing on the bed beside him.

"Oh my God!" Sophia cried as she tried to catch her breath.

Marcus rolled over onto his side and pulled Sophia closer to him so that they were lying face to face. "Holy shit, Sophia, what have you done to me?" He tilted her chin up so her lips met his and softly kissed her again. "What have you done to me?"

July 20, 2015 – The Perfect Plan

Sophia had thought about this night long and hard for the past several months. She planned every last detail and now it was almost complete. Every possible emotion was going through her body at this moment, and it was impossible to process what she was actually feeling. There was a brief second where guilt began to creep in, but she just kept telling herself that it was the right thing to do, and that, in order to protect herself, this was honestly the only answer. Never in a million years did Sophia think she could become so cold and calculated, but the betrayal these two people had brought into her life was unforgivable, and she could not think of any other way to make it right.

She knew she needed to proceed to the next part of her plan soon, but her nerves were beginning to take hold of her and she was now genuinely starting to panic as the questions began to overrun her mind.

"What if this doesn't work? What if I missed something? Did I just make the biggest mistake of my life?" she worried. She tried to put all of these thoughts aside. She knew it was much too late to worry about any of that. It was finished, and there was no turning back now.

She did a thorough sweep around the room and made sure that the scene was laid out exactly how she intended it to be. She made sure each body was in place, she made sure the gloves she wore to pull the trigger were now on Cat's limp hands, and that the gun was lying at a perfect, fallen angle near her body. She hung the clothing that Cat had taken down back in her closet, placed her shoes back on the rack, and put her makeup away. As she headed for the door, she turned just one more time and studied the grisly scene she was walking away from.

She left the master bedroom door slightly ajar and continued down the stairs, into the kitchen. She quickly washed the two glasses that were still sitting on the island, and tucked the bottle of vodka back into the butler's pantry. Confident now that everything was how it should be, she grabbed her things, which she had hidden in the front closet, headed out the side door, and carefully crept out in the night.

There were no neighbors anywhere near their property, so she was fairly certain that she didn't have to worry about anyone witnessing her leaving her home at this hour of the night. She walked for what seemed like forever. She remained in the dark shadows off to the side of the road, and when she finally came to a crest, she stopped and tucked herself as far into the shadows as she could, and there she stood and waited.

Suddenly, she could feel every pulse of blood being pumped to her heart, and as she stood in the darkness, all of the night sounds surrounding her slowly took control of her mind. Every single sound – the wind rustling through the leaves, the crickets chirping, the cars off in the distance – made her jump, and made her heart race.

This was the perfect plan. It had to be. She couldn't risk having anyone find out the truth, because nobody would truly understand why she did this. Well, *almost* no one would understand.

She was a good person, she truly was. She'd dedicated herself for eleven years to both her husband and her best friend, and she'd stood by both of them through thick and through thin. Her loyalty to them never faltered, and even through each and every tumultuous year with Marcus, she had still remained dedicated to him. She had stood by Cat through every heartbreak, every triumph, every loss she'd suffered. She was there for her. And in the end, they both betrayed her in the worst ways possible. The secrets and the deceit that she had uncovered about both of them shook the very core of her soul, and the further she'd dug, the more she'd found out, and she'd quickly realized she needed to do something to protect herself.

She was just so thankful she didn't have to go through this all alone, because, honestly, if she had, the very idea of what she'd done tonight would have destroyed her. She didn't think she could have found the courage or the strength to execute this plan.

As she continued waiting off to the side of the road, thinking about what had happened up to this point, she could hear the faint purr of an engine coming up the hill. Suddenly, her palms were sweating, and she could feel her heart pounding in her throat. She was sure at any moment she was going to lose whatever was remaining in her stomach.

"Oh shit, oh shit, what if someone's coming?" she muttered to herself, while trying to remain as calm as possible.

She knew that this was where she was supposed to wait, but she was just praying that nobody had decided to go out for a stroll this early into the morning. She stood ever-so-still as the car got closer to her. The headlights were nearly blinding as the SUV pulled up to the side of the road. She didn't have a clue what kind of vehicle she should be expecting, but she knew it was coming. The final stages of the plan were in place. She just had to get through the next few hours and it would be done. She knew the next several months were going to be hard on her, she knew what to expect. They had been over it again and again, and now she needed to get through this last part.

As the black SUV came to a stop, Sophia went to the passenger side door and nervously reached for the handle. She softly opened the door so as not to make a sound. She was still fearful that someone could be around. You just never knew. She stepped up on the foot bar of the SUV and then slid into the seat. She sat silently for a brief second before pulling the seat belt securely over her shoulder. As she clicked it in place, she turned to face the driver and spoke with a tremble in her voice.

"It's almost over." She sighed deeply, and then repeated, "It's almost over."

July 16, 2004 – Whirlwind

The next couple months after their encounter at Marcus's fixed dinner party were nothing short of a whirlwind. They spent every moment they could together in between her catering events and his work with Alex at the studio. It was surreal, and Sophia could still not wrap her head around the man that had come into her life. Every day was a parade of flowers, jewelry, dinners at nice restaurants, parties, and, of course, passionate love-making every chance they could possibly get.

Sophia had introduced Marcus to her mother and, of course, to Cat, who was instantly won over by his sophisticated charm and banter. Her mother, of course, was slightly concerned that maybe things were moving a little bit too fast, but Sophia was constantly reassuring her that it was all okay, she was not going to do anything she was not ready for. That wasn't to say that Isabelle Vaughn didn't find Marcus's charm appealing. She was just concerned that maybe he was a bit too charming. She could see how incredibly happy her daughter was with him, and she did not want to interfere with her happiness, but she just wanted Sophia to be cautious, that was all.

On this night, Marcus had escorted Sophia and Cat to another fabulous industry party at one of the hottest clubs on the Sunset Strip, coincidentally called "The Strip". This time, they were celebrating the fact that Alex Preston had picked up yet another movie deal. This one, not unlike his previous film, was going to feature a lot of over-the-top shootouts, fast cars, and half-dressed women. Alex's desire to get into more interesting storylines was essentially non-existent, because he knew as long as there were men on this planet his movies would be Blockbusters. Marcus's plan was to one day be able to direct his own movies, maybe one or two that had some sort of thinking process behind the writing, and not just big blow ups, big muscles and big boobs.

The line up to the club looked miles long. Most people standing there knew they had no chance of getting into this exclusive party, but maybe, just maybe, they could catch a glimpse of one of the stars of the movie, or someone they could claim as famous. As the three walked up to the velvet rope, the bouncer guarding the door immediately lifted up the rope and smiled at them.

The bouncer knew Marcus instantly. Really, anyone so closely associated with Alex was known in this town, and that was one of the biggest reasons Marcus wanted to have a breakthrough and direct his own film, because he wanted to get out from under Alex's shadow. He was known as Alex's Assistant and, while he had learned a lot from Alex about directing a film, Marcus wanted to be his own person.

The club was bursting with energy. There seemed to be a thousand people in the building, and Sophia could feel the humidity when she walked in, from all the bodies that were being forced so close together. The music was blaring, some sort of house or techno music, Marcus led the two women to the back VIP room, where it was a little bit quieter. It was your typical Alex Preston event: drugs, women, and booze. They found a table near the back corner, which seemed to shelter them from some of the insanity going on, and as soon as they were seated, a petite, busty redhead came up to the table.

"What can I getcha?" She spoke loudly over the music.

"We will take a bottle of your finest top-shelf tequila, and three glasses, please."

"Good choice," she quickly replied, and headed off to take orders from the other tables.

"Straight tequila?" Sophia asked, with a sour look on her face.

"Oh, come on, Soph don't be such a stick in the mud. Neither one of us has to work tomorrow. Let your hair down, girl, and let's have some fun!" Cat chimed in.

"Trust me, Babe, this stuff is like candy. You will love it. Plus, it's all on Alex, so I ordered the best and most expensive for you ladies," Marcus said, trying to ease Sophia's mind.

As they were sitting at the table waiting for their drinks, Cat glanced up and, in a sarcastic tone, said, "Oh, great. Brace yourself, folks, here he comes."

Alex Preston was walking, or, actually, stumbling was a better description, up to the table. He clumsily sat at the open seat next to Cat and looked her right in the eye.

"Well now, who do we have here, Marcus?" he asked, while still holding his stare on Cat's.

"Alex, this is Cat Warner. You've already met her, you lush. You hired her and Sophia to cater your movie release party at your house a couple months ago. Don't tell me you have forgotten already?" Marcus teased.

"Oh, well I am certain I would never forget such a fucking fantastic pair of tits," he answered, now looking down at Cat's chest. "Are you sure we have met honey? Because I am sure I would not have forgotten you."

Cat laughed at Alex's inability to even somewhat hit on a woman.

"So I guess it's safe to assume that you don't recall coming into your kitchen, yelling at us while we were preparing for your party, and telling us that you didn't hire our 'tight little asses' to sit in your kitchen and gossip all Goddamn day? Well, that doesn't surprise me, you know? I guess you just had one too many lines of coke off some skank's ass. I understand. It must be pretty rough to be Alex Preston. I get how stressful it must be to be a royal dickwad. Oh, and if you ever call me honey again, I will kick you so hard in the balls you will be choking up nuts for the next week."

Marcus and Sophia both laughed hysterically at Cat's unexpected response. Not many women would stand up to Alex – they were usually too concerned about adding a "Hot Hollywood Director" notch on their bedpost. Alex himself was immediately speechless. He didn't know how to respond to a woman such as Cat, who had such confidence. In a way, though, it turned Alex on.

"Well, I can see your name matches your persona. You are a feisty one," Alex muttered, not sure what else to say to her. He definitely did not remember her from his party, and, yes, it was because he was way too stoned and drunk, but he knew that he wanted to get to know her now, that was for sure.

As their quick conversation came to an end, the waitress came and put down a bottle of Don Julio and four shot glasses, as she noticed Alex was now seated with them. When she bent over,

Alex's gaze immediately went to her chest. He sat and stared obviously as he started to slowly sway back and forth in his chair.

"You are such a disgusting pig." Cat fanned her hand in his face. "I cannot believe women actually fall for your shit."

Marcus, still chuckling, picked up the bottle and poured a round of the expensive liquor. He passed one to everyone at the table, including Alex, and lifted up his glass to give a quick toast.

"I am really not sure that you need any more, buddy, but I would like to give a toast to you, Sophia," he said pointing his glass in her direction. "You are the most amazing person that I have ever met, and I can't wait for each day with you. And, because I met you, I got to finally witness a woman hand Alex his balls on a platter, so for that I am thankful. Cheers!"

"Cheers!" the two women happily responded, while Alex, giving a mocking laugh, also raised his glass to meet the others'.

The rest of the night was filled with lots of dancing, laughter, and a lot of drinks. Sophia felt at ease and let her hair down for the night as she and Marcus moved on the dance floor and mingled with all the celebrities in attendance. Even though Sophia was generally unaware of who these stars were, she knew that most people would die to be in her shoes right now.

She and Marcus were stuck in the middle of a group of people, dancing to the beat of the music, when she glanced around, wondering where Cat was. She looked back to their table and was completely astonished by what she saw.

"Marcus, oh, my God, look, look over there at our table!" she exclaimed, as she pulled on his arm, and practically broke his neck as she turned his head towards the table.

Cat and Alex were making out like a pair of teenagers. She was practically straddling Alex with her long legs, and they were totally oblivious to anyone around them. Marcus belted out a contagious laugh.

"Well, that certainly didn't take him long, now did it? I don't know what it is about that Man, but, even with what a slime ball he is, he always seems to get women," Marcus stated, still laughing.

Sophia, starting to get worried for her friend, began heading back to the table to try and break this hot mess up. But as she turned to walk away, Marcus grabbed her by the arm and pulled her back.

"Where are you going?" he asked.

"I think that Cat may have had way too much to drink tonight. I know she will wake up in the morning and regret this. What kind of friend would I be if I allowed her to sleep with that lowly excuse of a man?" Sophia replied.

She turned away from Marcus and headed back towards the table. She stood over the two and watched them for a moment, and then, realizing they really had no idea she was there, she tapped Cat on the shoulder.

"Cat." She poked, with no response. "Hey, Cat, come on, we're going to head out. It's getting late, and I think we all have had a bit too much to drink. Come on, let's go get a cab," Sophia coaxed.

Finally pulling herself free from Alex's face, Cat looked up at Sophia and responded, "No, you go. You guys go, I'm good. I will get home safe, I promise. Don't worry about me so much, Soph, I'm fine." Cat took a quick breath and then found Alex's lips again. After a quick second, Alex pulled himself away, and looked up at Sophia, and Marcus, who was now standing behind her.

"She's in good hands, love, don't you worry," Alex said, with an almost-creepy tone to his voice, and then turned back to Cat.

Marcus pulled Sophia to the side gently, by the waist.

"Come on, let's go. Don't worry about her, Sophia, she will be fine. Alex is a bit of a creepy douche, but he wouldn't hurt a fly. He will make sure she gets home safe, I promise." He pulled her to face him and he looked her in the eye. "I promise."

"Okay, fine, Marcus, but I mean it: if he does anything to hurt her, I swear to God...."

Standing outside of the club, they waited near the curb for the first cab to come and pick them up. Both of them were quite drunk, but as they waited they stood hugging each other and swaying back and forth.

"I love you so much, Sophia," Marcus gushed. "I am so happy you came into my life." He then leaned in and kissed her softly on the mouth.

"I love you, too, Marcus" she whispered in between his kisses.

Just then, a cab pulled up and they both hopped in. Marcus gave his address as they sped off. During the entire cab ride, Marcus could not keep his hands to himself. They kissed passionately and held each other tightly, as if they feared, if they were to let go, they would slip away from each other. The cabbie glanced occasionally into his rear view mirror and smiled to himself. This was something that he got to see nearly every night in his cab, and sometimes he got to see too much. The cab pulled up in front of Marcus's house, and the cabbie turned back over his shoulder.

"Here we are, folks," he interrupted.

Marcus, finally able to pull himself out of Sophia's grasp, reached into his pocket and removed a $50 bill and handed it to the cab driver.

"Thanks, buddy, keep the change."

Marcus thanked him again when he got out of the cab, and walked around to Sophia's side and opened the door for her. She slipped out of the cab and grabbed Marcus's hand as they walked to his front door. He fumbled with his keys, as Sophia had her arms wrapped around him from behind, and finally, he was able to locate his house key and he opened the door and let them in. With the door barely closed behind them, Marcus turned and pulled Sophia into him and kissed her, softly, but passionately.

He suddenly lifted her up, so that she circled him with her arms and legs, and he carried her up the stairs to his bedroom. By the time they actually reached the bed, he already had Sophia's top and her bra off, and when he knew it was safe to put her down, he laid her gently on the bed and began undressing himself while she laid there in the dark room and watched the outline of his body in the moonlight filtering through the window. Once he was fully undressed, he slowly pulled off the rest of her clothes and fell on top of her. As he slowly led himself into her, he did not pull his intense gaze from hers.

"I love you," he whispered. "More than you can possibly know." He then maneuvered himself so she was straddling him, sitting at the edge of his bed. She continued moving with his rhythm, and before she could even try to control herself, she could feel that familiar tingle creeping up her legs and down her spine, and as the two sensations came together, it pushed Sophia over the edge and she began to climax with great intensity.

Marcus stood up quickly and again laid her down on the bed, and as he leaned over her, he found her again. He could feel her throbbing around him, and after only a few short moments he found himself letting go as well. Finally collapsing beside her, Marcus pulled her into his arms and turned to look at her.

"I never want to know what life is like without you Sophia. I don't want to wait, or need to wait, to know that I want to spend my life with you. Let's get married. Will you please marry me?" he asked her, unexpectedly. He could see a look of shock wash over her face, and for a second he was sure she was going to call him crazy. He waited for what seemed like an eternity for her to respond.

"Yes, Marcus, I will marry you. I don't want to wait either. I love you as well, and I don't need to take things slow to know that you were meant to be my husband. So, yes. Let's do it, let's go get married. I don't need a big fancy wedding with everyone watching, I just need me and you."

Marcus, heart filled with happiness and relief that she said yes, pulled her into him tightly and began to laugh with joy. They agreed to get some sleep, and as they lay in each other's arms, drifting to sleep, they knew at this time tomorrow they would be falling asleep as Mr. and Mrs. Marcus Donovan.

July 20, 2015 – The Time Draws Near

The black SUV pulled up outside of the villa at Malibu Resorts and Spa roughly around 5:30. The sun was just on the verge of making its appearance over the horizon, and Sophia knew she was cutting it close. She really wanted it to be dark when she was dropped off, and was hoping nobody was out for a morning run on the spa grounds. She turned to the driver with a childlike look on her face. She was scared now, and as it was coming to the final stages, she became more and more nervous. She undid her seatbelt and opened the door to get out.

Just as she was about to close the door, she quietly spoke. "Please, tell me we did the right thing?" Satisfied with a quiet nod in response to her question, she softly closed the door to the SUV and headed to the front door.

The Spa, which sat just outside of Malibu, was on the ocean-front, and it was beautiful. The small villas that sat on the grounds were cozy and cute. There were areas for all different types of services, such as massages, wraps, facials, mani's and pedi's, and, well, really anything she could imagine to pamper herself. Sophia had taken advantage of a few of them herself over the weekend while trying to prepare for the upcoming events. She had a handsome young man named Hector give her an amazing massage under a little cabana, right on the ocean, and between his hands and the ocean breeze over her skin, it was almost enough to make her forget what was yet to come. Almost.

Marcus had booked her reservations at the resort nearly two months ago for an early anniversary present, as he knew it was one of her favorite places to go with Cat. However, Cat was not with her this time when she checked in early Saturday morning.

She crept back through the front door and, after putting all of her things down on the table near the door, she walked directly into the bathroom and stripped off all of her clothes and drew herself a hot bath. As she waited for the big claw-foot tub to fill up, she examined herself in the mirror. It was almost as if a stranger were staring back at her. The dark circles, the red eyes, and the paleness of her skin…. She continued to stare, hoping that maybe she would start to recognize herself, but after this night, she was afraid she might never recognize herself again. How could someone go on with their life, and just pretend that everything was normal? How was she supposed to act now? How was she supposed to respond when people began mourning for her and her loss? Almost nobody knew the truth, and she could never tell them. This was something that had to go to her grave with her, and she was just praying that the plan was flawless. It had to be flawless.

She glanced over to the tub and noticed the water was nearing the rim. She reached over and turned off the faucets, and softly stuck one toe into the steaming water to make sure it was not too hot. She carefully lowered herself into the warmth and leaned her head back against the edge.

She closed her eyes and tried to block out what had taken place, but instead, with the silence surrounding her and the darkness with her eyes closed, the events came flooding back at a furious pace. Flashes of every moment: taking out the gun before Marcus came home, waiting in her closet for him to come into the bedroom, hearing him head to his Scotch table to pour himself a drink, and finally him collapsing on the bed and drifting into his drunken slumber. She could hear the ring of the gun over and over, and it was becoming deafening. Then, in a new flash, she saw Cat and the look on her face as she realized what was happening, a look that almost made Sophia rethink her choice, and then the sound of the gun again. As she played it over in her mind, she realized that she would now only ever look at herself as what she was: a murderer. She was a murderer. What if she couldn't live with this? She had to, though. It was this, in order to save her own life. She understood that to the core, and it's what would get her through. They both deserved this, and Sophia knew this was the way she wanted it to be. She was human, though, and she'd expected to go through these emotions. She just hoped she was strong enough, at this point, for such a ride.

She lay in the tub for what felt like an eternity, and she could feel herself starting to drift off. She glanced up at the large clock on the wall. It was now 6:30. She had about an hour and a half until she had to make the call. Stepping out of the tub, she reached for one of the soft, fluffy towels hanging on the rack and dried herself off, then slipped into the robe that was hanging on the back of the door. She walked back to the bed and decided she just really needed to lie down for an hour. She was exhausted, but it was not the time to sleep. Rest, yes, but it was almost time to get ready and pack her things and go home. She reached in her purse for her cell phone and set her alarm, just in case her body defied her and did not wake up when she needed it to. As she laid her head back on the pillow, she closed her eyes, and within what felt like minutes, her iPhone's alarm woke her out of a dead sleep.

Slowly, as her mind started to wake up, the memories of the hours before flooded her again. Her stomach was turning, and she knew she needed to eat something, anything, so she headed to the small kitchen area and grabbed an apple, trying her best to get it down. She managed to eat most of it. She tossed the remaining core into the garbage, and then went out and got herself dressed in a pair of white shorts and a simple pink tank-top. She applied a small amount of blush, mascara, and lip gloss before brushing her hair and throwing it into a messy bun. She glanced at herself one last time in the mirror before walking around the room and collecting all her belongings.

She double-checked that she had everything. It was now just after 8:00, and it was time. She picked up her phone and she searched for his number, and once the screen displayed his picture, she hit send. It rang several times, then finally his voicemail picked up.

"Hey, you've reached Marcus. You know what to do."

Sophia took one deep breath as she waited for her turn to begin speaking, and when the beep on the other end was complete, she began her message.

"Hey, honey, it's me. I just wanted to let you know that I'll be heading home shortly. I will be checking out and hitting the road in about 15 minutes. I hope you had a great weekend, and I look forward to seeing you soon. I missed you, Babe." She tried her absolute best to sound as happy and pleasant as possible, hoping there were no tremors in her voice.

She hung up the phone and again felt a wave of nausea wash over her, but she had to push through it and just continue on. The thought of going back to the house was almost paralyzing at this point, but she knew it was time to go. She headed to the main lobby to check out and clear up her bill, and then she got in her car and started back to where this all began.

July 17, 2005 – The First Year

The smell of freshly-brewed coffee filled Sophia's nose and the sound of pots and pans clanging in the kitchen woke her early that morning. As she slowly woke from her deep sleep, she could hear her husband whistling a tune she did not quite recognize, but it sounded lovely just the same. As she lay in the warmth of her big, fluffy duvet, she glanced out the French doors that led from their bedroom to the back patio and she could see the sun's rays shining on the surface of the pool, that pool where she and Marcus first made love. It was almost impossible to think that a whole year had already gone by since they decided to run off and get married in Vegas.

"A whole year already," she thought to herself. "Where does the time go?" As she was off in her own little world, thinking of what had evolved in their lives, she could hear Marcus coming down the hall. As he entered the bedroom, he saw that she was awake and he gave her a wide grin.

"Well, good morning my beautiful baby, how was your sleep?" he asked as he walked toward the bed, carrying a tray with a beautiful Gerber daisy in a small vase beside a plate of bacon and eggs, and a glass each of coffee and fresh-squeezed orange juice.

"I slept like a rock. You really wore me out last night, you know?" she replied with a smirk. "And how about you, Babe? Did you sleep alright?"

"I slept great," he stated as he placed the tray on Sophia's lap.

He quickly ran back out into the kitchen and returned almost instantly with his own cup of coffee, and then he settled himself back into his side of the bed and nuzzled up to Sophia as she began digging into the delicious breakfast.

"This looks so yummy, thank you so much," she said as she scooped a forkful of scrambled eggs into her mouth. Piling more onto her fork, she pointed it to Marcus, prompting him to open up. When he did, she quickly popped the fluffy eggs into his mouth.

"Happy one year anniversary, baby," Marcus said, turning to Sophia while finishing off the last of the eggs in his mouth. "This has been a great year, and I cannot wait to spend the next fifty years with you," he continued.

"I can't wait either, Marcus. This has been a great ride so far. I can't wait to find out what the rest of our lives have in store for us," Sophia replied as she set her unfinished breakfast down on her nightstand.

"What do you want to do today, baby? Anything you want today is all yours. Well, almost all yours – I got us reservations at Koi for 6:30 this evening, so whatever you want to do 'til then, your wish is my command," Marcus teased.

"Oh, really?" she teased back. "Anything?" She rolled over and pulled him close to her and began to kiss him softly.

"Anything," he moaned in between her kisses.

Marcus finally managed to pull himself away from Sophia after about an hour, and he stood up from the bed and walked to the bathroom to take a shower. As he entered the bathroom, he stuck his head back around the door.

"Get that sweet little ass up and moving," he joked as he threw her towel at her, while she lay on her side, with her hand propping up her head, laughing back at him.

"I'm moving, I'm moving, just give me a moment."

She could hear the shower come alive, and as Marcus climbed in he began whistling that same tune again. She looked around their bedroom and still could not believe she was married to this man and had this life.

The last year had been amazing for them. Marcus was finally given the opportunity to step out from Alex's shadow and made his directing debut. It was a small, low-budget film, which didn't feature a lot of big name actors, but it was the perfect place for him to start showcasing his talents. The movie ended up doing so well at the box office that it not only got a young, up-and-coming actor by the name of Chase Stevens recognized, but also got Marcus recognized as more than just Alex Preston's assistant. With such great success on his first movie, the next opportunity fell easily into his lap. This time, it was a much bigger-budget movie, with A-list actors, but the lead role was going to none other than Chase, the hot new talent that had stolen the spotlight in his first motion picture appearance. Not unlike most of Alex's movies, this was going to be a big action blockbuster, and Sophia knew that when this movie made its premiere it was going to get Marcus's name on the list of Hollywood's hottest up-and-coming directors.

As for herself, she was still working, part-time now, for Fresh. With Marcus's success on his first film, she did not have to focus so much attention on the catering business. She was able to spend more time on her writing. It had mainly been for her personal satisfaction, but she knew she wanted to find something that would pay her for her passion. She knew, most definitely, she did not want to end up another Hollywood wife, who spent her days going for lunches with the other wives, drinking way too much before noon, and spending too much money on shit she didn't need. She actually wanted to have a purpose and contribute to their marriage, not take advantage of it. There were a few magazines she was trying to work her way into, but she was having a difficult time, even with a degree in journalism. She knew that Marcus was not pressuring her, but she was anxious to find something where she could feel settled and content.

After several moments, Sophia glanced at the clock and realized she should probably get up and get ready as well. She jumped out of the bed and walked into the bathroom. Marcus was still in the shower, and she opened the door and slid in behind him.

They pulled up outside of Koi about 6:20. The valet came to Sophia's side of the car and opened the door to let her out. She stepped out and graciously thanked the young man with the name Julio embroidered on his blazer. Marcus came around and met with Sophia, and handed Julio a $20 bill and thanked him again. Marcus took Sophia by the hand and led her into the restaurant and up to the hostess.

"Reservation for the Donovans for 6:30," he politely told the hostess.

"The Donovans... Oh yes, Mr. Donovan, I see you right here." She grabbed two menus and had them follow her through the dining room to their private table.

"Here you go, sir. Hope this table is suitable for you?" she asked shyly, while smiling up at Marcus. Sophia witnessed it all the time, the effect that he had on women, and this young woman was no different.

"This is perfect, thank you very much," he replied as he slowly pushed Sophia's chair toward the table. He then walked over to his own chair and sat. As he was adjusting his chair, a nice-looking young man came up to the table with a bottle of red wine.

"Good evening, my name is Tony and I will be your waiter tonight. Can I start you off with a glass of wine, perhaps?"

"Wine would be perfect, Tony," Marcus responded politely. Tony took out his corkscrew and efficiently opened the bottle of wine. He poured just a small amount into Marcus's glass, allowing him to make sure it was to his liking. Marcus picked up his glass and swirled the liquid around a few times, gave it a quick smell, and took a small sip, savouring the flavours in his mouth.

"That is lovely; you can actually just leave the bottle with us, please." Marcus requested.

"Absolutely. I will give you two a few moments with the menu. Please do not hesitate to call me if you need anything," he offered, then turned and headed away.

Sophia and Marcus held hands across the table. The wine was delicious, the soft music was romantic, and the company was perfect.

"Well," Marcus raised his glass to Sophia's, "a toast: to my beautiful wife of one year, I look forward to each and every moment with you, and I am looking forward to spending the next 50 years with you. I love you, Sophia." They softly tapped wine glasses.

"And I love you Marcus, and I am so proud of what you have accomplished over this last year. I am so very proud to be your wife," Sophia replied.

They sat holding hands and laughing at the memories of their last year together. If anyone did not know them already, it would be easy to think this young couple was here having one of their first dates the way that they looked at each other. You could see the electricity between them from across the restaurant, and it was easy to see the love that they shared. Just as Marcus said something that made Sophia burst out laughing, she was interrupted.

"Sophia? Sophia Vaughn, is that you?"

A gentle-looking young man was standing at their table, waiting for Sophia's response. As she looked up from Marcus, a look of utter surprise crossed her face.

"Oh, my God, Adam! What are you doing here?" she exclaimed as she jumped out of her seat and grabbed him for a tight hug. "Oh, my God, Adam, it has been years!"

Adam was tall and slim and had dirty-blond hair that fell just above his bright blue eyes. He had a sweet smile and a softness to him that was hard to explain. He hugged Sophia tightly, shocked to see her here after all these years. When he pulled away, he held her at arm's length and replied, "I moved here last year from Dallas. Well, I actually moved to San Francisco, but I am down in LA for a few days for a business meeting. What are you doing here? You still lived in San Diego, the last I heard."

"Oh man, it has been way too long," Sophia teased as she quickly hugged him again. "I moved out here about two years ago. Mom is still back home, but I came out here and started working for a catering company, and to do some writing." Sophia glanced over at Marcus and was instantly aware of a look of displeasure on his face. She thought to herself, "Oh, geez, he must be upset that I haven't introduced him yet."

"Oh, Adam, I would love to introduce you to my husband, Marcus Donovan. Marcus, this is Adam Doucette. Our families were very close while we were growing up. He and his family used to live in Imperial Beach when we were younger." As Sophia spoke, Marcus reached, almost reluctantly, for Adam's extended hand.

"Nice to meet you, Adam," Marcus said coldly.

Adam could feel the tension resonate from Marcus, and he couldn't quite put his finger on the uneasy feeling Marcus gave him, but it was an odd sensation when first meeting someone new. He managed to shrug it off, and turned back to Sophia and grabbed her hands.

"I wish I could stay and chat more. Oh, it was so good to see you, but I do have to run. I have to meet friends in a few minutes, but please tell me you are free for lunch this week, we need to catch up. I can't believe it's been so long." He reached into his jacket pocket, pulled out one of his business cards and handed it to Sophia. "Give me a call tomorrow, let's go grab lunch and catch up," he said as he pulled her in for another quick hug.

"Yes, for sure, I will call you tomorrow. Oh, Adam, it was so good to see you. Have a great night, I can't wait to catch up," Sophia replied before he quickly said another goodbye and turned to head out of the restaurant. Sophia watched till she could no longer see him, and was still reeling over running into one of her oldest friends after nearly fifteen years as she sat down in her chair and took a deep breath.

"Wow, I can't believe I just ran into him. Oh, it'll be so nice to catch up with him, it has been so long," Sophia sighed.

Marcus stared at her, looking almost angry. She had never seen this look on his face before, and was wondering why he would be so upset. She reached for his hand.

"Is everything okay, honey?" she asked.

"It's fine, Sophia, but to be honest, I'm not sure lunch is such a good idea."

Sophia looked at Marcus in utter confusion. "Why not? It's only Adam. He's a very dear friend of mine, whom I haven't seen in years, and I would love to spend some time catching up with him. What are you so concerned about?" she asked him softly.

"Sophia, I said it's not a good idea. I will not have you going out with some man I don't know for lunch, do you understand me?"

"But Marcus, it's fine. It's just Adam. He is not a stranger, he is my fri–" Sophia was unable to finish her sentence before Marcus abruptly cut her off.

"I said you will not be going out for lunch with him, Sophia, now do not bring it up again. I do not want to hear another word about Adam, Sophia. End of conversation," he proclaimed harshly.

Sophia slowly released his hand from hers, and an unfamiliar sense of uneasiness crept over her just as Tony glided back up to the table to take their order. She sat quiet and still, and her utter disbelief over what happened began to overwhelm her. Slowly, the sounds of Marcus and Tony's voices faded into silence.

July 20, 2015 – Act One

"9-1-1, what is your emergency?" the operator at the other end of the line asked.

"My name is Sophia Donovan. Oh, my God, please send help, please. My husband is dead, please help me!" Sophia screamed into the phone through desperate sobs.

"Ma'am, calm down, please. Tell me your address and I will get someone there right away," the operator replied calmly.

"Fifteen Canyon Hill. Please hurry – someone shot them, please hurry!" she continued crying into the phone.

"I have someone on their way right now, ma'am, I just need you to stay calm. I need you to tell me if you are alone in the house."

Sophia inhaled a deep breath to answer the operator. "Yes, I think so, just please hurry. Oh, my God, who would do this to them?"

"Ma'am, who is 'them'? How many people?"

"Two. Someone shot them, they shot both of them. I need help now."

"Ma'am, I am going to need you to stay on the phone with me, okay? I need you to stay on the line until help arrives, they are on their way. Please just try and stay calm, okay?" the operator calmly asked again.

After several moments, which felt more like hours to Sophia, she could hear the sirens in the distance, coming towards her house in the hills.

"I can hear them. Oh, I can hear them!" Sophia gasped into the phone while running to the window. She could soon see the flashing lights of the first cop car, followed by an ambulance. She quickly ran out of the room and down the stairs, with the phone still in her hand. She could hear the operator saying something, but, knowing help was here, she just hung up and tossed the phone to the side. She pulled open the door and ran out onto the drive, not even allowing the vehicles enough time to come to a stop or turn off the sirens. The first cop car came to a sudden stop and the officer driving stepped out, and instantly ordered Sophia to remain where she was as he reached for his gun with one hand, and held up the other hand.

"Ma'am, please stay where you are, and tell us what's going on," the officer ordered.

"Please!" she cried. "Please help me, someone shot them. Please help me."

The other officer was now standing outside the car, and the ambulance came to a stop while silencing the alarms. The paramedics pulled the gurney out of the back and stood by as the officer driving the patrol car ran past Sophia and entered the house. Sophia turned to follow him in, but was quickly deterred by the other officer.

"Ma'am, please wait out here with us," she ordered firmly as she softly pulled Sophia back by her arm. Moments later, the radio attached to her chest blared loudly.

"All clear," the officer reported from inside the house. At the officer's confirmation, the paramedics gathered their gurney and rushed through the front door and up the staircase.

"Are they alive? Please tell me they're alive!" she wailed as she ran up the stairs after them and followed them into the room.

"Please, ma'am, we need you to wait outside the bedroom."

The officers came up the stairs and followed the paramedics in to further examine the scene. It didn't take long to determine that both Marcus and Cat were no longer alive, and with that, both of the paramedics knew that their job was done. They packed up their supplies and gurney and headed out of the room.

"Where are you guys going?" Sophia shouted at the two men. "You have to do something, help them! Where are you going?"

The older of the two men stopped and turned to Sophia with a compassionate look on his face. Unfortunately, in his line of work, he had seen this all too often, and had experienced all levels of grief from the loved ones.

"Ma'am, I am so sorry for your loss, but there is nothing we can do. The officers will help you. Again, I'm sorry, ma'am." The paramedic continued down the stairs and out the front door to load up the ambulance and await their next call.

Sophia turned to the officer that had been driving the patrol car with desperation in her eyes, and asked him, "Who would do this? How did this happen?"

The officer she spoke to was Brady, and his partner was Officer Pratt. Brady was in his fifteenth year on the force, and it showed in the lines of his face. He seemed, at first glimpse, to be somewhat callous and cold, but his partner offset that with her sympathetic nature. Pratt was roughly thirty years old, but this was only her second year on the force, and her first year as Brady's partner. She was petite, blonde-haired and, honestly, not how Sophia had pictured cops. She was kind and had a warm heart, and had probably, with those traits, chosen the wrong career, but she chose it to help people and keep them safe, and that was what she was here to do now.

Officer Pratt came up to Sophia and softly requested they go downstairs into the living room. Sophia settled herself on her couch, across from Pratt, and silently looked at her, waiting for the questions to start coming. The first was the most obvious.

"Ma'am, can I please get your full name?" Pratt asked.

"Sophia," she croaked. "Um, Sophia Donovan. My name is Sophia Donovan."

"Thank you, Sophia. Listen, I know this is hard, but I'm going to need you to tell me what happened here. I need you to tell me everything that you can possibly remember right now, okay?" Pratt continued. "Can you confirm for me who the two individuals upstairs are?"

Sophia sat with her hands cradled in her lap, observing them for a moment before she took a deep breath to answer Officer Pratt.

"My husband, Marcus Donovan, and Catarina Warner," she replied as she began to cry softly again.

"Okay, Sophia, thank-you. And can you tell me how you know Catarina Warner? Who is she, in relation to you and your husband?"

"Cat is my best friend," she muttered quietly. "Cat *was* my best friend," she corrected.

Officer Pratt jotted down all the information that Sophia was relaying to her, as detailed as she could, and while she continued to question Sophia downstairs, Officer Brady was upstairs placing the call that a homicide had taken place at the home of Marcus Donovan, and requesting the homicide division be immediately dispatched.

December 24, 2007 – A Family Affair

Sophia stood back and admired all her hard work. The house looked beautiful. The Christmas tree towered in the corner with its array of gorgeous ornaments, lights, and, of course, the star that sat perfectly on top. The fireplace was adorned with festive garland, softly glowing candles, and two large stockings hanging from the mantle. It all looked so perfect, and she needed it to look perfect, as this was their first time hosting Christmas in their new home. They had sold Marcus's house on Mulholland and purchased this amazing home about six months before. Sophia had never pictured herself living in the Hollywood hills, never mind in a house this size, but Marcus had become quite successful from his last three movies. At first, she hadn't wanted to buy something so large, but Marcus had convinced her that this was their dream home, where they were going to raise their future family. They had talked about a family a lot in the last few years, and shortly after moving into their new home they decided to take the plunge and start trying. Unfortunately, no baby yet, but these things could take time, Sophia knew that. As she sat back, admiring her beautifully-decorated living room, Marcus came in through the opposite entrance, holding a glass of bourbon.

"Are you sure you're ready for this?" he asked, concerned.

"Of course. This is going to be great: your family, my mom, Cat and Cat's, um, friend?" she asked, although fully aware Marcus didn't know who Cat was bringing either. "I can't wait to host Christmas Eve in our home. This is the first time I've been able to do this, and I think it's going to be great," she continued.

"Okay, if you say so. You know how my family is, Sophia. I just don't want you to be disappointed if this doesn't meet your expectations, that's all," he replied as he walked over to the mantle to examine the decorations. Reaching out, he adjusted the garland to make sure it was perfectly straight, and he also adjusted how the stockings were framing the fireplace. Once he was satisfied, he turned to face Sophia and said, condescendingly, "Soph, I would think that if you cared so much about how this evening was going to go, you might also want to make sure that it doesn't look like a child did all of the decorating. You know how much better things look when they are done properly."

His comment was harsh, and probably uncalled for, but she knew he was tired and had been working an excessive number of hours over the last few months on his new project, so she was sure he hadn't meant it the way it sounded. She took a quick breath and allowed his comment to roll off her back. She really didn't want to cause an argument right now, not tonight. She wanted it to be perfect, and she had been working hard all day to make that happen. She walked over to Marcus and put her arms around his neck and gave him a sweet, soft smile.

"I'm sorry, honey. My mind is just a bit frazzled, and I'm just trying to make this perfect. This is our first event with everyone all together, and I just don't want anything to go wrong. I hope that everyone gets along. They're family now, and I want it to go smoothly." She reached up on her tip-toes to give him a peck on the cheek, and then walked back to the kitchen to check the turkey that she had placed in the oven a few hours ago.

Sophia puttered away in the kitchen, making sure she had everything started for the Christmas Eve dinner that night. She made sure the turkey was basted, the potatoes were peeled and washed, the stuffing was prepared and ready to go, and she checked the bar again to make sure they were fully stocked on a good selection of wines, bourbons, and scotches. Satisfied at how everything was coming along, she took a seat on one of the stools at the island and reached for a copy of LA Today that was lying on the counter. Thumbing through the pages, she glanced over all the newest celebrity gossip for the week. Who's dating who? Who's divorcing who? And who's wearing what? She continued flipping the pages until she came to the back of the magazine, and there it was, her weekly column. It was there like clockwork every week, same page, same section, just different topics. This was definitely not her choice of a dream job, writing a relationship column for a gossip magazine, but this was where she was starting, this was who had decided to give her a foot in the door, and it really wasn't so bad. After all, she got to work from home, and she got paid decently for her columns. But, honestly, it wasn't what she envisioned for herself. Sophia also knew that Marcus had a huge hand in getting her this job: the editor's daughter just happened to be a part of the film crew on Marcus's last movie. It was a small favor, of sorts, and now, a year later, it had become quite a popular section of the magazine, thanks to Sophia.

She sometimes reflected on the fact that she gave relationship advice for a living, and questioned her qualifications on the subject. Her marriage was not perfect, by any stretch of the imagination, so how was she supposed to give legitimate advice to couples on their own personal issues? Didn't it make her a bit of a hypocrite, telling women to do one thing when she was doing the exact opposite in her own marriage? Their marriage definitely had its great moments, and she loved her husband. She was still attracted to Marcus, very attracted to him, but there had been a lot of hurdles. Marcus was a perfectionist, and it showed in his work, but sometimes it flowed through into their home, and sometimes Sophia felt that she could never have things well enough for his liking. He liked her to look good all the time, he liked the house to be clean, and he liked order in all things. It had been and it still was a bit of an adjustment, but she didn't want to fault him for liking things to be nice.

The biggest adjustment, though, was adapting to a life of fame, and having a famous husband. He worked long hours, alongside beautiful women, and she quickly had to learn how to decipher the truth from gossip when she started reading horrible stories about how their marriage was over on the cover of magazines in line at the grocery store. Over the last few years, she'd become insecure and jealous, and she began questioning Marcus on every ugly rumor she read, and, rightly so, Marcus would get furious with her and her lack of trust. A lot of it was her fault, he was right, and what kind of marriage could they have if they couldn't trust each other? Marcus was a bit on the jealous side, too. Sophia remembered, not long after they were married, running into her friend Adam, and how Marcus had refused to let her have lunch with him. She understood Marcus's reaction now. After all, would she be okay with him having lunch with another woman? Probably not.

As she sat at the island in her own little daydream, she heard the doorbell ring. She tossed the magazine to the side, stood up, and ran to the main entrance. Marcus walked up behind her as she opened the door for Marcus's parents, Bruce and Adele Donovan, as well as his younger sister, Olivia.

"Mom, Dad, Livy!" Marcus walked past Sophia to hug his family. "Merry Christmas! It is so good to see you guys, come on, come in," he said as he led them in the front door. Sophia stood off to the side, waiting for them to finish greeting each other, and then Adele turned to her.

"Sophia, my darling, come here, give me a hug." Adele reached out and hugged her tightly.

"Oh, honey, you are so skinny, have you not been eating well?" Adele asked as they pulled away from each other.

"Oh, Adele, of course, I've been eating well. Your son is a great cook." She winked up at Marcus. "It's just been really busy around here. I guess I've just forgotten a few meals here and there."

"Hi, Sophia, hope you are well," Bruce said as he came up to her and gave her a loose hug.

"Bruce, I am very well, thank you. I hope you're doing good as well," Sophia replied. Sophia, even after nearly three years of marriage to his son, was not at all comfortable around Bruce Donovan. She constantly felt like he was judging her, and thinking she was not quite good enough for his son. Adele, in turn, seemed to compensate for her husband's indifference with a rather obvious over-kindness. Olivia, on the other hand, who had already made her way into the living room.... Well, Sophia just never knew with her. It all really depended on her mood that day, if she was going to welcome Sophia or not. The two women were certainly not close, and Sophia actually preferred not to be around her, but she knew his family was important to Marcus, so she always made an effort with Olivia.

"Come, guys, come in," Sophia prompted as they all walked through the large entryway into the kitchen. "What can I get for you to drink?" she asked politely.

"Scotch on the rocks," Bruce barked.

"Oh, I will have a glass of red, please and thank you," Adele asked.

"Olivia, what about you?" Sophia called out as she retrieved the wine and scotch for her mother- and father-in-law.

"Wine will be fine," Olivia answered as she joined the rest of them in the kitchen. Sophia filled everyone's glasses and handed them out. Just then, the doorbell rang again, and Sophia quickly and happily ran to answer it. She was relieved to find some familiar and comforting faces. Her mother, Isabelle, stood with Cat, and a tall and attractive man holding a bottle of wine in one hand and a bouquet of flowers in the other.

"I am so happy to see you guys, get in here!" Sophia exclaimed as she ushered all three into the entry-way. She helped them with their jackets, putting them in the closet, and took the bottle of wine and flowers from Cat's friend.

"Sophia, this is Josh. Josh, Sophia." Cat introduced them as they reached out to shake each other's hand.

"So nice to meet you, Josh, come on in, guys, come on in, let me get you drink," Sophia said as she led them into the kitchen. As the four of them walked into the room, everyone stopped talking and stood, waiting for an introduction.

"Mom, this is Bruce and Adele Donovan, and this is Marcus's younger sister, Olivia."

Isabelle shook their hands while smiling.

"So nice to meet you all. It's about time, I guess, hey?" She laughed uncomfortably.

"Everyone, this is my best friend Cat, and her friend Josh," Sophia continued. After she finished the formalities of making sure everyone knew everyone's name, Sophia offered everyone else a drink, and then they continued to visit as she finalized the meal. After about another half hour, they were seated at the big formal dining table and digging into their first meal together as a family.

The conversation flowed rather nicely throughout dinner, and the drinks flowed just as easily. Everyone seemed in good spirits and to be getting along great. Sophia was feeling thankful that the evening was going just as planned. After they finished dessert, they all retired into the large living room and continued on with their conversation. They had, of course, all been interested in Marcus's new movie and who was going to be in it, especially Olivia. Having a famous brother definitely helped her love life, even if it only meant they were dating her because of who her brother was. Sophia stood up and excused herself to the kitchen to make some coffee for everyone, and just as she was about to start the pot, the doorbell rang.

"Who is that?" she asked herself softly as she headed to find out who could be there, on Christmas Eve.

She opened the door and saw Alex leaning against the entryway. She could tell he had been drinking, and was most likely high, as well. Sophia and Marcus had invited Alex and his wife, Taylor, over for dinner, but they declined without giving a reason as to why. Right away, Sophia thought their plans must have changed.

"Alex, hey, I am glad you guys could make it. Where is Taylor?" Sophia asked as she peeked out the door.

"Where is he, Soph?" Alex slurred heavily.

"Where is who?"

"Where is your son of a bitch husband, that's who. Where the fuck is he?" he asked again, this time pushing past Sophia and walking into the house.

Alex stumbled down the hall and found himself the center of attention as he came into the living room. As soon as Alex laid his eyes on Marcus, he leapt towards him, tackling Marcus out of his chair.

"You, son of a bitch, how could you? You, worthless piece of shit, I gave you everything!" Alex yelled while punching Marcus in the face. As soon as Marcus regained his composure, he managed to get Alex on the ground with one quick swoop, and he punched him in return.

"What the fuck is wrong with you, you piece of shit?" Marcus gave him one last punch, and was suddenly pulled off of Alex by Bruce and Josh. "What the hell is your Goddamn problem, Alex?" Marcus shouted, staring down at him.

Alex glared up at Marcus, with blood running out his nose and from a small cut above his eyebrow.

"You fucking make me sick you fucking bastard. I hope you rot in hell. You and I are done! We are over, you hear me? And if you ever look at, think about, or fuck my wife again, I swear to God, I am going to kill you."

The silence that suddenly filled the room was deafening, and everyone's attention shifted from Alex back to Marcus. He stood frozen to the ground, knowing everyone's eyes were on him, waiting for him to say something, but no words came to him, and it remained silent until Sophia spoke.

"Marcus?" Sophia asked with worry in her voice. "Marcus?" she said again. "What in the hell is he talking about?"

July 20, 2015 – Parade of Strangers

Within an hour, Sophia's house was filled with all sorts of people coming and going. The coroner had arrived and made his way upstairs to investigate the bodies, the crime scene unit was there to begin investigating the scene, and a bunch of people in suits were there for reasons Sophia couldn't guess. She was still sitting in her living room and had just finished speaking with Officer Pratt, recounting the events leading up to this morning. Sophia felt at ease speaking with her. Pratt was sympathetic to the situation, and Sophia was happy she was able to have the conversation with her instead of with Officer Brady. He intimidated her a lot, and right now she needed to maintain her composure and not let anything or anyone rattle her. She felt like she was in a circus. There were so many people, and cameras going off everywhere. She knew her home had become an official crime scene at this point, and it was terrifying her. She was doing her absolute best to stay in the frame of mind she was supposed to be in. As she sat silently, crying on the couch, a man and a woman entered the living room.

The woman, who wore her black hair pulled back in a tight bun, was dressed in a simple grey pantsuit over a white silk blouse. She was a smaller woman, standing only about five feet tall, but she had a serious look to her, and Sophia instantly knew she was not going to be as kind and welcoming as Officer Pratt had been. She walked up to Sophia and spoke in an abrupt tone.

"Mrs. Donovan?"

Sophia glanced up, suddenly feeling small and timid as the woman stood over her.

"Yes, I am Mrs. Donovan," she responded in between her silent tears.

"Mrs. Donovan, my name is Detective Jill Keller, and this is Detective Caleb Stone," she announced, and she turned to point to her partner.

Sophia stared up at Detective Keller as she made her introductions, and then shifted her attention to Detective Stone and studied him for a brief moment.

Detective Stone was about six feet tall, with dirty-blond hair that was combed back out of his hazel eyes. He wore a neatly trimmed beard, which enhanced his masculine facial features, especially his strong jawline. He wore an expensive-looking dark blue suit with a matching tie, and he carried a small notebook in the left breast pocket, which he reached for as he sat on the couch next to Sophia.

"Mrs. Donovan," he began, and Sophia quickly interrupted.

"Sophia, please. Call me Sophia."

Detective Stone nodded his head in acceptance to her request. "Sophia." He started again. "I know you have already been through everything with Officer Pratt, and I know this is very difficult, but I'm afraid we are going to have to ask you some more questions," He spoke softly.

Sophia's eyes were red and swollen, and she gave him a look of pure defeat as she slowly shifted her position on the couch.

"Of course, I understand," she replied, just as Detective Keller was pulling up a chair to sit facing Sophia and Detective Stone. Keller then also pulled out a small notebook and flipped open to a clean page, and retrieved a pen out of her breast pocket.

"Sophia, can you please tell us what time you arrived home to find your husband, Marcus, and Ms. Warner?" she asked as she began to write something on her pad. Sophia inhaled a quick, sharp breath and answered her.

"I got home about nine this morning."

"And where was it that you were coming from this morning?" Detective Keller continued.

"I was actually staying at the Malibu Seas Spa Resort, Marcus had given me an early anniversary present to go pamper myself for the weekend while he was in New York," she answered while wiping away more tears from her eyes. "I checked out this morning around eight and then I headed home."

As Detective Keller continued to jot down the information that Sophia was relaying, Detective Stone stepped in and asked her some follow-up questions.

"Sophia, may I ask you what your relationship with Ms. Warner was? How exactly did she fit it into yours and your husband's life?" Detective Stone asked as he got his pen ready

"Cat and I have been best friends for about eleven years. She has been part of our family for eleven years. I met Cat around the same time as I met Marcus and we have been best friends since. She and Marcus have always gotten along and been close as well, but I cannot understand what happened here. Detective Stone, what happened? Can you please tell me what is going on?" Sophia searched for answers as she looked at him with her big dark eyes, where tears welled again and fell down her cheeks.

"I understand this is confusing and scary, and you don't know what is going on, and that's why we're here, Sophia. We are going to find out what happened and who, exactly, is responsible for this. We're just going to need you to help us, and give us any information that you can, okay?" he asked her as he reached behind him and grabbed a Kleenex out of the holder to hand her.

"I don't know what you want me to tell you. None of this is making any damn sense to me. There is no reason either one of them would ever want to hurt each other, no." She shook her head. "No, this just is not happening, this is some kind of joke that someone is playing on me, right? Who would do this, and why? Why in the hell would someone do this?" Sophia was now raising her voice and becoming agitated. She stood from the couch and paced in front of the living room window.

"Mrs. Donovan, we just need you to stay calm, please. Any information you can give us will be helpful, whether you think it is or not. We will find out what went on here last night, and we will find out who did this, but, again, we are going to need you to give us your full cooperation and give us all the possible information you may have." Detective Keller stood and walked over to Sophia. "Mrs. Donovan?" Sophia kept pacing in front of the window, not giving her an answer. "Sophia?" she asked one more time. Sophia finally stopped pacing and turned to face the two detectives watching her.

"We're going to need you to come down to the station with us, please. We have a lot to go over, and we need to clear the scene to begin the investigation." Keller spoke seriously.

Sophia nodded her head in understanding and finally started to calm down.

"What about my things? Can I get some of my things?" Sophia asked, sounding like a lost child in search of their mom.

"This is now an official crime scene. Unfortunately, you won't be able to get any of your belongings until the investigation is complete. Do you have somewhere you can go for a little while? Friends, family?" Stone asked her, sounding concerned.

"Uh, I, uh, think so, yes. My God, I have to call his parents and his sister, I have to call my mom and Cat's father!" She began to panic again.

"Mrs. Donovan," Detective Stone began, then corrected himself. "Sophia, listen, we will take care of everything. Don't worry about all that right now. Right now we just need you to come with us, alright?"

Sophia again managed to calm herself down enough so she could answer him.

"Okay," she sighed deeply, nodding her head.

She was fully aware this was going to be part of the process, and she knew she was going to have to cooperate in everything that they asked of her, so she walked over to the table at the end of the couch and picked up her purse from where she had dropped it that morning.

Keller led the way out of the house, to where a black sedan was waiting in the driveway. Detective Keller opened the back door for her and waited till Sophia was seated in the back of the car before closing the door. Keller reached for her own handle, but not before glancing at Detective Stone over the roof of the car and giving him *that* look. That look, Caleb Stone knew, was the look Jill Keller got on her face when she thought she had the case figured out before it even began.

December 30, 2007 – Unapologetic

It had been nearly a week since the Christmas Eve disaster, and the Donovan household had been tense, to say the least. Marcus adamantly denied everything Alex had accused him of and told Sophia that he had no idea where any of this complete nonsense was coming from. She didn't know whether to believe him or not, but, regardless, Marcus had been spending every night in the guest suite to give her some space. Sophia needed time to figure out whether Marcus was telling her the truth, and if she should truly trust her husband. She desperately wanted to believe him, but there was a small part of her that wasn't sure if she should.

"Why would Taylor make this up?" she would often think to herself. She was not close to Alex's wife, by any means. They were two different people, and Sophia honestly thought that Taylor was with Alex for all of the wrong reasons, but, regardless, what would she have to gain from creating such a lie?

She spoke at length with Cat and her Mom about what she should do, and she would get conflicting advice. Her mother had already thought the relationship progressed much too quickly, and she often tried explaining to Sophia that it takes time to really get to know a person. Now, after witnessing what took place that night, she did not trust Marcus at all and was certain he must have cheated. Cat, on the other hand, was much more understanding. She told Sophia to trust her husband and what he was telling her, but then Cat also knew Marcus on a different level than Isabelle.

Marcus was in the living room watching football on this Sunday evening, while Sophia was in her bathroom, soaking in the tub, replaying the events of Christmas Eve over and over in her mind. She was desperately trying to comprehend what could possibly have happened to lead to that debacle, when suddenly she heard the doorbell chime downstairs. She had no idea who would be stopping over this late on a Sunday evening, but she slowly stepped out of the tub and put on her fuzzy housecoat, and decided to go down and see who it was. As she reached the top of the stairs, she could see Marcus with the door open, and when she made it halfway down the stairs she could see Alex standing outside with an envelope in his right hand. She walked up behind her Husband.

"Alex? What are you doing here?" she asked curiously.

"Sophia, Hey. listen, I was just telling Marcus that I owe you both an enormous apology for what happened here the other night. I am hoping I can come in and explain a few things and share with you what is going on," Alex replied, sounding sorrowful.

Marcus stepped back and glanced at his wife, waiting for her to be the one to decide if they should allow this man into their home again and hear what he had to say. Sophia peered up at Marcus for a quick moment, and then stepped aside.

"Come in, Alex." She motioned for him to enter the house and offered to take his jacket.

"Let's go in the kitchen and have some tea," she stated as she began heading into the kitchen to put on a kettle of water.

When the three of them were seated at the round table in the kitchen, they looked awkwardly at each other, waiting for someone to start speaking, to break the uneasy silence.

"Listen, you guys, I am so sorry. Marcus, man, I understand if you never want to forgive me, but just hear me out, okay?" He spoke nervously.

"Go ahead, then, explain why it is that you walked into my house on Christmas Eve and attacked me in front of my family, while accusing me of fucking your wife. I would really love to hear it, Alex." Marcus spoke angrily, and Sophia looked over at him and shook her head.

"Marcus, stop," she scolded, then turned to Alex again. "Alex, what is it?"

"Well, you guys know Taylor and I have not been, well, on the best of terms over the last little while. Christ, I know we got married way too fast and for the all the wrong reasons, but, regardless, she is my wife, and I do love her, or loved her.... Damn it, I don't even know anymore. Anyway, I think a part of me always knew that she was screwing around, but I just never wanted to admit it to myself. But then, on Christmas Eve, we were having a few drinks together and we ended up getting into a huge fight.

P a g e | **70**

Things got pretty nasty, to say the least, and that's when she told me that she slept with you, Marcus." Alex inhaled a deep breath and continued.

"When she told me that, I told her right away that I didn't believe her. I even called her a lying bitch and told her she was crazy, but she swore to me that you guys were sleeping together. She also insisted on going into every detail, which just enraged me more, and before I knew it I was here at your house causing a fucking mess on Christmas Eve."

Marcus quickly interrupted, "Alex where are you going with this?"

Alex closed his eyes and slowly nodded his head and continued, "Well, after I left here, I decided to go get a hotel room for a few days. I knew I wasn't ready to go home and face her, because I had no idea what I even wanted to do about the situation. She tried texting and calling me, telling me that we really needed to talk, but I didn't know what to say to her, so I just ignored her. I was furious, man." He paused and looked at Marcus, expecting some sort of reaction, then continued. "So I decided to head back home on Friday night, and I was ready to talk to her about it all, and I was willing to work on things and see what we could do to save our marriage. Shit, I knew with how I handled the situation with you, and with the information I had at the time, I was sure our friendship was going to be over, but I knew I had to try and fix my marriage first, and I hope you can understand that." Alex paused, and he pulled the letter out of the envelope and he handed it to Marcus to read. He took the letter out of the envelope and slid closer to Sophia so they could both see what was in the letter.

Alex,
I have to apologize for what happened the other night. I lied to you. I never slept with Marcus, he has never even tried to flirt with me, let alone sleep with me, but I knew how much it would hurt you to say that it was him. I think you know that I have not been faithful to you and in that moment, when you were accusing and demanding to know who it was, I just decided to tell you the one person who I know would hit you the hardest. I tried, Alex, but I have to be honest, I am just not in love

70

with you. Trust me, my leaving is for the best, otherwise, someone is going to end up getting hurt even more than they already have.
  Goodbye

When Marcus and Sophia were both finished reading the letter, he slowly folded it back up and handed it back to Alex. The three of them sat silently at the table for several long moments before Alex spoke again.

  "Like I said, she was my wife and I loved her. I never thought she would just make something like this up to hurt me, and, plus, it didn't help that when she told me I was drunk and didn't care to think about my actions. When I got home Friday evening, all of her shit – and a lot of my shit – was gone, with this fucking letter lying on my pillow." Alex tossed the letter on the table. "But, Marcus, you have to believe me when I tell you how sorry I am that I trusted this bitch's word without even getting your side of the story. Not only that, I feel like a complete asshole for coming over here and ruining your guys' family dinner." He sat back in the chair and rubbed his hands through his hair and then looked from Marcus to Sophia.

  Sophia and Marcus turned and looked at each other after Alex had finally finished speaking, and Sophia could see her husband was trying to process all that he just heard. Hell, she was trying to process what she just heard. Marcus knew Alex better than almost anyone, and he also knew he was extremely impulsive and rarely thought out his actions. He also knew that if Sophia had ever told him something like this, he would have done the exact same thing as Alex, only worse. Marcus sighed deeply, and reached over and patted Alex on the shoulder.

  "Hey, man, it's all good. I don't blame you. I would have done the same thing. I just don't know why she would fabricate such bullshit just to piss you off. She really must have been out to hurt you. Hey, if you ask me, man, you are much better off without that woman in your life, Alex. You should probably be thankful she left," Marcus chuckled, and turned to look at his wife.

  Alex looked relieved at Marcus's reaction. He was, frankly, not sure if Marcus was going to believe him or accept his apology.

He certainly didn't think he would understand, let alone forgive him so quickly.

"I'm glad to hear it, man. I was really worried about coming here after what I did, but when I found this little note of hers, my mind was blown to shit. I don't know what I was thinking with her. I knew I couldn't trust her. Jesus, I knew she was fucking around, but I didn't think she would bring you into her lies," Alex responded with a sigh of relief.

Sophia sat and listened to the two men talking, and was somewhat confused at what was taking place. She knew how upset Marcus had been at the whole situation, and didn't think he was going to ever forgive Alex. She knew Alex was sincere – in fact, she had never witnessed such sincerity out of this man. It was just unclear to her why his wife would say these things and then up and leave him days later. Was Marcus lying? Was Alex lying? Or was Taylor lying? Sophia honestly didn't know, but what she did know was that something didn't seem right.

She should trust her husband, though, she thought. She trusted him when it came to all the gossip in the magazines, so why not this? As she sat, trying to sort out the conflicting emotions going on her mind, Marcus snapped her back to attention.

"Well?" he asked her.

"Well?" Sophia responded, obviously not having heard him the first time.

"So can you please tell me this means we are okay? I told you I didn't sleep with her. Why would I ever sleep with her, let alone anyone else, and jeopardize our marriage and what we have? You know I love you, Babe," Marcus said while reaching for Sophia's hand across the table.

She gave a soft smile at him and allowed him to briefly hold her hand, just as the teapot began to whistle. She got up from the table and grabbed three mugs from the cupboard. As she filled the glasses and placed a tea bag into each steaming mug, she couldn't seem to shake the cold, uneasy feeling that was washing over her. She turned and walked back to the table, carefully balancing the hot mugs, and then set them down on the table and took her seat again.

"Soph," Alex began, "I'm sorry I had to put you through this. I just hope you can also forgive me, and please don't hold any of this against Marcus. This was a huge misunderstanding. I know how much he loves you, and he would never do anything like this to you."

"Come on, Babe, you know I wouldn't hurt you like that. Why would I do that to you? I just need to know we are okay. I love you, Soph, I just want you to know that."

Reaching across the table, she grabbed her husband's hand and gave it a tight, little squeeze.

"I love you, too," she replied softly.

Marcus sighed a deep breath of relief as he leaned back in his chair. He never wanted to hurt Sophia, or Alex for that matter, and hated what they both had to be put through these last several days. But, he had done what was necessary to resolve the situation. He was just thankful that Taylor, unlike Sophia, was easy to manipulate into doing what he needed her to do.

July 20, 2015 – Lie to Me

The interrogation room was hot and muggy, and the coffee was bitter and stale. For the last few hours, Sophia sat and answered more questions than she could even care to remember. They asked her everything she was prepared for, as well as questions that she was not expecting, but she thought she had remained amazingly calm throughout the entire process. Her nerves were rattled, and she was exhausted. She had never been so exhausted in her life.

Detectives Keller and Stone were both sitting across the metal table from her, with their pens and notepads, taking detailed notes on everything she had to share with them. Finally, Jill Keller took the last sip of coffee from her Styrofoam mug and closed her notebook.

"Thank you, Mrs. Donovan, you were very cooperative. I hope you understand that this is going to be a very high profile case, because of who your husband was, and I just want you to be prepared for a lot more questioning and, even more, publicity. This is going to hit the media fast, and we do need to ask that you not leave the area for the next little while, in case we need to reach you." Detective Keller spoke matter-of-factly. She was usually blunt and showed little sympathy towards Sophia – or anyone, in any of her cases, for that matter.

"I understand," Sophia replied quietly.

"Like I said earlier, your home is now an official crime scene. We will advise you when the investigation is complete, and at that point, you can do with the property what you will."

"I know this is going to be extremely difficult for you. Do you have friends and family that will pull together and help you out in the meantime?" Detective Stone asked.

She replied to Stone, "Yes, of course, my mother should be here shortly. I called her as soon as we arrived at the station."

All three of them then stood up from the table and Detective Stone walked to the door, holding it open for the two women. Detective Keller left the room first, and Sophia followed behind her. As she passed Detective Stone, she looked up at him with an expression of childlike fear and he gave her a warm smile before closing the door behind them. Sophia made her way to the front, with Stone trailing behind her, and as she came around the corner, Sophia saw her mother sitting in the waiting area. She had her jacket wrapped around her arm, in her lap, while she chewed nervously at her fingernails. She glanced up at the sound of the door opening, and as soon as she saw her daughter, she stood up, rushed toward her, and pulled her into her arms.

"Oh, my God! Sophia, baby, are you alright?" she cried as she buried her face in Sophia's hair.

Sophia instantly had tears rush to her eyes at the sight of her mother, and being held made her feel like a young girl again. Having her mother with her was the most at ease she had felt during this entire process.

"I'm okay, Mom, but Marcus and Cat are dead. They are both dead." She wept as her mother held her.

"I know, sweetie, I know. Listen to me, we're going to get through this, do you understand? We are going to get through this," Isabelle soothed her daughter, as Sophia continued to cry in her arms.

Detective Stone stood and watched the two women, and he could feel his heart breaking for Sophia. He knew this was the most difficult thing she was probably ever going to go through, and he knew what the next few months were going to look like for her. Her husband was a major player in the Hollywood scene, and this was not going to be quietly swept under the rug.

Detective Keller came up behind him. "Is that the mother?" she asked curtly.

"Yes, it is," he replied.

Detective Keller walked up to the two women, but gave them a moment, not wanting to interrupt them.

"I'm sorry." Sophia wiped her eyes as she pulled away from her mother. "Mom, this is Detective Keller. She's one of the investigating officers on the case. This is my mother, Isabelle Vaughn."

"Mrs. Vaughn, I am sorry to have to meet you under these circumstances. However, I trust that Mrs. Donovan can be entrusted into your care, and as we explained to her earlier, we are going to need her to remain in the area during the course of this investigation, in case we need to speak further with her. I just want to make sure you are both in full understanding of that."

"Detective Keller," Isabelle began, "I am going to take care of my daughter. I will be here with her, by her side, until you guys figure out what in the hell happened in that house last night and you can assure me that my daughter is not in any sort of danger." Isabelle pulled Sophia tightly to her side while fixing her stare on the Detective.

"Come, baby, let's go. Let's get you home to rest." She led Sophia towards the front entrance, as Detective Keller followed them out of the station.

Sophia stopped and turned to Detective Keller. "Detective Keller, none of this is making any damn sense to me right now, so please just tell me that you are going to figure out what happened?" She looked at Keller desperately. Detective Keller folded her arms in front of her chest and inhaled deeply before answering.

"Mrs. Donovan, I can promise you I am going to find out exactly what went on in your home last night. I eat, sleep and breathe my job, and if there is one thing I will not tolerate, it is leaving a case unsolved. I will find out what happened to your husband and Ms. Warner. I will find out the truth no matter who tries to get in my way."

Sophia and Jill Keller stood looking each other dead in the eyes, and Sophia felt a chill crawl slowly up her spine. She'd had a feeling, the first moment she met this detective, that she was going to be a problem. Sophia just prayed she did not become too much of a problem. Isabelle, suddenly feeling her daughter's discomfort, shot Detective Keller a piercing stare and pulled Sophia gently by the arm.

"Come, Sophia, let's get you home," she uttered, pulling her daughter in her arms again.

May 7, 2008 – Forgiven

Sophia sat in her office and stared blankly at her computer screen, unable to get any words from her brain to the keyboard. Her office sat tucked in the far back corner of the fifth floor, which was entirely occupied by LA Today. Sophia's advice column had been a huge success over the last couple of years, and she had since been put in charge of a new feature, which they called "Inside LA". Every week, she covered a different celebrity's home, so the fans could get an up-close-and-personal, inside look into the houses of LA's elite. Actors, athletes, celebrity chefs, politicians and even other authors were given the opportunity to showcase the inner workings of their lives and to put their beautiful homes on display. With two major articles every week, Sophia found herself with a hectic and busy full-time career. She still enjoyed writing the advice column, but she quickly fell in love with "Inside LA". She got to meet some amazing people – and some not-so-amazing people, but it kept things interesting – and she did get to see a lot of gorgeous homes. Today, though, she was focusing on her advice column, and her mind was blank as she stared at the screen.

"Hey, you got a minute?" Samuel Ellis asked, while softly knocking on Sophia's open door.

Sophia looked up from her screen and was happy to see Sam standing in her doorway. Samuel Ellis was one of the Chief Editors at LA Today. He was a captivating individual, always fashionably dressed, his dark hair impeccably styled, and he always had a smile on his handsome, tanned face. He had a way about him that cheered a person up, just by walking into the room, no matter what kind of shitty day they were having. He was the one who offered Sophia the "Inside LA" section of the Magazine after he saw how much the readers loved her "Love in LA" column.

"Good Morning Sam. Yes, come on in. You know I always have a minute for you.

He placed a manila folder on her desk, then took a seat across from her.

"I just got this week's list of available potentials. Let me know who you want, and I will get it set up for you. I swear to God,

I don't know how some of these people make the list each week. Victoria Porter? Really? Since when are The Housewives of Newport considered elite? I am not sure who's putting these potentials lists together, but I think we have differing views on elite." Sam laughed sarcastically, then picked up the folder and scanned the list.

"Well, maybe you're just getting too old to know who's hot and who's not," Sophia teased Sam with a laugh.

"I must be. Jesus, what is the city coming to?" he laughed back at Sophia. "So how are things at home? Is the wretched sister-in-law still staying with you? You know, I don't understand how you two haven't thrown that little snot out on her ass by now."

Sophia smirked at Sam's description of Olivia and nodded.

"Yes, she's still here, and Marcus and I have had so many fights about it lately. I told him that it's time for her to go. She was only supposed to stay with us for a few days, and it's been three weeks now. God, I honestly don't know how he got through sixteen years living in the same house as her! She's impossible to deal with, her mood swings are unpredictable, she's spoiled and she's lazy, and I have had it with her."

Sam smiled and shook his head, amazed that Sophia had allowed the woman to stay in her home for so long. He knew Sophia wanted to make Marcus happy, but, like Sam had told her numerous times before, it was time to step up and tell Olivia to find someone else to torment.

"Listen, Honey, I am telling you: you need to kick that sister to the curb. Marcus, well, he's just going to have to deal with it. You know the saying, 'happy wife, happy life', and is it ever true. Hey, why don't you join me and Devon for dinner tonight? We would love it if you could. Get away from Medusa for a while," Sam offered excitedly.

Sophia took a second to think about whether there was any reason she couldn't sneak away for a little bit that evening. It would be nice, not having to go home right after work to deal with Olivia, and she was sure Marcus wouldn't mind. He never cared when she and Sam got together, especially not if Sam's boyfriend was with them.

"Sure, you know what? I would love to join you guys. I haven't seen Devon in a little while, and I could use a few drinks, and a few laughs, and you two, well I know you're definitely good for that."

Sam was thrilled that she accepted, and stood up from his chair. "Fantastic, I will let Devon know. He will be so excited to see you." Sam turned to head out, but then came back to Sophia's desk. He placed both hands on the edge of the desk, looking serious suddenly. "But...."

He paused for a second, and Sophia looked up at him, confused. "But what?" she asked.

"Honey, you need to promise me that tonight, you are going to go home after dinner, and you are going to tell your husband that you want his crazy sister out of your house by the weekend. You have to promise me you're going to do that, okay?"

Sophia laughed and reached over to touch Sam's arm, and replied, "Okay, Sam, for you, I will. I promise."

He left her office, and she reached for her cell phone to call Marcus and let him know she would be home late.

She pulled up outside of her house about nine that evening, after a fantastic dinner. She sat in her car for a few moments, enjoying the silence, preparing herself for the circus that had recently become her home. She'd promised to talk to Marcus tonight about asking Olivia to leave, but she knew it was going to cause another fight. She stared at the lights glowing inside the house as she remembered how the last conversation went, about a week before:

"Sophia, she's my sister. I'm not just going to throw her out on the street, not when she needs us right now." Marcus raised his voice to her.

"Marcus, damn it, she was only supposed to be here for a few days, and it's been almost two weeks. Christ! She is moody, rude, and she hasn't done a damn thing to help around this place since she got here. It would be one thing if she showed some goddamn gratitude, but she doesn't give a shit, Marcus. You need to grow a pair of fucking balls and tell her she needs to get out of our house, and soon. This is bullshit, and I'm not going to continue being uncomfortable in my own house!" Sophia responded, her voice also rising.

Marcus did a double-take, shocked at the way she was speaking to him. He stepped towards her, his finger pointed at her. She could see the anger that was beginning to take over, and she took a step back from him.

"This is not your decision, do you hear me? I will not have you tell me what I need to do in my own home, and I will certainly not have you try to come in between me and my family, do you understand? I don't know at what point you climbed up on to your fucking high horse and became such a selfish bitch, but you can be damn sure that I am not going allow you to tell me what I have to do, and if you ever speak to me that way again, Sophia, I swear to God you will regret it."

Those words still stung Sophia, even a week later, and even though Marcus did apologize for the way he spoke to her, she could not forget the anger she saw in his eyes that night. The words rang in her ears for days, even though he swore to her that he didn't mean anything he said. They had definitely had their share of arguments, but this one was different. It was as if a switch had gone off, and he had become someone she was unfamiliar with, and it scared her. She was nervous about approaching the subject again with him, but he had told her, afterward, that they could talk about it again if Olivia had not found her own place.

She stepped out of her vehicle and entered the house through the main door. She headed into the kitchen, hoping to find Marcus. Instead, Olivia was seated at the island, drinking a beer while she chatted on her cell phone. Sophia was not surprised to see the mess that surrounded her: dirty plates, and empty beer bottles. Olivia noticed Sophia and quickly got off of her call.

"Oh, hey," Olivia said as she hung up her phone.

"Hey," Sophia responded, with clear frustration, before continuing, "So any leads today on a place?"

"Nah, you know how it is. All shit out there, or too damn expensive." Olivia cocked her head to the side, then said, "You seem pretty concerned about me finding a place. I didn't realize I was on a timeline." She glared up at Sophia.

"Olivia, I'm not getting into this with you right now. I'm exhausted."

"Get into what? There's nothing to get into. Marcus invited me to stay till I could get my feet on the ground, and that's what I'm doing. As far as I'm concerned, it's not your decision when it's time for me to leave, so maybe you should just keep your nose out of my business unless I ask for your opinion."

Sophia knew exactly what Olivia was trying to do, and she wasn't going to buy into it. She just shook her head at Olivia, grabbed her purse, and headed up the stairs to find Marcus, who was lying on the bed, watching ESPN while sipping a glass of Scotch. When he saw her enter, he sat up and hit the mute button.

"Hey, baby, what's up? You don't look happy at all," he said, concerned.

"Look, Marcus I don't want to fight with you about this again, but I cannot handle her here anymore. The place is a mess downstairs, she is drinking us out of our booze, and the lack of respect for me is unbelievable. Honey, please, I don't want to fight about this, but we really need to talk about telling her it is time to leave," Sophia pleaded.

Marcus shook his head gently while motioning for her to sit on the bed. Sophia did, and Marcus pulled her into him.

"Babe, I told you how sorry I am about the other night, and I am. I'm so sorry. I had no right to speak to you like that. I was just tired and stressed, and I just got really defensive, but you know what? You're right. It is time for her to go. She has worn out her welcome, and she is disrespectful to you, and it's time I ask her to go. I promise she will be gone by this weekend," he said, then kissed the top of her head. Sophia turned to face him.

"Really? Really?" She was almost certain she must have heard him wrong. Marcus nodded in response, and she lunged at him, spilling his scotch over the side of his glass. He placed the glass on the nightstand and pulled her on top of him.

"Well, if I'd known I was going to get this response, I would have asked her to leave a long time ago," he laughed as he pulled his wife closer.

She wrapped her arms tight around his neck and kissed him deeply on the mouth, and, after the tension in the house over the last week, it immediately awoke both of their desires. Marcus flipped Sophia onto her back and ripped at the button on her jeans, pulling them down onto the floor. He stood and quickly undressed, and as he did, Sophia pulled her shirt over her head and tossed it to the floor. Before falling back on top of her, Marcus yanked off her panties and threw them over his shoulder. He took her face gently in between his hands and kissed her passionately, tracing her lips and her tongue with his.

"I am sorry, I love you so much," he whispered in her ear as he pushed himself deep inside her. She threw her head back with a loud moan as he entered her, and as he continued to push deeper, she gripped his back, as if he might slide away from her. Before she knew it, he had flipped her over on her stomach, and entered her from behind as he pulled on her hair. She dug her hands into the duvet under her and, as he sped up, she bit her pillow to try and stifle her moans. The intensity of it was too much for him and he let himself go, instantly becoming weak in the knees, and he then fell down beside Sophia, who was still trying to catch her breath. Still lying on her stomach, she turned her head to look at Marcus, who was also breathing deeply. He smiled and said, "Jesus, maybe we need to fight like that more often."

July 20, 2015 – Mommy Dearest

Isabelle and Sophia pulled up outside of the beach house around three o'clock that afternoon. There was not much spoken between the two women on the drive out to Malibu, but Isabelle knew her daughter just needed some time before she was ready to talk about it. Inside the house, all of the curtains had been drawn, and it was clear that the housekeeper had recently been there to clean. The aroma of pine mixed with the smell of the saltwater in the air. Isabelle opened the curtains and the windows to let the sunshine and the summer breeze flow into the house, then walked into the kitchen and inspected the contents of the near-empty refrigerator. She made a note to herself to run out to the grocery store once Sophia finally fell asleep. She walked back into the living room and noticed her daughter was sitting on the edge of the sofa with her hands folded in her lap. Tears were slowly falling down Sophia's cheeks, so Isabelle immediately walked over and sat down next to her.

"Oh, honey, I'm so sorry you have to go through this. Is there anything I can do for you?"

Sophia looked up and met her mother's eyes. "Oh, Mom, I don't know what to do." She continued weeping as she reached to pull her mother towards her.

Isabelle held her tightly in her arms, rocking her back and forth as she whispered, "It's okay, baby, it's okay. I'm here for you."

Sophia reluctantly pulled away from her mother, and reached into her purse for her cell phone. She held it in her lap, knowing what she had to do next.

"Mom, I have to call Marcus's family. I have to see how they are. My God, Mom I don't know what I'm going to say to them. Adele is going to be devastated. I wish there was something I could say to all of them to help give them answers. I know they're going to want answers, but, Mom, I don't have any."

Isabelle touched Sophia's arm. "I know this is hard, honey, but they need you now. I know you don't have any answers for them, but, sweetheart, it's so important that you're all here for one another right now. It's time to call them, sweetheart."

Taking a deep breath, Sophia scrolled through her contacts until she came to Adele and Bruce Donovan. For a moment she sat, just staring at her phone, unable to bring herself to hit send. Finally, she hit the button and waited for someone to pick up. It rang three times, and Sophia thought for a moment that she wasn't going to get an answer, but then she heard Marcus's dad on the other end.

"Hello?" Bruce's voice was deep and hollow. Sophia could hear his pain through the line and it genuinely broke her heart.

"Bruce, this is Sophia."

"Sophia. Oh, my God, Sophia."

"Bruce I am so sorry. How is Adele?" Sophia responded, her voice quivering.

"Sophia, can you please tell us what happened? Who did this to our son?"

Sophia tried desperately to remain composed, but hearing the devastation in Bruce's voice was too much. She realized how severely she underestimated how difficult this part was going to be. She wiped the heavily-flowing tears from her eyes and reached for a tissue off of the coffee table.

"I don't know, Bruce, I don't understand who would do this to them," Sophia lied. "I found them this morning when I got back from the weekend. I don't know how to make any sense out of this, Bruce, I just don't know who would do this. Oh, my God, how are Adele and Olivia?"

There was silence on the other end of the phone, and she thought that the call got disconnected, but suddenly Adele Donovan was on the line.

"Sophia?"

"Adele, yes it's me. I am so terribly sorry." Sophia cried into the phone at the sound of Adele's voice.

"What happened to my baby? Sophia, please, who would want to hurt my Marcus? You have to know something, anything."

"Please, Adele, I wish I knew something. The house is being investigated and nobody has given me any answers. I'm at the beach house for now," Sophia replied, certain Adele would be able to sense her guilt.

"We're on our way there," Adele exclaimed frantically, before suddenly hanging up the phone. Sophia sat with the phone up to her ear for several seconds before realizing the line had gone dead. She put her phone down on the coffee table and fell back against the couch. She placed her palm over her forehead, covering her eyes. Her heart sank, knowing she was the one responsible for this unbearable pain she had caused, but she reminded herself of why she had done this.

"They're on their way here, Mom."

"You did great, sweetie. You told them all you know, and that's all you could do. They're in shock right now, and when things calm down it will be okay. We can all wait together to find out what happened. That's all we can really do right now."

Marcus's parents had settled in Riverside, which was about an hour north of LA, a couple of years before to be closer to Marcus and Olivia. Sophia knew they had hoped that grandkids would have been in the picture by now, but as hard as she and Marcus tried over the last several years, there was just no baby. She was desperate to have a baby, but Marcus had refused to seek medical intervention. He insisted it was not his fault, and he would at times make Sophia feel guilty that they had not yet gotten pregnant. It seemed every time they fought, he would jump at the opportunity to ask her what kind of wife she was when she couldn't even bear him a child. She knew now it wasn't her fault, but parts of her still felt for his parents, especially Adele, who seemed to be waiting for a miracle. And when Sophia discovered the secrets about her husband, she knew she would never have a family, at least not with Marcus.

"They're going to be here in, like, an hour, Mom. I just don't know if I have it in me to do this."

"Don't worry. You do only what you can handle right now. Let them come here, and explain to them what you know, but sweetie, you're really going to need to get some rest soon. You can't over-do it, not now. I understand they're going to be shocked and devastated, but I won't allow them to come in here and push you to your breaking point." Isabelle reached for her daughter's hand again.

"Oh, Mom, I'm so glad I have you right now. I don't know what I would do without you." Sophia glanced down at her phone, and then back at her mother. "I don't even know where to begin looking for Paul. My God, Cat hasn't spoken to him in at least a couple of years."

She scrolled through her phone, searching for the last number she had for Cat's father, Paul. He had left Cat's mom, Tatianna, when Cat was only about five years old. Paul was a lost cause. He chose to give up his family to chase the easiest and quickest high. He could never hold a job, and God forbid he knew how to stay faithful to his wife, so it was probably the best thing for everyone when he disappeared. Tatianna Warner struggled to raise her daughter on her own, but she did the best she could until she eventually passed away of cancer when Cat was twenty-two. When Cat was about twenty-four, her father decided that he wanted to be a part of her life again. Things were okay for them for a little while, but eventually, Cat realized that he had not changed at all. When he was around, he was hitting her up for money or a place to crash, but he was never there for her when she needed him, and it affected her greatly. Sophia believed deep down that Cat's unhealthy relationship with her father was a contributing factor in the path that she eventually took.

Sophia pressed the send button when she found the number she had for Paul. It rang a few times, and then a recording sounded on the other end. "We're sorry. The number you are trying to call is currently out of service. If you feel you have reached this recording in error, please check the number and try your call again."

"Damn it," Sophia muttered, and tossed the phone on the coffee table. "That's the only number I have for him. I wouldn't even know how else to reach him."

"Sophia, if he's anywhere near a TV, the news is going to reach him. Sadly, this is going to spread fast. Don't worry about him right now. Please, just worry about yourself." Isabelle's concern for her daughter was heavy on her face.

Sophia spent the next hour-and-a-half telling her mother what happened. She explained how, when she returned home from the resort, she found Marcus and Cat. She explained to her the phone call to the police, the officers, and everyone coming into her home, and then she told her about the interrogation from Detective Stone and Detective Keller. Isabelle's heart was heavy as she listened to what her daughter had gone through, and she would have done anything to take away her pain.

Just as Sophia was finishing her story, there was a loud knock at the door. She jumped in her seat. Even though she was fully expecting them, the abrupt knock startled her. Looking to her mother for reassurance, she knew she had to get this over with, so she got up and went to open the door. Bruce, Adele, and Olivia stood, silent and deathly pale. As soon as Adele saw her daughter-in-law, she began to cry hysterically. Bruce put his arm around his wife and, just as Sophia was about to invite them in, Olivia barged through the front door, pushing Sophia out of the way. She quickly swung around, facing Sophia with a vengeance in her eyes.

"You bitch," Olivia spat towards Sophia. "Tell me what happened to my fucking brother. Now!"

September 1, 2009 – The Watcher

"God, Cat, I don't know what's wrong. I can't figure out why I'm having such a hard time getting pregnant. My doctor says everything is fine, so I just don't get it," Sophia exclaimed in frustration before taking a sip of her iced tea. They were sitting outside, having lunch at a chic little café on Melrose Ave.

"Well, maybe you're just putting too much pressure on yourselves. You know, stress can do funky things to the body. You just need to stop trying so hard, and just, I don't know, try enjoying the sex part. You know, it's going to start becoming a chore soon if you keep getting disappointed that there's no baby every time you fuck your husband."

Stuffing a forkful of salad in her mouth, Sophia nearly choked at Cat's blunt remark. "Ugh. Maybe you're right, though. I am thinking too much about it, and I'm putting too much pressure on the whole situation. I'm just getting so tired of counting the days, to know when I'm menstruating, and when I'm ovulating, trying to find out when I'm fertile and not fertile, and you know what? It is, it's starting to become like a chore. We used to be so spontaneous, and we could make love anywhere, but lately, unless it's approved by my calendar it's like it just doesn't happen. I just want a baby," she whined as she stuck her bottom lip out.

Cat smiled at her friend with sympathy.

"I know you do, babe, and you will get one. It just takes time, sometimes, but before you know it you will have a sweet little bundle of joy keeping you up all hours of the night because it's hungry or thirsty or, I don't know, because it needs its shitty diaper changed or something." Cat laughed loudly, then continued, "Come on, Soph, you know it will happen. You will have a baby, just be patient. Has Marcus gone to the doctor to see if his baby-makers are up and running?"

Sophia had nearly spat out her iced tea as she listened to Cat's description of motherhood. She finished swallowing, then answered, "Oh, I tried getting him to go, but he insists he's fine. I don't know if he's scared or what, but he keeps saying it will happen when it happens. He thinks if we have to start exploring medical help to have a baby, then maybe it's just not meant to be. I don't know. What if I just don't have one? I could get too old you know? And it could just very well never happen. I'm thirty-two years old, Cat. I don't know how much longer I'm willing to push it. I guess I just need to let destiny take the reins, and what shall be, shall be."

"Exactly," Cat agreed.

"So, remember, the premiere starts at seven tomorrow. Do you know which lucky gentleman you're bringing with you yet?" Sophia half-teased.

"Ah, you know what? I think I would rather just fly solo tomorrow night. You know how many hot guys are going to be there. Jesus, it would be like bringing sand to a beach! Yeah, you know what? I think I'm going to just be a third wheel, if you don't mind? At least until the party starts." Cat winked at Sophia. "I can't believe Marcus has another movie coming out already. Too bad he can't pump out baby juice at the rate he pumps out new movies." Cat, instantly realizing what she said, clasped her hand over her mouth.

"Catarina Warner!" Sophia scolded. She tried to keep a straight face, but she knew Cat's sick sense of humour, and both women instantly broke out laughing. Sophia crumpled up her napkin and tossed it at Cat's face.

"You are so bad, you know that?" Sophia continued, laughing.

"Oh, honey, you have no idea," Cat joked in return.

Sophia continued chuckling softly to herself, but stopped when she noticed a familiar face walking in the direction of the café.

"Oh, my God," she whispered to Cat over the table.

"What? What it is it? Why are we whispering?" Cat hunched over the table, getting closer to hear Sophia.

Sophia, realizing how silly she must sound, began speaking in a regular tone.

"It's Adam. You remember, I told you about him. He's the one that I ran into when Marcus and I were out for our anniversary dinner," Sophia explained.

"Oh, Adam," Cat gasped. "You mean the guy that Marcus had a hissy fit over because he wanted to have lunch with you? That Adam?"

"Yes, that Adam." Sophia wasn't sure if he was going to notice her sitting there, but as he got closer, he looked up from his phone and instantly recognized her.

"Sophia? Hey!" Sounding as surprised as he looked, he walked up to the table.

"Adam! Oh, my God, hey! I'm so happy to see you again," Sophia exclaimed, and she stood up to give him a hug.

Cat smiled up at them. She could see the friendship that still lingered between them, even after years of not seeing each other. She didn't understand why Marcus had such an issue with Adam. He seemed like a sweet guy.

"Adam, this is my friend Cat Warner. Cat, this is Adam. Don't worry, she's already heard plenty about you. My mom loves to share old stories about us growing up." Sophia giggled as she touched his arm.

"Hey, Cat, it's so nice to meet you." Adam reached for her hand.

"You as well, Adam, and she's right, you know. I do know an awful lot about you, and that could be a good thing or a bad thing, you know?" Cat gave him a wink.

"Hey, listen, Adam, I never did get the chance to apologize for the last time we ran into each other. You know, so much came up and things got super crazy. I'm so sorry I couldn't make lunch; I hope you understand."

Adam nodded and waved his hand in the air. "Oh, I understand. I know you have a very busy life, Soph. I know who your husband is, and I get it. I can't imagine how much you guys have on the go. Please, don't worry about it all." He reached into his pocket and handed her another card. "Here, hang on to this, and please give me a call, and hopefully over the next little while things will slow down enough for us to be able to go for lunch, or grab a drink." He glanced over at Cat and continued, "And, hey, you should join us. You got to hear lots of stories about me. I think it's only fair I get to be privy to some of the wild shit you two have gotten into."

"Sounds like a deal to me," Cat said as he reached to shake her hand again.

Adam grabbed Sophia and gave her another tight hug, then a soft kiss on the cheek.

"Try not to get too busy to call me this time, would ya?" he said as he pulled away from her. He turned to Cat one more time. "It was a pleasure meeting you, Cat. I hope to see you again soon."

"Oh, you will," she responded with a flirtatious grin.

Adam continued down the street, and turned around to give both women a final wave, and when he was out of sight, Cat immediately turned to Sophia and said, "Well you could have told me he was so damn cute! Oh, come on, hand over that business card. You don't mind if I call him, do you?"

"No, of course not. I kind of got the vibe that he was into you. Here, put his number in your phone." Sophia handed Cat the card.

"Well, who knows? Maybe I won't go to the premiere solo, after all." She looked at the card and continued, "Maybe Mr. Doucette wouldn't mind escorting me."

Across the street, Marcus sat behind the tinted windows of his Escalade, watching his wife toss her head back in laughter. It was a good thing he had called her office to find out where she was having lunch today, otherwise, he was sure Sophia would have failed to mention she was with the man that he specifically asked her to stay away from. As he inhaled a deep breath, to try and remain calm, he started the engine of his SUV and headed out onto Melrose, driving in the direction that Adam Doucette had walked.

July 21, 2015 – The Dawning of Reality

Sophia's eyes barely wanted to open as her body slowly began to wake. She felt like she had been hit by a train. Every muscle in her body ached, her head was pounding, and the sheer exhaustion she felt was nearly too much to take. She could hear the waves crashing on the shore outside of her window, and the warm summer breeze was blowing through the open patio doors. Had it been any other, regular summer morning, it would have been absolutely gorgeous. But with the weight of the last twenty-four hours sitting heavily in her chest, Sophia wanted nothing more than to curl into a ball and die. She thought back to the events of the day before, and the extensive interrogation that followed, and then the encounter with Marcus' family. It still wasn't over. Now she had to prepare herself for the Hollywood shit storm that was about to break out.

She tried to focus on her bedside alarm clock, and had to rub the sleep from her eyes before the numbers became clear. It was almost four in the afternoon.

"Jesus," Sophia whispered to herself, and she slowly slid into a sitting position, leaning against her headboard.

It had been nearly eighteen hours since her mother tucked her in. She knew she'd been tired, but she didn't think she would sleep straight through to the next afternoon. But, after the long, drawn-out process of telling Marcus's parents and sister what happened, she was surprised she woke up at all. His mother just sat and cried hysterically the whole time, while Bruce cradled her in his arms. Olivia, on the other hand, was nearly out of control as she stormed around demanding answers. Even after explaining to her what happened Sophia could sense Olivia was not satisfied with the answers she was given. Olivia continued to pace back and forth across the living room, demanding to know more details, until she finally gave up and headed to the liquor cabinet to pour herself a glass of vodka. It wasn't much later than that when Bruce knew it was time to take his daughter back to the hotel that they had gotten in LA. He told Sophia he wanted to be near the scene and close to the investigation, as if he could offer anything to this case.

Sophia sighed deeply and turned her head to stare out at the ocean waves crashing against the beach. She could see people out walking in the sand enjoying the warmth of the day. She wished desperately at this moment that she could just be one of those people out walking with no worries or cares. Moments later, Sophia heard a soft rap at the door. She glanced over to see her mother peering in.

"Hey, sweetheart, is it okay if I come in?" Isabelle asked.

"Of course, Mom, come in," Sophia replied, turning her gaze back out the window.

Isabelle walked around to Sophia's side of the bed and sat facing her daughter. She gently reached over to push some stray hairs out of Sophia's eyes. Sophia smiled softly at her mother.

"Thank you, Mom, thank you for being here for me. I'm sorry I slept so long."

"Oh, honey, you have nothing to apologize for. This is traumatic for you, and I would never be anywhere other than here with you now, do you hear me?" Tears slowly welled in Isabelle's eyes. Her heart was broken for her daughter in this moment, and seeing the pain that she was feeling was tearing her up. "Listen, honey, I think you should try and eat something. You need to stay strong, and you haven't eaten for hours. How about I make you some of my famous homemade chicken noodle soup?" Isabelle raised her eyebrows at her daughter.

Sophia knew she should eat. The only thing she had eaten over the last day was an apple at her room in the Spa and a stale cup of coffee at the station. She wasn't sure she would be able to keep anything down, but she knew she had to get some strength back, because this wasn't over yet.

"Sure, Mom, that would be great. It would probably do me good to get something in my belly."

"Okay, honey." Isabelle reached for her daughter's face again, wiped away a stray lash that was lying on her cheek, and then continued, "Sophia, when your father died, a part of me died with him. I know the pain you're feeling right now. I just need you to understand that this isn't your fault. None of this is your fault. Whatever was going on with Marcus and Cat, or whoever else is responsible for this, it has nothing to do with you. I just want to make sure you're safe, and I will be here for you as long as you need. I am your mother and I love you more than anything in this world, and whenever or whatever you want to talk to me about, I'm here to listen. I will always be on your side, and I would never let you go through anything alone."

She then stood up and bent down to give Sophia a kiss on her cheek before heading back out into the kitchen to make dinner. Sophia watched her as she walked out of the room, and suddenly the intense sense of guilt she felt made it hard to breathe. Guilt, not because of what she did, but that she couldn't tell her mother the truth. Guilt, because she knew no matter how close they were she was going to have to lie to her about this for the rest of her life. Sophia knew that, no matter how badly she wanted to turn to her mom and tell her the truth, this was something that she must never find out.

September 2, 2009 – The Premiere

Sophia sat at her vanity applying the last of her lipstick as she got ready for Marcus's premiere. She fussed with the uncooperative wisps of hair that insisted on falling out of place and gave her hair one last spray to set everything in place. She knew she looked beautiful in this moment. Her hair, her makeup, the jewelry, and, of course, the dress – she looked stunning. Yet, as she sat looking at her reflection in the mirror, she struggled to admire the woman looking back at her. She reached her perfectly manicured fingers up to her cheek, and she could still feel the sting on her skin. A part of her felt to blame for what happened yesterday. She should have known better, but she wasn't expecting Marcus to see her while she was having lunch with Cat. God, she knew how he felt about Adam. He made it pretty clear the first time they ran into one another. She really shouldn't have been so blasé about it when she ran into him again. As she stared into her own eyes, she thought about what had taken place the afternoon before:

"Honey, I'm home!" Sophia walked from the kitchen to the living room as she continued to call him. "Babe? Are you here?" She assumed he was, as she saw his Escalade parked out on the drive. She saw the door to his office was open slightly, and she peeked into the room. Her husband was sitting on one of his leather chairs, with one leg crossed over the other, sipping on a drink. She slowly opened the door and walked in.

"Hey, honey, here you are," she sang happily as she walked towards him. She leaned over and gave him a quick peck on the cheek. Marcus looked up at her, and she could instantly see displeasure sweeping across his face.

"How was your day? Did you guys make good leeway on set today?" She kept talking in hopes that he would somehow change his mood.

Marcus took a slow sip of his drink and looked up at her. "It was fine, Sophia," he replied shortly, then continued, "And how was your day? Anything interesting happen?"

Sophia paused for a moment, trying to think whether anything of interest had happened that she should share with her husband. "Hmm, nope, not really. Pretty typical day at the office. Oh, I did find out that I get to do a feature on Macey Thorpe's house next week." Sophia sounded excited as she continued explaining to Marcus, "She's the host of 'Celebrity Cooking Wars', and apparently her house is something to see. Samuel thinks that I'm going to fall in love with her house and then will try getting you to build me a replica." She giggled, only to realize she was the only one laughing. "Marcus, what's wrong? Did something happen at work today? You want to talk about anything?" Sophia asked her husband, concerned now.

"I don't know, Sophia," he snapped. "Why don't you tell me if there's something that you would like to talk about? I asked you if anything interesting happened today and all you have to share is that you get to do some stupid feature at some wanna-be Celebrity's house. You think that's what I meant when I asked you if anything interesting had happened? Because I'm sorry Soph, but that is the least interesting thing I have heard all week. So how about you try again. Anything interesting you would like to share?"

Sophia looked down at her husband, taken aback by his sudden response. She could not, for the life of her, figure out why he was acting like this, and couldn't understand where he was trying to go with this conversation. She stood back on her heels and crossed her arms over her chest as she thought how to respond.

"Marcus, I'm not sure what you are talking about. What's going on? Why do I get the sense that you aren't happy with me? Did I do something to upset you?" she inquired.

Marcus shot her a look of pure contempt, baffled by his wife's response. She was standing right in front of him, lying to his face, and she had the audacity to ask if she did something to upset him.

"Did you do anything to upset me?" He gave a sarcastic laugh. "I don't know, Sophia, maybe you're just too stupid and you need me to help you figure it out. You don't recall lunch today with Cat, on Melrose, at Dolce? You don't recall your lunch today, sitting out in the open streets of Melrose for all to see you?"

Sophia shook her head, then replied, "Yes, of course, I met with Cat today for lunch. I don't see how that's supposed to be a problem." She paused for a brief instant, thinking maybe she missed a lunch date with him, but was confident in her conclusion.

"A problem? You don't see how you lying to my face is a problem? Jesus, Sophia, why don't you pull your head out of your ass? So I suppose you're going to have the gall to sit here and tell me that you don't think it was a problem that you were with that little Adam fuck that I specifically asked you not to have lunch with? You sat out in broad daylight, hugging him and touching him, and you don't see how that is a bit of a problem for me?" He stood up and stepped angrily towards his wife.

Completely unsure how to respond to Marcus's accusations, she knew the best thing would be to not upset him any further. She swallowed the lump that was beginning to form in her throat and answered, "Honey, I'm sorry, I wasn't lying to you. He just showed up. He saw us sitting, having lunch, and he stopped and talked to us. I introduced him to Cat and apologized to him for not being able to meet him for lunch the last time I ran into him." Sophia looked up at her husband, and when their eyes met, for a brief second she felt like he was calming down, and that he knew she was not lying to him. Her heart rate slowed, but just as she started to relax, she was struck by the most painful sensation she'd ever felt. It took her a moment to understand what had happened, although she instantly felt warmth running from her nose. She grabbed her face in astonishment as she looked up to Marcus.

"Don't you ever lie to me. I will not tolerate being lied to, especially by my own wife. When I ask you a fucking question you are to tell me the truth. I will not be disrespected by some self-righteous whore, not in my home, do you understand me?" he yelled as he towered over her, then he pushed past her and walked out of his office, slamming the door behind him.

Sophia, still holding her cheek, realized her nose was bleeding and quickly grabbed a tissue off his desk and placed it firmly under the flow. As the reality of what just happened began to take form, Sophia crumbled to the floor and began sobbing uncontrollably. She was shaking, her limbs losing all feeling, and she curled up on Marcus's office floor, where she lay until she had no more tears to shed. Even then, she stayed silently on the floor, her cheek still stinging, her eyes fixed on, but not really seeing, the closed door.

She heard the click of the door, and she looked up to see the handle turning slowly. Fear instantly filled her, as she was sure Marcus was going to continue with his rage. She pulled her legs up to her chest as she watched his feet enter the room. He walked slowly and carefully up to her, and before she knew it he was sitting on the floor beside her, crying uncontrollably.

"Oh, my God, Sophia, I am so sorry. I don't know what in the hell took over me. Baby, please, you know that was not me, you know I would never hurt you like that." Sophia instantly began to cry again as she realized that Marcus was here not to hurt her, but to apologize. He tried to pull her gently towards him, and he could feel her resistance at first, but she slowly allowed him to cradle her.

"Please, Sophia, you have no idea how sorry I am. You don't have to forgive me. I had no right to accuse you of anything. I just saw you with him, and I was so scared that you were lying to me, and I lost it. Baby, please, you have to believe me." The tears flowed heavily as he pushed Sophia's hair out of her tear-soaked eyes. She could feel his body tremble, and she was shocked. She had never seen her husband in this state.

She sat up slowly and wiped her nose one more time with her tissue, and then whispered, "How could you do that? I was telling you the truth. You have to know that I was telling you the truth. I would never want to do anything to hurt you, Marcus." She looked him in the eyes.

"I know, I know that, Sophia. I just got jealous, and I was afraid. I can't lose you. I don't ever want to have to worry about losing you. Please, baby, I'll do anything, please just forgive me. It will never happen again, I swear," he cried in desperation as he reached for his wife again.

Sophia's emotions were going crazy. She was still in shock over the fact that Marcus actually put his hands on her, but as she sat there and saw the pain that he was in, and the regret that overtook him, she couldn't help herself. She fell into his arms and surrendered herself to his grasp.

Sophia's reflection didn't show any remaining signs of what took place that prior afternoon. Anything that was there she was able to hide easily with her makeup.

She had been fighting an internal battle since it happened, and she was still unable to believe that Marcus had actually hit her. She never thought he would go to those lengths, but she also knew she wasn't innocent in the whole thing. She should have told him right away that she had seen Adam. She shouldn't have kept that from him, or tried to keep that from him. She had seen the regret in Marcus's eyes when he came to apologize, and she truly wanted to believe that he would, in fact, never do that again. She had to believe that.

What would she tell someone writing into her column to do? Well, probably to leave, to run away, but now that she was in the situation, it was entirely different. She had to trust that her husband was sorry, and to try, on her part, a little bit harder to not upset him to that point.

Marcus walked into the bedroom and Sophia sat looking at him in the vanity mirror. He looked extraordinarily handsome in his Armani suit. His dark hair was brushed away from his face, and when Sophia saw him in the mirror all of her doubts seemed to vanish. She remembered at that moment why she loved him so much.

"You look stunning," Marcus spoke from the door.

Sophia turned around to look at him, and she gave him a shy smile. "You as well. I don't remember ever seeing you look as handsome as you do in this moment."

Marcus knelt down in front of his wife and ran his fingers softly over the cheek where he not long ago left the sting of his hand. "I can't tell you how deeply sorry I am for what I did yesterday. I will never let myself forget how horrible that felt. You don't deserve to be treated that way, and I swear to you I will never hurt you again." He then bent closer to her, placing his lips ever so softly on her cheek. He stood up and walked over to the little bar, where he kept all of his Scotch neatly arranged and poured himself a small glass.

Sophia turned to face herself in her vanity mirror again, then spoke. "Marcus, I'm sorry I lied to you. I just want you to know that you have nothing to worry about, with anybody. I would never betray you, and I would never allow another man to come in between us. And I certainly want you to know that Adam will never be a problem again, I promise you."

Marcus watched his wife finish applying her make-up as he took a small sip from his glass. He savoured the warm liquid in his mouth, then nodded and swallowed before replying.

"Oh, I know, sweetheart. I know he will never be a problem for us ever again."

July 24, 2015 – Fanfare

Marcus and Cat's murder had hit the media with a vengeance. It was the main story in every major newspaper and magazine. Sophia dreaded even turning on her TV every day, as the faces of her husband and best friend filled the screen no matter what channel she tuned to. Paparazzi, reporters, and solemn fans stood outside of the Donovan house daily, hoping to get answers as the investigation continued. Flowers and candles were placed around the property, and each day the crowds would linger closer and closer to the house, hoping to hear some news. Sophia was thankful their beach house wasn't known to the public, and they managed to keep it secluded. Otherwise, she was certain, any remaining peace she had would vanish. Her mother was still with her and for that, she was thankful, because if she hadn't had someone to talk to over these last few days, she was sure she would have gone crazy.

Leaving the house was not the best idea. She didn't want to be spotted, not right now. At times like these, the paparazzi were bloodthirsty, and she knew she needed to keep her distance for a little while and let some of the dust settle. Sophia poured herself a cup of tea, then headed into the living room, where she decided to quickly turn on the TV and see what was going on, just to appease her curiosity. She pointed the remote at the sixty-inch mounted on the wall above the fireplace, and sure enough, a picture of her and Marcus at one of the last red carpets was displayed on the screen. A pretty Asian woman reported the story.

"Marcus Donovan was a highly sought-after and successful film director who was found murdered in his Hollywood hills home early Monday morning. Along with the body of Marcus Donovan, the body of a Ms. Catarina Warner was also discovered at the scene. Donovan's wife, Sophia, was the first to discover the gruesome scene, when she returned from a weekend getaway in Malibu. It looks at this time that it may have been a murder-suicide, however, further details will not be released until the investigation comes to a close."

They flashed a few more pictures of Marcus across the screen, followed by the pictures the media was able to gather of

Cat. She had attended most of Marcus's events with them, so it wasn't difficult to find pictures they could litter all over the tabloids. Just as the broadcast cut to a commercial break, Sophia's mother entered the living room. Sophia turned to see her reaching for her purse on the table.

"Honey, you need to stop watching so much of that. We just need to focus on our family and what we need to do to grieve. You know better than anyone that the media is going to be in a frenzy with this, and half the stuff they're going to release will be trash." Isabelle tossed her purse over her shoulder and gazed at her daughter.

"I know, Mom. I just can't help it. Nobody has said anything yet, and it's getting frustrating. Those detectives haven't even called me or anything. I just want to know what's going on. I want to know what they've figured out. I just hate being in the dark about this." Sophia pointed the remote at the TV again, turning the screen back to black.

Isabelle met her daughter in the middle of the room and gave her a hug, then held her at arm's length. "I know this is hard, and it will be for a while, but we just have to be patient and we have to let the police do their jobs. They'll have answers for us soon, I promise. In the meantime, just try not to pay attention to any of that media garbage. Listen, honey, I'm going to run out to get a few more things. Is there anything that you need me to get?"

Sophia shook her head "No, I think I'm good, Mom. I'll text you if I think of anything while you're gone. Thank you, though."

Isabelle headed out of the front door, hopped into her vehicle, and backed out of the drive. Sophia stood watching her out the window until she could no longer see the car, then headed through the living room to the patio that overlooked the ocean. She stood, cupping her mug in both hands, as she watched the waves dance on the shore. Just as she was about to take a sip of her drink, she was startled by the doorbell. She set her mug onto the table and walked backed through the living room.

When she opened the door, she was surprised to see Detectives Keller and Stone. She met eyes with Detective Stone for a brief instance, wondering why they were here, and then she met the harsh stare of Detective Keller.

"Mrs. Donovan," Keller began, "we're sorry to barge in like this, but we just wanted to have a few words with you about the investigation. I hope you don't mind us just stopping in like this."

"No, of course not. I don't mind. I just hope that I'll be able to help, and you're able to give me some information on what's going on." She stepped to the side, inviting them both in. Keller walked right past her and let herself into the living room, admiring the view laid before her. As Sophia closed the door behind them, she caught Detective Stone looking at her with worry in his eyes. She smiled softly up at him, and then they both followed Keller into the living room.

"Wow, this is quite an impressive beach house, Mrs. Donovan. It looks like you guys must have done very well for yourselves. This place is five times bigger, and nicer, than my house in the city," Keller said as she turned back to Sophia and Detective Stone.

"Thank you, Detective. We were very grateful to be able to have the things we have. This has always been a nice get-away for us when we needed to escape the hustle and bustle of LA," Sophia replied.

Keller then motioned for Sophia to take a seat, and she and Detective Stone sat down with her. Keller took out her trusty notepad and pen.

"Mrs. Donovan," she began, but Sophia politely interrupted her.

"Sophia, please. You can call me Sophia. I don't mind," she said, smiling at Keller.

"If you don't mind, I prefer not to address you by your first name. We are here on business, not pleasure," she almost barked in response.

"Oh," Sophia whispered, fidgeting uncomfortably in her seat. Detective Stone stepped in, sensing the tension that was beginning to present itself.

"Sophia," he began, hoping to make her feel more at ease, "we have a few more things we need to discuss. I promise we won't take up much of your time, but a few things have come to light and we just have some things to clarify with you."

Sophia felt a familiar tinge of panic, as she was not entirely certain what he was talking about. She prepared herself, gathering all the necessary information in her mind, hoping she had the right answers ready.

"You said that Catarina Warner was a close family friend, is that correct?" Detective Stone began.

"Yes. Like I said, she and I met, actually, on the same day that I met my husband. We have been best friends since, and she has been a very close part of my family," Sophia answered, feeling calm.

"Mrs. Donovan," Keller continued questioning, "did you, at any time, suspect anything unusual between Ms. Warner and your husband?"

Sophia looked confused, and replied, "Unusual how?"

"Did you ever suspect there was anything inappropriate going on between them, Mrs. Donovan? Any concerns that there was something going on with them, beyond the point of friendship?" Detective Keller answered.

Sophia could feel tears welling up as her nerves began to take hold of her, and she rapidly shook her head.

"No, never! Of course not. That would never happen. I trusted both of them with my life. That's crazy. Why would you ask me something like that?" Sophia replied, offended.

"Listen, Sophia, we are making sure we have all the information we require to complete this investigation. I warned you this was going to be difficult, and some things may be brought to light that you don't want to hear. I'm sorry this is hard but...." Detective Stone tried to ease Sophia, but was cut off harshly by Keller's icy stare.

"Have you ever suspected your husband of being unfaithful in the past, Mrs. Donovan?" Keller continued.

"No, Marcus was never unfaithful to me. He was an amazing husband, and I had a terrific marriage. Listen, I don't know where these absurd questions are coming from, and I understand you are trying to do your job, Detective, but I am still grieving the freshly-open wound of losing my husband and my best friend, and I would highly appreciate it if you could refrain from walking into my home and accusing my dead husband of cheating on me. At least, give me the courtesy of waiting till his body is cold." Sophia shot Detective Keller a look of anger as tears escaped again.

Detective Keller smirked at Sophia's reaction, but pressed harder, determined to get her suspect to crack, like she always did. She answered Sophia's glare with one of her own. "So you're sure, then? You have no explanation as to why your best friend was found in your bedroom, with your husband? You can't seem to think of any other reason, and yet you're so sure that they would never betray you. So tell me, Mrs. Donovan, do you think Ms. Warner was the one who shot your husband, only then to turn the gun on herself? Or do you have some other conclusion?"

Detective Stone again felt he needed to interrupt. "Detective Keller, that's enough," He spoke sharply. "We didn't come here to intimidate or try and coerce her into giving us her theory of what she thinks has happened." He turned back to Sophia.

"We're going to be accessing all of your and your husband's financials. That means bank, credit, safety deposits, any and all info. It's much easier to do this with your approval, otherwise we'll have to obtain a warrant, so I hope that you understand that this will be much less painful for everyone with your full cooperation. Do we have that Sophia? Do we have your cooperation?" Detective Stone looked at her seriously, waiting for her response.

"Yes, Detective, of course. You can search into whatever the hell you need to. Just find out what the hell happened. I want answers more than you can possibly know, so please just do whatever you have to, I need to know what happened, I need to find out who did this to my husband and my friend. God, just please figure this out."

After he jotted a few notes down on his pad, he turned to Keller and gave her a quick nod indicating that he had what he needed before flipping his pad shut. He smiled softly at Sophia as he stood up.

Detective Keller followed behind Detective Stone, and Sophia walked them both to the door, they both turned to face her again. "Your cooperation is appreciated Sophia, and I promise you we are doing everything we can to figure out what happened to your husband."

"Thank you." Sophia nodded in response.

As the door closed behind them, Caleb turned to Jill. "Jesus Jill, what in the hell is wrong with you? You know damn well you can't try to intimidate a witness like that. She is cooperating fully, in this case, so what is your problem?" he demanded.

Jill stormed off toward their vehicle and got into the passenger side, slamming the door. Caleb got into the driver's seat and turned to her, still expecting a response.

"I know you think this case seems pretty cut-and-dry. You know as well as I do that Catarina Warner was fucking Marcus Donovan, and it seems pretty obvious that this is a murder-suicide, but Christ, Caleb, I'm just not getting a good feeling about this. I know her alibi is sealed tighter than a nun's honey pot, and she's acting pretty damn convincing, but my gut just keeps telling me she knows something," Jill answered.

"Well, you know what, Jill? That's great. Follow your gut, let's get this fucking case figured out. But as the head investigator of this division, I am telling you: don't let me ever catch you trying to fuck with a witness again, or I promise you the only cases you'll be dealing with are the useless dumpster hooker cases that nobody could give a shit about, do you understand me?"

Jill gave one of her sarcastic grins in Caleb's direction and responded, "Shit Cal, you got a hard on for this chick already, or what? Don't let her distract you."

Caleb turned on the car and put the engine into drive. "I don't get distracted, Keller. I do the distracting."

September 3, 2009 – Unexpected Goodbye

Sophia walked into her office and threw her purse and briefcase onto the comfy couch she had across the room from her desk. She could not believe how absolutely exhausted she was from the premiere party the evening before. It was not yet nine thirty, and she already wanted to fall into her couch and have a nap. The premiere was a success and, as she suspected, Marcus's new film was going to be another huge hit.

Everyone from the studio was there to support him, including Alex and his new girlfriend, Gabriella. It certainly hadn't taken Alex long to recover from his wife up and leaving him: he was back in the saddle only a few short weeks after she left. Gabriella seemed like a sweet girl. She was a bit younger than Taylor had been, but she seemed to actually like Alex for Alex, and not for his stardom. She was not in the industry. In fact, she owned her own little bakery, which was modestly successful, and had met Alex when, one morning, he randomly stopped in to grab a coffee and was instantly taken with her.

Cat was also there, solo, just like she had said she would be. Sophia had told her it was not the best idea for her to invite Adam after the fight with Marcus. She shared with Cat the whole fight, the harsh words, and the name-calling, but she left out the fact that Marcus hit her. She didn't see how sharing that with Cat would have helped the situation any.

Now, back at work, Sophia headed out to the lunchroom to grab herself a cup of coffee, where she found Sam chatting happily with one of the interns.

"Well, good morning sunshine!" Sam exclaimed when he noticed her walk into the room.

Sophia walked right past them, straight to the coffee maker, and poured herself a generous cup of coffee. She turned back to them and smiled tiredly. "Good morning, Sam." She then turned to the young brunette. "Good morning, Hailey."

Hailey gave her an energetic wave and smiled widely. "Good morning, Sophia."

"Listen, honey, don't take offence to this, but you look like shit today. I take it the party went well last night? I'm almost bummed we had to miss it now," Sam said.

Sophia laughed softly at Sam's honesty, and replied, "It was great, of course. Marcus's film is going to be another huge success, and the after-party was amazing. However, I feel far from amazing today. It was a late night, and I'm exhausted. If I didn't have to finalize the schedule for the Macey Thorpe feature today, I would definitely still be at home sleeping,"

"I'm super excited to be able to help you on the feature, Sophia," Hailey jumped in. "God, I love Macey Thorpe, she is just so wild, and after hearing about her house, I can't wait to see it for myself."

Hailey was a fairly new intern to the magazine and was just finishing up her journalism degree at USC. She was bubbly, enthusiastic, and always aiming to please. Sophia had asked for her help on the Macey Thorpe feature, and it was as if she had offered her the world. Hailey was over-the-moon that she was going to have the opportunity to get a sneak peek into the residence of one her most beloved celebrities. Sophia just hoped she made the right choice and that her fandom would not compromise her ability to complete the job.

"Well, I'm happy that you're so excited about it, because today one of us has to be. There's a lot of work to get done before Monday. Give me about a half hour to get myself settled, then why don't you come to my office so we can finalize the last of the details?" Sophia asked.

Hailey took a quick sip of her espresso and nodded her head happily at Sophia.

"Of course, Sophia, sounds good. I'll see you right away, then." She bounced out of the kitchen, singing to herself.

Sam laughed at Sophia again. "You prepared for the little ball of energy today? This is all she has been able to talk about for the last couple days."

"I don't know, I'm not sure how much perky I can take today. I honestly can't wait till this feature is over so I don't have to hear the name Macey Thorpe again for a long time," Sophia said before blowing softly into her mug.

"Well, you better rest up for the rest of the week, because I won't have you missing Devon's birthday this weekend. I don't care how tired you are; you are going to drag that ass of yours to this party. Oh man, Devon is going to be thirty on Saturday. Shit, does that mean I am going to have to trade him in soon, get a newer, gayer model?" Sam joked, trying to liven up his friend.

Sophia laughed loudly, and slapped Sam gently on the shoulder.

"Oh, give it up Sam. What in the hell would you do without that man? I think you know as well as I do that your trading-in days are over. You will be riding this model for the rest of your life." Sophia continued to giggle. "And, of course, I wouldn't miss your party for anything. I can't miss poor Devon crying into his birthday cake at the fact that he's no longer in his twenties. Nope, I wouldn't miss that for the world."

Sam reached over and gave Sophia a quick kiss on the cheek before he turned to head out of the kitchen.

"Time to get to work, you have a date in twenty minutes with Hailey Mcbubbly," he remarked, then continued back to his office. Sophia shook her head, then gathered up all her patience to face the next few hours with Hailey and all her energy.

As Sophia sat at her desk, arranging all the files and photos to go over with Hailey, her cell phone began to ring a familiar tone. Knowing it was her mother, she stopped what she was doing to pick it up.

"Hey, Mom, what's up?" Sophia answered the call sounding much perkier.

"Honey. Hi, Honey." Isabelle began. Sophia could hear something was wrong in the tone of her mother's voice, which was usually pleasant.

"Mom, are you okay? You don't sound very good. Are you feeling okay?" Sophia asked, worried.

"Oh, sweetie, I am so sorry. I just got a call from Alice Doucette, Adam's Mother."

"Oh, yeah, I actually just ran into Adam the other day. He wanted to get together for lunch here soon, but things have been so hectic. I told him I would try and find a good time soon. How's Alice? I haven't spoken to her in forever."

Sophia was suddenly interrupted by her mother. "Honey, there was an accident." Isabelle began to softly cry into the phone.

"What do you mean? Is Alice okay?"

"Alice is fine. It's Adam. He had an accident while he was out jogging the other evening through Runyon Canon. Alice says he must have tripped or something, and he hit his head on the curb or a park bench or something, I'm not too sure yet, but, sweetheart..."

Isabelle was suddenly cut off by her daughter. "He's fine, Mom? It was a stupid accident, he's a huge klutz, but you're calling to tell me that he's just fine, right Mom? Adam is okay, isn't he?"

Sophia knew the answer already, but a part of her thought if the words didn't actually escape her Mother's mouth then it wouldn't be true.

"Baby, I am so sorry, I didn't want to have to tell you this. Sophia, Adam died. I am so terribly sorry."

Sophia sat, stunned, not sure what to say. She had just seen him the other day. He was fine. How could someone possibly just trip and fall, and hit their head and die, she thought to herself, trying to make sense out of what she was being told.

"No, Mom, listen, I just saw him the other day and he was fine. This is obviously a mistake. I mean, are they sure it's Adam? No, probably not – this is just going to be some silly mix up, Mom, just you wait. I mean, Adam can't possibly be dead, I just saw him on Tuesday," Sophia repeated.

Isabelle could feel her daughter's pain through the phone, and she knew there were no words that would help at this moment. Sophia and Adam had once been such dear friends, and she'd known that this news was going to be difficult for Sophia to hear. It was difficult for Isabelle herself to hear when Alice had told her. Adam had been like a son to her and Sophia's father, John. Isabelle smiled as she recalled how Adam and Sophia used to jump on John's lap, begging him for money if they promised to help do all the chores.

"Honey, I don't know what else to say but how sorry I am. Alice promised to call us back with the details of the funeral, and I told her that of course we would be there. If there's anything you need, you know I am here, whatever you need." Isabelle wasn't sure what else to say. The two women sat in silence for several seconds as Sophia struggled with her denial.

She finally replied softly to her mother, "I just can't believe this is happening. It makes no sense." Sophia cradled her head in her hand. "Call me as soon as you know the details, okay mom?"

"Of course, baby. I love you," Isabelle replied before she hung up the phone.

Sophia sat at her desk, desperately trying to make sense of what had happened to Adam. Was this just some freak accident? He must have had a heart attack, and fell and hit his head. Something must have happened. Jesus, how could someone go out for a jog and die on the trail, just like that? The tears began to fall as she thought about what his last moments must have been like. She prayed that he didn't feel any pain, and that they would be able to give poor Alice some answers. She sat recounting what turned out to be their last conversation, and a deeply disturbing thought came to her, a thought she knew she had to immediately push out of her mind. But no matter how hard she tried to ignore it, the only thing she could hear were Marcus's words ringing in her ears:

"Oh, I know, Sweetheart. He will never be a problem for us again."

July 31, 2015 – Sisterly Love

The week that followed Sophia's encounter with Detectives Keller and Stone was quiet, to say the least. She was still trying to avoid the public, as she knew the rumors and the stories were spreading like wildfire at this point. She knew that all of her and Marcus's personal records had been ransacked, and the police would be going through everything with a fine-toothed comb. She'd known that this was going to happen, but it still made her a little uneasy, her whole life being put under a microscope. She was just desperately hoping that all of her tracks were covered, and that seeds were being planted properly.

Her poor mother would come home nearly every day, in tears, after reading the cover of some gossip magazine, including LA Today. The headline on one would read, "Fatal Love Triangle Ends in Murder," while another read, "Why don't you Love Me? A Mistress's Bloody Revenge". Today was no different. Isabelle walked through the front doors of the Beach House and slammed her purse and keys on the table.

"Damn it, Sophia, why can't they just leave you alone? What in the hell is wrong with these people that they can't let you alone to grieve the loss of your husband and best friend? What makes them think that they know all the answers when the damn police haven't even given any details into the case? Why do they have to continue smearing all these lies all over the media?" She sobbed with frustration as Sophia walked over to calm her down.

"Mom, listen to me, you know better than anyone that this is just what they do. They're bloodhounds, and they don't care what they have to do or say as long as they can get their stories on the cover of any magazine that will get noticed. You just have to ignore it, okay?"

Isabelle shrugged her shoulders and wiped the tears from her eyes, then responded to her daughter. "I know, I know, but when it's your own family it is so much harder. I just want them to finish this investigation up, I mean what in the hell is taking so long? It seems to me a pretty open-and-closed case."

Sophia knew what her mother believed had happened. As much as she hated to think that her best friend of eleven years would betray her daughter, she was confident that Marcus would not have any issues sinking to such levels. Everyone knew that her son-in-law was not one of her favorite people, and after the road that he and Sophia had travelled over the years, it wasn't hard to blame Isabelle for how she felt.

"Mom, I know that you think it's a simple case, but I still can't believe that Cat would be having an affair with Marcus. I don't think she would ever do anything like that to hurt me. The police are doing their best to figure it out, and maybe soon they will be able to provide us with some answers," she replied, while walking to the kitchen to dump out what was remaining in her water glass. "Are you going to be okay? I have to go meet Bruce, Adele, and Olivia for lunch. Do you want to come with me?" Sophia asked her mother softly.

Isabelle shook her head and replied, "No, no. I just want to lie down for a bit. Unless you feel you need me there with you. I know how hard it was when you were last with them."

"I'll be fine, mom. Now that emotions have settled a bit, I've agreed to sit down with them and to tell them everything I know. It's not a lot, but I'm hoping that something I say will help a little bit with this. I know Olivia and Adele are really struggling. To be honest, I'm just a bit worried about Olivia. I never know how things are going to go down with that one." Sophia sighed deeply.

"Okay, sweetie, if you're sure that you'll be okay. I'm just feeling overly-exhausted today, and I just really need a rest. You let me know if you need anything at all, though, okay?"

Sophia walked over to her mother and gave her a warm hug. "Mom, you have been so amazing through this. I don't think I would have ever been able to stay so strong through this if it wasn't for you. You go and get some rest, and I'll talk to you more when I get back."

Sophia grabbed her purse off of the table and headed out to the driveway, where she stepped into her Mercedes.

Sophia walked into the front Lobby of the Esquire Hotel, where Marcus's Family had been staying since they arrived into town a little over a week ago. Sophia had agreed to meet them, but she didn't want to be out at some busy restaurant where everyone

one would recognize her, so they agreed to meet at the quiet lobby bar in the hotel. As she walked into the lounge, she could see Bruce, Adele, and Olivia seated at a secluded table near the back. Bruce looked over at his daughter-in-law, and stood when she got to the table.

"Sophia." He spoke curtly, then continued, "How are you?"

For a moment, Sophia thought he was going to reach for her and give her a hug, but she quickly realized he'd stood to pull her chair out for her. When Sophia was situated at the table, Adele instantly started crying again. Sophia reached for her hand across the table.

"Oh, Adele." Sophia began to cry, too. "I am so terribly sorry that you guys have to go through this with me. I don't know what else to say right now. This has been a complete nightmare, sitting and waiting for someone to give me some answers as to what happened that night. I feel helpless, and I hate that there's nothing that any of us can do at this point." Sophia turned to Bruce, and she could see his features soften as tears began to flood his eyes as well. This was not something she had ever witnessed before. Bruce Donovan wasn't an emotional man, so she knew the amount of pain he had to be in right now. Silently, she struggled with the knowledge that his pain was because of her, but they could never know that. She turned to look at Olivia, and she could feel the daggers of hate burn into her eyes as Olivia glared at her.

"You know, Sophia, if you and Marcus were so damn in love and had such a wonderful fucking marriage, then how in the hell did you not know that your husband was fucking your own Goddamn best friend? Huh? Answer me that. You're going to sit here and try telling us that you are Mrs. Innocent in this whole thing and you have no idea what happened? That is such bullshit, and you know it." Olivia's words cut into Sophia like knives.

"Olivia!" Bruce scolded. "That is about enough out of you, young lady. Whatever you may think you know or don't know, you will keep your mouth shut, do you understand me? This family is suffering enough right now without having you and your intolerable behaviors adding to the fire."

Sophia was shocked that Bruce jumped to her defense so quickly, and hoped it meant that he didn't share Olivia's viewpoint on the topic. The last thing Sophia needed was the whole family questioning things. It was bad enough that she had to contend with Detective Keller and her suspicions. Sophia wiped her eyes and gently blew her nose.

"Bruce, it's okay. I understand, Olivia, I know you're hurting, and so am I. God knows, I am hurting. I understand that you want answers to what happened, and that you are angry. I get that, I do. But, I can only tell you that this is all as shocking and appalling to me as it is to you, and I want nothing more than to know what happened to my husband and my best friend. None of this is making any sense to me, but I'm trying my best to get through this until we know the truth."

Olivia's glare didn't soften at Sophia's response. If anything, it grew colder. Sophia knew how Olivia felt about her. It had been a constant battle between the two women and this was only going to deepen the hate.

Adele finally broke the uncomfortable silence. "Sophia, please tell us anything you know. Do you know anything at all that would have led to this? Was Marcus acting strange? Was Cat acting strange? There has to be something that you're not telling us that would help with this case," she pleaded.

"Of course, Mom. Of course, there's stuff she isn't telling us. If you're going to blame anyone for Marcus's death, then blame her." Olivia began raising her voice as she pointed at Sophia.

"Olivia!" Bruce barked. "I told you that was enough. If you can't keep your Goddamn mouth shut, then I suggest you go back to the room, because nobody wants to hear this nonsense." Olivia shot her father a look of disgust and stood up from the table.

"You know what? You guys can believe what you want. You can believe that she's all innocent in this and that she knows nothing. I'm not stupid, though. There's something that this little bitch isn't telling us, and when we find out what it is, and that it could have kept Marcus alive, well, then maybe you'll feel like assholes. I hope you do. Until then, Sophia, I want nothing to do with you, do you hear me? Nothing!" Olivia yelled before she stormed off.

Unfortunately, Olivia's little outburst drew much-unwanted attention to the table, and they were instantly recognized by the small crowd in the lounge. Sophia could hear the murmurs and she could see the stares being cast in their direction. This was why she hadn't wanted to be in public, not yet. It was too soon. As Adele began to realize what just happened, she started sobbing hysterically, and Bruce slid his chair over to try and soothe her. Sophia looked at both of them.

"You guys have to believe me. I don't know what happened. I don't know what the hell was going on, and I still don't know what the hell is going on. Finding my husband and my friend in my bedroom, dead, was the worst thing that has ever happened to me in my life, and I want answers so badly it's killing me. When I came home from the resort, I wanted my life to be over. My world was over. I understand Olivia's angry and frustrated, and so am I, but I'm telling you the truth. If I knew anything that could help with this case I would tell you, but I don't know anything except what I've already told you. Listen, I'll be here for you guys in any way that I can, and I hope that you will do the same for me, but I can't give you any more information, because I don't know anything else."

Bruce and Adele looked at Sophia with a softness to their eyes, a look that finally said to Sophia that they believed her, and that they knew that she was going through the same thing that they were. They all just wanted answers.

Sophia knew that soon they would have the answers they were looking for, but, of course, none of it was going to be the truth. That, only she would know.

September 26, 2009 – A Step Ahead

"I'm so sorry I had to miss your party, Devon. I hope you understand?" Sophia spoke as she reached to give Devon a hug. He and Sam stood at their front door, welcoming Sophia into their home. Devon hugged her tightly.

"Oh, honey, you do not apologize. I don't want to hear such nonsense. I am so sorry about your friend." Devon pulled away and looked into Sophia's dark, sunken eyes.

Devon was Samuel's incredible, devoted, and loyal boyfriend of six years. He had the kindest soul, and the love that he and Sam shared was one to admire. He had a unique and charming style about him – he just loved to dress different and be different. Everything about him was always so warm and welcoming that it was difficult for nearly anyone to not fall in love with Devon Atwood.

"Thank you so much, sweetie," Sophia replied as Devon and Sam led her into the house. Sam took her coat and her purse and tucked them into the front closet as Devon led her back through to the living room.

"Please, tell me that you need a glass of wine as badly as I do?" Devon asked Sophia as he headed over to the bar near the back of the room.

"Shit, yes, please. A very big glass of whatever you got will do," Sophia laughed softly.

Sam sat down beside Sophia and gave her another quick hug. He kissed her quickly on the cheek, and then sank back into the couch.

"Sophia, what happened to Adam? Do you know anything?" he asked.

Sophia shook her head and shrugged.

"No, they concluded that it was an accident. The autopsy showed there was no heart attack or stroke or anything like that, just the force to the head, which they say coincides with where he was lying. It looks like he fell and hit his head on the corner of one of the park benches. He was out for a late evening run, and nobody found him for, like an hour or so after it happened. God, I just can't believe it." Sophia reached for the large glass of wine Devon was carefully handing her.

"Well, sweetheart, if there's anything that Sam and I can do, you just name it, okay? This is horrible that you have to go through this. I hate seeing such a good person in so much turmoil. How is Marcus with it all?" Devon asked before he took a big sip of his wine.

Sophia thought for a moment whether she should answer that question honestly, or just with what she was expected to say. She decided to go with the latter. "Oh, well, he didn't know Adam, so it hasn't been too difficult on him. What has been difficult is seeing how it's affecting me. He has been good and supportive, and I am thankful that I have him right now."

"That's great. It's great that you have such a good man in your life. Geez, I don't know what I would do without Sam during a loss like this. I don't know what I would do without him, period," he remarked as he looked up at Sam, giving him a loving smile. Sophia watched as they exchanged glances and was suddenly feeling happy that these two had each other. She almost felt jealous for a moment.

Sophia decided to change the subject, and interrupted their loving glances across the room at each other.

"Well, so anyway, how was the party? Please tell me that I missed a crazy time," Sophia teased.

"Well, let's see. My friend Troy decided to jump out of my birthday cake half naked, Sam here ended up in the hot tub with three naked drag queens, and I woke up in the morning in the bathtub. So I would love to say that you missed a bunch of crazy stuff, but, honestly, I don't really remember what you missed," Devon laughed.

Sophia found herself unable to restrain her laugh, as well. Devon had the most contagious smile and laugh, and she could easily imagine all of the things that he had just explained.

"Well, I am sad I missed it. You know I'll be here for the next one."

"Listen, Sophia, I just want you to know that if you need any time off, it's not a big deal. I can get someone to cover for you. You just let me know, whatever you need," Sam offered.

Sophia smiled at Sam's generosity and nodded. "I appreciate that, I do. I just need to keep myself busy, though. That's the best thing for me. Between work and home, it keeps me going, and it doesn't give me too much time to think about it all. I'll let you know, though, if I need to take you up on that," she replied graciously.

The three sat and chatted over wine for the next couple hours, and then Sophia realized what time it was and, even though she always hated cutting her time with these two short, she placed her empty glass down on the coffee table.

"I hate to say it, but I really ought to be going. I wasn't expecting to be out this late, and I really should get home," Sophia apologized as she stood up. Devon and Sam both stood with her and walked her to the front door. Devon gave her another hug as Sam retrieved her things from the closet. He held her coat as Sophia slipped her arms in, and then he handed her back her purse. Then he, too, gave her a big hug.

"Oh, I am so thankful I have you two in my life," Sophia gushed.

"We wouldn't have it any other way. You are family to us, Sophia. We love you, and remember, if you need anything, don't hesitate to ask," Sam replied as he released her from his grasp. He turned and opened the door for her, and watched her walk to her vehicle.

As Sophia pulled away from Sam and Devon's, she glanced in her rearview mirror and immediately noticed a black Escalade parked along the street behind her. At first, it remained where it was, but when she came to the first stop sign, she noticed it pulling out. The first thing that came to her mind was that it looked exactly like Marcus's, but then realized that many people in this city drove black Escalades. When she glanced back up and didn't see it behind her, she knew it must have been all in her head.

As she continued out of Sam's neighbourhood, she glanced one more time in her mirror and instantly noticed the SUV again. This time, the broken left light caught her attention. Marcus kept saying he had to get it replaced soon, but he still hadn't, and it was at that moment that she realized that her suspicions were right: it was, in fact, Marcus in the SUV.

"Why in the hell would he be following me to Sam and Devon's?" she asked herself out loud.

Sophia continued home and, finally, when she came to their house, she pulled into the driveway. She sat in her vehicle for a few moments, waiting to see if he would pull up behind her, but after a little bit, she decided to head inside. Not two minutes after she got into the house, she could see his headlights pull up in the driveway outside. She sat at the island and waited for him to come into the kitchen. Hearing the front door close, he called for her as he came in the door.

"Hey, babe. I'm home!" he shouted.

"I'm in the kitchen," she responded. He walked into the kitchen and gave her a kiss on the cheek.

"How was your day?" he asked.

Sophia looked at her husband, and he could instantly sense that something was not right. She was looking at him accusingly and he instinctively got defensive.

"What's wrong, babe?" he asked.

"Marcus, by chance, were you following me home?" she asked, quite nonchalant.

He laughed snidely. "Following you home? I just got home. What are you talking about, Soph?"

She took in a deep breath before she answered. "Marcus, is your bottom light still broken?" she asked bluntly.

He looked at her with a raised brow and nodded slowly. "Yes, is that what this is about? You're concerned I haven't gotten my light fixed yet?" he asked sarcastically.

"Marcus, I was leaving Sam and Devon's, I didn't notice it was you at first, but I saw a black SUV following me and then I saw the broken light and I knew it was you. I'm just asking you why. Why did you follow me to their house?" she asked him, trying to keep the accusation out of her voice.

She could see that Marcus was getting very angry and she could also tell that he was trying to decide whether to lie or tell her the truth.

He decided to go with the truth. "Jesus, Sophia, do you think that I enjoy feeling like I have to check up on you once in a while? I don't like that I have to do it, but what other choice do you leave me?"

Sophia looked at her husband, stunned, and felt like shaking her head in hopes it would help her understand what he just said to her.

"Check up on me? What the hell are you talking about, Marcus? What do you mean by 'I gave you no choice'? Exactly how often do you feel the need to follow me?"

"Sophia, come on. You lied to me. When I asked you to be honest with me, before, you lied to me, which in turn says I can't trust you. How am I supposed to believe anything you tell me now? The only way I'll know if you're telling me the truth is if I find out for myself. It's really no big deal. Just drop it," Marcus demanded.

Sophia gaped at him.

"Just drop it? You've been following me. You followed me to lunch the day you saw me with Adam, and now you say you have been following me since, and exactly how often did you follow me before all that? I'm sorry, Marcus, but this is not right, I haven't given you any reason not to trust me, and I am not okay with any of this."

Marcus glared venomously at his wife.

"I am sorry, Sophia, but I don't recall asking your permission. If you wouldn't lie to me, then I wouldn't feel the need to follow you. This is all your fault, so don't you dare try and twist this on me. I have never done anything to you." He began to feel the heat on his face.

Sophia considered for a moment whether the words that were in her head should be released from her lips, but with the outrage she was feeling, she knew she couldn't keep anything in, so she met Marcus's gaze with her own and let the words spill out.

"You didn't do anything to me, Marcus, but are you sure you didn't do anything to Adam?"

The second the words were out, she wished she could take them back. Within seconds, Marcus had her by her throat, slammed up against the wall. The blackness in his eyes was like coal, and she could feel the heat of his anger through the hand wrapped around her throat.

"What the fuck did you just say to me?" he spat in her face.

"I'm sorry, I'm sorry, Marcus, I didn't mean it." She began to cry.

"Is that what you think? You think I did something to that worthless piece of shit? If I ever hear you utter those words again, or, in fact, utter my name in the same Goddamn sentence as that little rat, I will make you regret that you are even able to speak. How dare you ever speak to me like that, you stupid bitch." He released his hold on her neck, dropping her to the floor. "You fucking disgust me!" he shouted as he stared down at her, then he walked around her and left the room.

Once again, Sophia was left in shock. She reached for her throat, trying to gasp for breath. As she sat on the floor, trying desperately to calm her breathing, the voices began to battle in her mind. Once again, Marcus managed to make her feel guilty for causing him to get so angry that he had to put his hands on her. She questioned herself, and why she would allow herself to say those things. What did she expect? Why would she even think to challenge him like that?

Then, there was the other side, the side of her that became fully aware at that moment that maybe, just maybe, her deep-seeded suspicions were not so crazy after all. As she sat against the wall, with her hand on her neck, she struggled with which side she should choose to believe.

August 5, 2015 – Daddy's Girl

Paul Warner sat across the table from Detectives Keller and Stone in the stuffy interrogation room. He was still reeling at the news he'd received when they found him slumped over the bar, sipping on a cold beer. The guilt was overwhelming, and he couldn't help but feel that he failed his daughter. He was sure that if he had stayed in her life none of this would have happened. She needed her Daddy, and he was just not there for her. He reached into his front shirt pocket. Pulling out a nearly empty pack of Marlboros, he quickly lifted the pack up to his mouth and retrieved a cigarette using only his teeth. He desperately began patting himself down, looking for something to light it with before he looked up to Detective Keller. "Do you have a fuckin' lighter?"

"I'm sorry, Mr. Warner, but you cannot smoke in here. This is a federal building. It's going to have wait," Detective Keller replied annoyed at his ignorance.

"This is bullshit," He exclaimed as he tossed the unlit cigarette onto the table. "What the fuck happened to my daughter? You must know something by now, so tell me what in the hell happened to my daughter?"

"Mr. Warner, we have the best team working on this case. We're going to figure out what happened at the Donovan home that evening, but we need to ask you a few questions first. What was your relationship like with your daughter, Mr. Warner?"

Paul picked up the Marlboro from the table and began spinning it between his thumb and index finger, watching as the loose tobacco began to spill out onto the metal table.

"What relationship? Cat wanted nothing to do with me. I tried to have a relationship with her, but she made it clear she didn't want me to be a part of her life, so I left. What else could I do?"

Detective Keller took notes while Detective Stone stepped in with a few questions of his own.

"I know you weren't a part of your daughter's life for long, but in the short time that you were involved with her, did you become aware of anyone that may possibly want to hurt her? Any bad relationships? Bitter boyfriends?" Detective Stone asked him as he chewed on the back of his pen.

Paul thought to himself whether anyone stuck out to him, becoming more and more agitated that he knew so little about his own baby girl.

"No. I mean, I know she had a lot of friends and she dated a lot, but I didn't meet any of them. I met Sophia and her husband Marcus many times, but there was nothing suspicious there. They were all great friends. Sophia and her were like sisters."

Stone took a deep breath before continuing. "Mr. Warner, do you think it is possible that Catarina and Marcus Donovan could have been having an affair?"

Paul was caught off-guard by the Detective's question, and was immediately offended.

"What the fuck are you talking about? Cat wasn't a home-wrecker, she would never do that to her best friend. Of course not."

Detective Keller studied Paul's reaction, and although he was still partly drunk from earlier in the day, she knew he was not hiding anything from them. He knew nothing about this. They'd known that when they brought him in, but he was Cat's only surviving family member, and they were hoping he would be able to shed some light on it all.

"Mr. Warner, were you aware that your daughter underwent an abortion quite recently? Do you know anything about that?"

"Christ, no," he answered sadly. He felt horrible that he had no idea, that she'd made a decision like that without him even knowing about it, but then was suddenly furious at how personal this detective was getting.

"I'm sorry, but isn't that her personal business? How the hell does that have anything to do with anything? That was her choice, so what fucking right do you two have to go digging into her life like that?"

Caleb knew this was becoming a lot for Paul to take. He had just found out his daughter was dead, so Stone completely understood his anger. He cleared his throat before addressing Paul's concerns.

"Mr. Warner, you have to understand this is a murder investigation. We have to uncover the lives of Ms. Warner and Mr. Donovan to help us discover what might have led to this. We need to find out what was going on that would have led Ms. Warner to..." Detective Stone was cut off by Paul.

"Find out what led her to what? To kill that son of a bitch? Is that what you were gonna say? So you admit it: you think she killed him, then killed herself. You think my sweet little Cat is capable of murder? Well, you guys don't know what in the fuck you are talking about. You're both useless. Everyone working on this case is bloody useless if they think that is what happened."

Detective Keller was beginning to get annoyed with Paul as she listened to him trying to undermine her abilities as an experienced Detective.

"Mr. Warner, you need to calm down now," she ordered. "We know what we're working with here. We just wanted to get some feedback from you about your daughter, and we thank you for coming in, however, I think this conversation is over and we will keep you posted on this case."

Keller slammed her notebook closed and stood up from the table. She headed out the door, leaving the two men sitting at the table alone. Detective Stone stared at Paul, and Paul instantly knew he had better calm down, or he could get his ass thrown behind bars.

"Mr. Warner I know this is very difficult, finding out the way you did about your daughter, and it's totally unfair, and I can understand your pain. However, you need to let us do our jobs and keep your opinions to yourself, do you understand me? Now, if you think of anything that can help us in this matter, please call us, but in the meantime, please just stay clear of this investigation and let us do our damn jobs. You're free to leave, Mr. Warner." Stone stood up and let himself out of the room, leaving Paul sitting alone.

He headed into Jill's office, where she was sitting at her desk, facing a young, blonde girl. As Caleb walked into the office, Jill glanced up with a serious look on her face.

"Caleb, come in," she said as she motioned to him to join them. As he walked over to the desk, the blond girl turned to look up at him. He gave her a warm smile.

"Caleb, this is Gabriella Preston," Keller introduced as Caleb reached for Gabriella's hand.

"Gabriella, this is Detective Caleb Stone. He is my partner, in this case, and he is the head detective of the Homicide Division."

"Nice to meet you, sir," Gabriella spoke timidly.

"Caleb, Mrs. Preston is here because she thinks she has some information that can help with our case."

"You do? Mrs. Preston, did you know the victims, Catarina Warner, and Marcus Donovan?"

Gabriella ran her fingers through her mass of blond curls nervously. As Caleb waited for her response, he thought that she looked familiar, but could not seem to place it. In this city, everyone looked like they could be somebody, but Gabriella he swore he had seen somewhere before. Finally, Gabriella got up the nerve to answer his question.

"I knew both of the victims very well. I'm married to Marcus Donovan's best friend, Alex Preston."

Caleb's eyebrows rose as he turned to look at Jill, who sat and waited for Gabriella to continue. Now Caleb knew why she looked so familiar. As Alex Preston's wife, she would have been at every major event, and her face would have been all over all the entertainment and gossip magazines. Caleb pulled a chair up beside Gabriella.

"Mrs. Preston, what type of information do you have for us?" Keller asked her from across the desk.

Gabriella inhaled a deep breath and began fidgeting with her hands in her lap. She looked up at Keller, then to Stone, then stated boldly, "I know for a fact that Marcus and Cat were having an affair."

Caleb and Jill turned to look at each other, both with curiosity in their eyes. Gabriella continued, "I know this because I caught them together at one of our parties in my home."

Caleb waited a moment to see if she was going to continue speaking, but she seemed to have nothing more to say, so he decided to step in.

"When was this Mrs. Preston?"

"A few months ago."

"And did you share any of this with Sophia Donovan? Does she know any of this?" Keller asked.

"No," Gabriella replied shortly.

"Why not?" Keller pushed. "You are friends with Sophia, are you not? You don't think that this is information that she should be privy to?"

Gabriella looked down at her hands in her lap, and then up at Keller. Keller repeated her question. "Why didn't you tell Sophia Donovan that her husband was having an affair with her best friend, in your home no less?"

Gabriella responded to Keller while holding her intense stare. "Because he told me that if I ever told anyone what I saw, he was going to kill me."

June 6, 2011 – The Beginning

Sophia walked into Cat's office and noticed she was still on the phone. Cat mouthed the words "I'm sorry," and held up one finger, telling her friend she would only be on the phone for another minute or so.

Sophia slowly walked around Cat's office, looking at the logos she had plastered all over her walls, and then she turned her attention to the many awards lining one of her bookcases in the corner of the room. She was so proud of Cat. After she'd left the catering gig, she managed to get her foot in the door at a prestigious advertising agency in downtown LA called Creative Underground. She had to start as one of the ad exec's mules, and he was a real asshole, but after only a couple of years she managed to steal the show with her creativity, and she was finally given her own campaign. Now she was the Creative Supervisor for the agency and she loved her job.

" 'Kay, listen I got to go, I have a lunch meeting. Send me the files in the morning and I will take a look at it." Cat paused a second on the phone then continued. "Okay, sure. Yes, sounds good. Talk to you later." She hung up the phone and turned to Sophia. "Hey, babe, I'm sorry about that."

"Oh, don't be silly, I'm a bit early anyways." Sophia walked over to Cat's desk and set down the paper bag that contained their salads from one of their favorite delis down the road.

"I'm fricking starving. I could seriously eat a small child right now," Cat joked. Sophia laughed and handed Cat her salad and Diet Coke.

"Come, let's go sit over here," she said as she pointed to the table near the wall of windows overlooking the hustle-and-bustle down on 7th street. Sophia got herself settled at the table, popped her straw into her Pepsi and took a sip.

"So, busy day today?" Sophia asked.

Cat waved her fork in the air as she chewed a mouthful of salad. When she had washed it down with a gulp of her Diet Coke, she answered Sophia. "Yeah, we're pretty busy. We just picked up a huge client, so things have been a bit hectic around here. My assistant has been out sick this week, too, so that hasn't helped matters much. I'm glad you could sneak over here for lunch, though. I know things are pretty crazy at work for you as well."

Sophia sat and poked her salad with her fork, pushing a tomato from one side of the bowl to the other. She was in a bit of a daze, and Cat interrupted her daydream into her salad.

"Hey, Earth to Soph. What's going on, girl? You seem a little bummed."

Sophia looked up at Cat and tears began to well in her eyes. She grabbed a napkin off of the table to dry up the tears that suddenly began to fall. Cat put down her fork and reached for Sophia's arm.

"Hey, hey, hey, what is going on? What's with the tears?" she asked, concerned.

Sophia wiped her eyes again and sighed deeply.

"Shit, Cat, it's nothing, really. I'm probably just being over-sensitive. It's just Marcus. God, we have been fighting too much lately, and, I don't know, I just keep getting this feeling that something is going on. He's been staying at the studio a lot lately, and he gets all these late night calls on his cell phone, and it seems like all we do is fight lately. I don't know, I just think that maybe something is going on. I think maybe he's having an affair or something." Sophia began to pick at her salad again.

Cat looked at her friend and was unsure what she could say to put her mind at ease. She picked up her fork and took another bite of her lunch.

"Sophia, you're being crazy. I know Marcus has proven to be a bit of an asshole, but I don't think he would ever do that to you. He loves you, Soph, you know that. And, well, he is a man, and men are meant to be assholes from time to time. I think it is built into their DNA or something. Don't worry, babe, you know that he is not cheating on you."

Sophia wondered if her friend was right. She took a sip of her Pepsi and then replied, "I hope so. I mean, I know we have been through a lot over these last few years. I just hope that it has not led him to find someone else. Cat, he has these sexy women around him all the time for this movie, and honestly I think it's starting to make me a bit insecure."

Cat gasped at Sophia in amazement. "Insecure? Insecure about what? Sophia, you are beautiful, you are hot, you are sexy as shit. Hell, if I was a lesbo I would do ya in a heartbeat." Cat laughed at her own remark and continued speaking. "Soph, trust me when I say you have no reason to be insecure. Those nasty bimbos have nothing on you and, hell, if Marcus doesn't see that then, well, what the fuck good is he anyways?"

Sophia found herself, oddly, feeling better. Cat always had a way of doing that. Even if what she was saying wasn't true, she still felt better. She managed to put a forkful of salad into her mouth and finally she felt like eating again. She had been so bothered the last couple days about this that she had actually lost her appetite.

"It's gonna be fine, I promise." Cat reassured her one more time. "I promise."

Cat sat in her BMW outside of Marcus and Sophia's house, thinking to herself before going inside. She didn't know for sure if Marcus was screwing around on Sophia, but Sophia had been pretty fragile the last little while. Really, since Adam died, Cat noticed that she had become over-sensitive. Sophia shared a lot with her, about the fights she and Marcus had been having, but Cat felt there were some details that she was purposely leaving out. Cat was sure she wasn't getting the full story most of the time.

Cat didn't like to admit it to Sophia, but she didn't think that Sophia knew how lucky she really was with Marcus. Yeah, he could be a dick from what Sophia shared with her, but like she'd told her earlier, what man wasn't? She felt bad for her friend, though. Sophia was so sure that Marcus was being unfaithful to her, and she was just so afraid to talk to him about it.

Cat quickly adjusted the rearview mirror and, as always, made sure she looked her best before stepping out of the car. She walked to the big front door and put her finger on the doorbell. After a few seconds, she could hear footsteps heading towards her. The door swung open and Marcus stood in front of her, bare-chested, in a pair of sweat pants that hung loosely off his hips.

"Cat, hey, how's it going?" Marcus seemed surprised to see her at the door. "Sophia's not home tonight. She had that meeting for next week's feature," he continued.

Cat shook her head and replied, "Oh, yeah, I know. She told me that at lunch today. Actually, I'm not here to see Sophia. I actually wanted to talk to you, Marcus."

Marcus looked a little baffled that Cat would show up, unexpected, wanting to talk to him, but smiled and opened the door wider for her to walk through.

"Uh-oh, what did I do?" he joked as Cat came into the front entrance.

She smiled up at him as she took off her sweater and put down her purse, and replied, "Nothing, nothing at all. I just, well, can we maybe go into the kitchen and grab a beer or something?" Cat asked him, knowing what his response would be.

He led her back through to the kitchen and headed straight for the fridge. He pulled out two chilled bottles of Corona, popped the cap off of both bottles, and handed one to Cat. She graciously accepted, and then began, "Look, Marcus, Sophia came and had lunch with me today at my office and, well, she seemed pretty... out of sorts, I guess, would be the best way to describe her."

"Out of sorts?" he asked, confused.

"Yeah, she was pretty upset. You know, she said that you guys have been fighting a lot lately, and she was really worried that maybe things were not going well with you guys, and, well, she thinks that maybe you're fucking around." Cat paused and waited for a reaction from him.

He gave a deep laugh and shook his head, rubbing his hands through his hair.

"Jesus Christ, that woman. When in the hell did she become so insecure, Cat? I don't know how many times I've had to tell her that I'm not fucking around on her. I don't know what she wants me to do, damn it. Yeah, she's right, we have not been getting along the greatest lately, but that doesn't mean I'm going to run and jump into the sack with some other chick."

Cat knew that Marcus was going to respond the way he did. She knew he was a good man, and wasn't screwing around on Sophia. Sometimes she wondered, quietly, what exactly Marcus saw in Sophia, if she was so insecure. A man like Marcus liked confidence, and integrity, and lately her best friend had been lacking those traits.

She gave a sarcastic laugh. "I told her that, dude. I told her she's crazy, but I don't know if she believed me or not. She seems pretty torn up about shit. You know, I don't know if you have noticed as much as I have, but does she seem different since Adam's death? She seems, I don't know, distant, and much more sensitive to shit. Is that just me?" Cat asked Marcus before she took a swig of her beer.

Marcus shook his head and replied immediately, "No, you're right, Cat. I've noticed it for a long time, and you know what? I've tried talking to her about it, but it always ends up in a fight. Shit, I'm surprised she hasn't been running to you, telling you what an asshole I am. I don't know, her jealously and insecurity has become almost more than I can take. Honestly, Cat, I have no idea what I'm supposed to do. I feel like I'm being analyzed and constantly being questioned about shit, and it's causing a real problem. Christ, you know I love her and I would do anything for her, but I'm not sure what I'm supposed to do. I'm always open and honest with her, which is more than I can say for her, so I'm at a loss."

Cat had never really gotten to hear Marcus's side of things before. They were definitely friends, because of Sophia. But she had never known what was going through his head during all this. She had never heard his side about Adam, and how that all made him feel. After the incident a few years back, on Christmas Eve, Cat told Sophia she needed to just trust him, and she knew that Sophia didn't. She still questioned him, even after Alex came and explained the whole situation. Cat got how frustrating this must have been for Marcus, always being questioned and being made to feel like a liar.

"You know, Cat, sometimes I wish she could just be more like you." He gave her a quick wink over his beer.

Cat laughed awkwardly. "Like me? Really? And what on earth would make you say that?"

Marcus set his beer on the counter and set his gaze on Cat's as he sat beside her on the island stools.

"Because, you are confident and secure, and you don't put up with shit from anyone. That confidence is the sexiest thing a woman can possess, and trust me, your confidence is the first thing that I noticed about you." Marcus's eyes didn't let go of Cat's, and she felt like she was in a trance.

"You are an amazing woman in so many ways. Shit, the fact that you are here, talking to me because my own wife doesn't want to approach the subject, well what does that say? You're a good friend to her, and to me as well, and one day one lucky son-of-a-bitch is gonna get to call you his."

Cat couldn't shake the feeling that was overcoming her as Marcus stared at her with those eyes and told her how amazing she was. This was her best friend's husband. Why was he having such a desirable effect on her? Well, she knew why. Marcus was gorgeous and charming, but Marcus was also married to her best friend.

When he slid a little bit closer to her, she could smell his muskiness and it was intoxicating. She had been around Marcus a thousand times but never like this, not this close, and she couldn't deny the feelings that were beginning to overwhelm her. She threw herself into his arms and kissed him hungrily. In a matter of seconds, they both stood up, kicking the stools out from under them, and Marcus had Cat sitting up on top of the island. He stood between her legs as they devoured each other with their lips. He reached up and quickly unzipped the front of her shirt, exposing her black lace bra, and he pushed it aside, freeing one of her breasts. He then wrapped his mouth and tongue around her erect nipple. As soon as she felt the warmth of his tongue exploring her nipple, she let out a cry of ecstasy while throwing her head back.

He yanked her skirt up to her waist so he could see the black stockings that were being held up by her silky lace garter belt with two little pink bows. He began kissing her inner thighs and he could feel her body tremble as he trailed his fingers up to meet her, then suddenly he reached up and tore her panties off her with one quick motion. He pulled her forcefully to the edge of the countertop and easily slid himself deep inside her. Cat tried to stifle the loud cry of pleasure that escaped her lips, but the sensation of feeling every ounce of him inside her was too much to take.

As he continued to push himself into her, he continued to explore her breasts with his tongue, and she dug her fingers through his thick dark hair. Marcus lifted her off the counter and turned her around, and then pushed her face-down onto the island, exposing her ass. Again he pushed himself into her, holding her shoulders with both hands. Cat's hands reached in front of her, grasping onto the edges of the counter, and every time she felt him pushing inside her she knew she was going to lose control soon. As Marcus gave one final, forceful thrust into Cat, she could feel him release inside her and she finally let herself succumb to him.

Marcus stood behind her, beginning to go soft as he remained inside her, and Cat lay on her stomach, still on the counter. The reality of what she just did came flooding to her now that she had been released from the ecstasy she was just entwined in. She leaned up on her elbows and Marcus quickly pulled himself out of her, yanking up his sweat pants. She turned to face him.

"Jesus Christ, Cat, what the hell?" he exclaimed.

"I'm sorry, Marcus. Shit, I don't know what happened. Fuck, shit, what we do now?" she asked him, panicking.

"Nothing. Look, it was a mistake. We both got wrapped up in the moment. Nothing has to happen, and she doesn't need to know about this. We need to promise each other that this doesn't leave this kitchen," Marcus replied as he picked up her ripped panties, putting them in her hands.

"You have to get out of here. I'm sorry, Cat, but you have to leave." He began walking to the front door.

Cat zipped up her blouse and crumpled her panties up in a ball in her fist. She walked to the front door, where she grabbed her purse and pushed them into an empty pocket. She was unsure what to say, but as she opened the door, she turned to Marcus one last time.

"I'm sorry, Marcus." She then headed out the door.

Marcus stood and watched her, and just before she got in the car he called to her. "Cat!"

She turned to him. He gave her a sexy smirk and exclaimed, "You were fucking fantastic, by the way."

Cat stood and stared at him as he disappeared behind the large oak door.

August 5, 2015 – Unexpected Surprises

The soft, fluffy sand wedged its way in between Sophia's toes as she sat on the white sand beach, overlooking the ocean waves breaking on the shore. As she dug her fingers in the sand, she could feel every morsel. She could also feel the breeze gliding gently through her hair. She couldn't remember a time in the last several months, or years to be more accurate, that she felt at such peace. There was no one bothering her here, and she could pretend that everything was fine. So far, everything was going smoothly. She just hoped that it continued this way. She picked up her cell phone, looking down at the screen, half-expecting it to ring at any moment. She would love for it to ring. She wanted nothing more than to hear his voice right now, but she understood they could not be communicating, not now. It was not safe. Right now the only thing that kept getting her through day after day was knowing, at the end of this all, she could wrap herself in his arms and never let him go.

As she stared up at the fluffy white clouds portraying themselves as random objects against the backdrop of the blue sky, she heard someone walking up behind her. She turned around to see Alex trudging through the sand towards her. She immediately stood up, wiping the sand off her backside, and walked to meet him. As soon as he was close enough, he pulled her into him and began to cry.

"Oh, Sophia, I am so sorry. I got back to town as soon as I could."

Sophia held him tightly and let him cry into her shoulder for as long as he needed. She could feel his body shaking as she rubbed his back, and then finally he looked up and met her eyes with his.

"Soph, I don't know what to say, what am I supposed to say to something like this? When I heard the news in Sydney I thought it was some kind of mistake, but Gabby assured me there was no mistake." He wiped his eyes with the sleeve of his shirt then continued, "Damn it, Sophia, I am sorry that they had to do this to you."

Sophia took Alex by the arm and led him back to her house, and they both took a seat on the chairs that were nestled comfortably on the patio to overlook the ocean.

"Alex, they are still investigating this whole thing. We still don't know what happened for sure. It can be really anything at this point, but I can't bring myself to believe that Cat murdered him. It makes no sense."

Alex seemed confused at Sophia's statement. He knew that Gabby had just come from the station, where she sat down with a couple of detectives to tell them what she knew. He was sure Sophia would have known that.

"Sophia, I'm sorry, but I'm a bit confused here. Haven't you spoken to Gabby since any of this has happened? I just assumed you would have." .

Sophia shook her head and replied, "No. Well, Gabby has called and left me a couple messages, but I just haven't been ready to talk to a lot of people yet. Why do you ask, though?"

"Shit, Soph, I'm not sure if I'm supposed to be saying anything to you about this, but Gab was down at the station today. I guess she went in to talk to a couple investigators regarding the case."

Sophia was completely unaware of Gabriella being a part of this case or having any information. She was actually surprised to hear that she'd gone to the station. I guess I should be expecting a few curve balls here and there, Sophia thought to herself. She should have returned Gabby's messages last week.

"Listen, Soph, I really don't know how to say this, but Gabby just shared this with me when I got home. Apparently, a few months ago, when we had that party to celebrate Gabby's new bakery, she walked in on Cat and Marcus. They were right in the middle of, well... well, you know?"

Sophia was not surprised by this news, although she was completely unaware that Gabriella had walked in on them. It made sense that they would have been together, as she was unable to make it to the party that evening because she had been in Catalina for the weekend. However, it was important that she seemed shocked and upset by the news that Alex was sharing with her.

"What do you mean, Alex? Gabby walked in on them what? What is it that you are trying to say, Alex?"

Alex put his face into his palms and shook his head and tried his best to answer. "Soph, you know what I am trying to say. Gabby told me everything, and she wanted to tell you, she really wanted to tell me, but she just couldn't, not until now."

"So wait a minute. My husband and my best friend are both dead, and now you are going to sit here and tell me that they were fucking each other and that your wife knew about it this whole time and didn't have the decency to tell me? She just decided to keep me in the dark? For what? Was she just trying to spare my feelings? Alex, how could she not tell me? Is that what she was calling for, because now that Marcus is dead, well, now it would be a good time to tell me?" Sophia stood up from her chair and began to pace.

"Jesus, shit, Sophia, she didn't tell you because Marcus threatened to kill her if she did!" Alex blurted out.

Sophia stopped in her tracks and turned back to look at Alex with a look of genuine shock on her face. Another surprise. She truly didn't know anything about this happening to Gabby, and as terrible as Sophia felt that she was forced into keeping this a secret, she was also very relieved. Even though Gabriella Preston was oblivious to it, she just helped Sophia in solidifying the final stages of her plan.

As Alex watched Sophia's reaction to what he just told her, he felt awful that she had to learn this from him. He had no idea that she didn't know, and he could see the devastation behind her eyes as he watched his best friend's wife desperately coming to the realization that, perhaps maybe, the man she had loved for so long was not the man she truly thought he was.

December 31, 2011 – Happy New Year

Sophia's eyes grew wide as she walked into the kitchen and discovered the huge bouquet of roses that sat in the middle of their large kitchen table. Those hadn't been here when she got home earlier, she was pretty certain of that, and just as she walked over to pull the card out of the foliage, she heard Marcus come in behind her. She turned around to face him and she was immediately impressed at how impeccable he looked in his Gucci tux. He stood smiling at her, and as she looked down at his hands she noticed he was holding a black velvet box.

"Marcus?"

"Sophia, honey you look exquisite. Damn, how did I get so lucky to get such an amazingly beautiful wife?" he complimented.

Sophia smiled bashfully at her husband and replied, "Marcus, these are beautiful." She bent over and inhaled the intoxicating scent of the flowers.

"But you didn't have to get me flowers. It's New Year's Eve, it's not like it's my birthday or anything." She paused, then jokingly waved her finger at him and continued. "Wait a minute, unless you did something wrong. Did you do something wrong Mr. Donovan?" she teased happily.

Marcus laughed at his wife's comment and walked over to her. He stood looking down at her, admiring the sparkle in her eyes.

"Go ahead Baby, open it up." He motioned towards the box.

Sophia smiled widely up at her husband, and in that brief moment, every horrible thing they had ever gone through, every fight, every argument, every tear shed, it all just disappeared. In that moment, she stood looking up at this man and she fell completely in love with him all over again. She slowly reached up and propped open the lid of the box and was astonished at what sat inside.

"Oh, my God, honey, it's breathtaking. Oh, Marcus, you didn't have to do this." She gasped with excitement as she admired the radiance of the diamond necklace lying perfectly atop its satin bed.

Marcus gently took the necklace out of the case and walked behind his wife as she pulled her hair off to the side to allow him access to her neck. He clasped the necklace together, then turned Sophia around so she was again facing him. The brilliance of the diamonds shone brightly against her tanned skin.

"You're right, Sophia, I didn't have to do this. I wanted to do this. You deserve nothing less than this, and I just wanted to start the beginning of this New Year right. I am so sorry for anything that we've had to go through. Things haven't always been easy for us, we've had our ups and our downs, but I've been a real ass and I'm sorry. I just wanted to do something to show you that it's a new year, and I want to start fresh with you. I just want us to be happy again. I love you so much."

Sophia's eyes glistened as tears began to surface, and she wrapped her arms around Marcus's neck and gave him a gentle kiss on the mouth before replying, "Marcus, I love you so much. Yes, we have had our ups and downs, but I'm not perfect either. I had as much to do with it as you did, and you have been so patient with me while I've struggled with my stupid insecurities and jealousy. I know things are going to be better for us, I just know they will. This is a new year. It's a time for new promises, and a renewal of our love. People admire us, Marcus, they see our relationship as everlasting and they strive for a love like ours. Yes, we have done an incredible job at keeping our issues private, but we will have that perfect love back. I just know it, honey. I know this year is going to be the start of our Happily Ever After."

The limo pulled up outside of Sam and Devon's home around eight that evening, and after it came to a stop, Marcus waited for the driver to come around to open his door.

"Happy New Year, baby," he said to her softly, just as the door was propped open by Jack, one of their most recent drivers. Sophia watched as Marcus climbed out of the back seat and then waited patiently until her side opened, and Marcus stood waiting with his hand extended. She reached up to grab it and slid out of the limo, being careful not to snag her dress. She then laced her hand through his arm and they headed into the festivities of Sam and Devon's New Year's Eve Bash.

As they walked through the door, they were welcomed with beautiful décor. A modestly-decorated tree stood off to the corner, but it towered to touch the top of the fifteen-foot ceilings. Soft jazz Christmas hits were playing softly in the background, loud enough to hear, but not so loud that you couldn't enjoy your conversations. Candles were glowing warmly throughout the entire home, and Sophia could smell the fragrant aroma of all sorts of delicious food wafting from the kitchen. As they stood at the entrance, admiring the beauty, Devon politely interrupted his conversation and ran up to greet them.

"Hello, hello, come in! Oh, I'm so glad you guys could make it. Sophia, you look amazing, as always. Marcus," Devon winked up at him, "you look yummy enough to eat, as always." He took Sophia's wrap and placed it in the main closet.

"Devon, your guys' place looks so beautiful! Don't tell me you did this all by yourself. If you say yes, I'm going to tell you that you need to quit your job as an architect and become a decorator," Sophia commented happily as they headed into the party.

Devon let out a boisterous laugh and then answered, "Bah, I don't think so, honey. Shit, if this was left up to me we would be washing buttered saltines down with cheap beer while listening to the acoustic stylings of City in Color. Oh, no, I didn't do this. This was all paid for, sweetie. Come, let's go find Sam. He'll be so happy you're here."

They made their way through the crowd, out into the back yard, and Devon spotted Sam, who was in the middle of a conversation with Nate Weston, one of the other Editors at LA Today. As they approached, both men were happy to see Sophia and Marcus.

"Sophia." Nate rushed to give her a hug and a kiss on the cheek. "You look gorgeous." He then reached his hand out to Marcus. "Marcus, good to see you, it's been awhile. I trust all is well with you?"

"Of course, Nate, everything is great. And how about you? How are those three little rug-rats of yours doing?" Marcus inquired.

"Ah, you know, three girls, all of whom think they're teenagers already. Let's just say I'm glad I don't have to deal with them all day like Katie does," Nate joked.

"How old are they now? Marcus asked.

"Six." Nate chuckled loudly. "And I wonder where they get it from?" he continued as he pointed over to his wife, who was near the bar, primping herself in her compact mirror.

Everyone laughed at the vision of his three little six-year-olds as he described their obsession with makeup, shoes, clothes, and shopping. After a few moments, he excused himself and headed over to his wife, who began giving the signal that she wanted another drink.

Marcus and Sophia stood and mingled with Devon and Sam for a little while longer, and just as they excused themselves from making the rounds of their guests, Sophia glanced over to the patio and was happy to see Cat walk through the doors. Cat instantly spotted Marcus and Sophia, giving them a quick wave while walking towards them.

"Hey, finally, what took you so long?" Sophia asked.

"I know, I'm sorry, my Dad called again. You know how those conversations always go." She sighed deeply.

"Yeah, right, Cat. It's okay, you can say what you were really doing. Having a quickie, perhaps, with Mr. Nobody?" Sophia teased.

Cat shot Sophia an uneasy glance, and then quickly looked up at Marcus to see a sweep of disdain wash over his face.

"Mr. Nobody", as it turned out, was Cat's secret lover, whose identity she was unable to share with Sophia, because she was pretty certain that if Sophia discovered Mr. Nobody was, in fact, her husband things would not go over so well.

"Nah, Soph, that's over. I don't know what I was thinking, letting that carry on for so long," Cat lied as she fidgeted with her dress strap.

"Over? What? How come you didn't tell me? Shoot, are you okay, Cat?"

"Yes, of course, I'm fine. Yeah, it's no biggie," Cat replied. She suddenly noticed Sophia's necklace and changed the subject.

"Um, holy fucking sparkles. When did you get that necklace, Soph?" Cat reached up to touch a diamond.

Sophia smiled up at Marcus before she answered, "This was a gift from my amazing husband. He decided to surprise me with this beautiful necklace and a gorgeous bouquet of roses this evening. Kind of a 'brand new year, fresh start' gift, I guess you can say. I am a pretty lucky woman," she gushed, looking up at her husband.

Cat's jealousy was almost evident in her eyes, and she did her best to hide it from Sophia. The heat began to rise to her cheeks, and she was thankful that at just that moment, Sophia saw one of her colleagues across the crowd and excused herself to go say hello. Cat stormed off to the bar to get herself a glass of champagne, and Marcus followed closely after her.

"Glass of champagne, please?" she barked at the bartender, just as Marcus came up beside her and ordered the same for himself. Cat turned angrily to Marcus.

"That's nice, Marcus, that is real fucking nice," she muttered under her breath.

Marcus reached for this glass of champagne before responding to Cat.

"Listen, Cat, she is still my wife. What do you expect me to do?"

Cat shot him a hateful look, then replied, "I don't know, Marcus, I don't fucking know. You know what? Just forget it. I don't know what the hell we were thinking anyways. I can't go on betraying my best friend like this. Every time I talk to her I get sick with guilt, so you know what? Maybe it's best if we just end this right now." She grabbed her glass of champagne and stormed off angrily into the crowd.

Marcus stood watching after her, and was suddenly startled as Sophia snuck up behind him and wrapped her arms around him. He put Cat's comments out of his mind for the time being, and turned around to pull his wife into his arms.

"Come on, baby, let's go dance." He kissed the top of Sophia's head and led her to the dance floor.

The next few hours sped by as the music played and the guests danced, drank and mingled. Everyone was in high spirits, and Sophia made the rounds, getting a chance to say hello to many of her friends and colleagues from the Magazine, and also to many friends she met through Samuel and Devon. The clock was nearing midnight, and as Sophia and Marcus swayed together to the smooth sounds of The Way You Look Tonight, they lovingly embraced each other and peered into each other's eyes.

The song was suddenly cut off as Devon came over the surround sound. "Okay, people, it's 11:59. Do we all have that special somebody we want to ring in the New Year with? If not, well, just grab anyone. Anyone will do. Are you ready? Here we go, and..."

"10, 9, 8, 7, 6, 5, 4, 3, 2, 1!" everyone shouted in unison. As the clock struck midnight, the whole crowd roared "Happy New Year!" and Auld Lang Syne began to play over the speakers.

Marcus pulled his wife in tight and whispered to her, "Happy New Year, baby. I love you so much."

Sophia looked up at him and replied, "Happy New Year, Marcus. I love you too."

Their lips met in a passionate kiss in the middle of the dance floor and they stood, holding each other, kissing for the duration of the song. It was the first time in a long time that Sophia felt they were finally back where they needed to be, and it was the best feeling she had ever had.

Cat stood near the bar and ordered herself another drink. She could not help but help seethe with jealously as she watched Marcus and Sophia embracing on the dance floor, sharing the New Year's kiss. She'd told Marcus that they had to end it, but she didn't mean it, and as she stood by and observed her lover with her best friend, she knew right there that this, this whole thing, it was far from over.

August 14, 2015 – The Unknown

Sophia's hair was whipping freely in the wind as she cruised down the Pacific Coast Highway. She thought to herself how good it felt just to drive with her top down and feel the breeze wash over her skin. The conversation she had shared with Alex just the other afternoon kept replaying itself over and over in her mind, and she still couldn't believe how Gabby's confession fell so perfectly in her lap. It was certainly the first she had heard of it, and she couldn't blame Gabby for not telling her, because she knew that Marcus's words weren't just some idle threat.

The days seemed to be getting somewhat easier, and the images of that night were slowly beginning to release their grasp from the corners of her mind. Sophia wanted nothing more than for this whole nightmare to come to an end, because she couldn't wait to be able to be with the man she loved, the man who saved her life.

As she approached her exit, she flipped on her signal light and merged onto the off-ramp. She knew the restaurant was nearby, so she kept her eyes peeled. Just ahead, to the left, she saw the sign for Malibu Honey. She pulled into the lot and found an easy stall to pull her car into. As she put the engine in park, Sam and Devon pulled up right beside her. Sam gave her a wide grin through his window, but she could see the sorrow hidden behind his eyes. She quickly got out of her vehicle and walked around the back of her car, just as Sam and Devon came to meet her. Sam reached out to her first, pulling her into his embrace. He kissed her softly on the cheek, and as he looked down at her, she could see the pain in his face.

"Sophia, honey, how are you doing?" he whispered to her.

"I don't know, Sam. I really don't know," she replied. Devon pulled her in for a hug of his own and held her tightly. This was the first time they had seen each other since it happened. As Sophia explained to them on the phone earlier, she just wasn't ready to see anyone prior to this.

"Soph, you know we're here for you. Whatever you need, anything at all." Finally releasing her from the hug, Devon stood, holding her hands in his. "Please, tell us they've found out what happened? Do you have any information yet, anything at all?" he inquired.

Sophia sighed deeply and led Devon by the hand as she turned and headed towards the restaurant. "Let's go inside," she replied.

Inside, they were met by a chipper hostess who showed them to a table and placed three menus on the table before turning to walk away. Sophia pushed the menu aside for a moment. Right now, she just wanted to be with her friends and fill them in on what she knew so far.

"Alex Preston came to see me the other day," she began as she fidgeted with her fingers. "He informed me of something that he thought I must have already known, but I haven't spoken to any of the investigators in a few days, so I wasn't aware." She paused, then summoned some of the few tears she had left.

"What did he say, Soph?" Devon asked impatiently.

Sophia pressed her lips tightly together and closed her eyes for a moment. "He said that Gabby went to talk to the detectives that are working on the case, and she shared some information with them, information that could help with the case. She told them that she walked in on Cat and Marcus at their last party, back in April. She said she walked in on them having sex." She dropped her head back down and continued focusing on her fingers.

Sam and Devon both sat in astonishment. They looked at each other, first, then back at Sophia.

"We were at that party, Sophia, both of us were there. Why in the hell wouldn't she have said anything? Why wouldn't she have told Alex, or us, or anyone for that matter? How could she keep this from you?" Sam asked angrily, in defense of his friend.

Sophia sat in silence for what seemed like forever before she finally looked up to her friends and gave them the same answer Alex had given her earlier. "Because she was scared."

Sam and Devon both tilted their heads in confusion, then Devon asked, "Scared of what? That you wouldn't believe her, or that Cat would kick her ass? What exactly was she so scared of?"

"Marcus. She was scared of Marcus. He threatened Gabby, that if she ever told anyone what she had seen that he was going to kill her," Sophia stated bluntly.

A look of shock spread over both of their faces and she could tell they were both internally trying to justify why Marcus would have done and said something like that. It didn't make sense to either of them, not the Marcus that they both knew.

"Do you believe that, Sophia? I mean, maybe she's making it up," Devon insisted, searching for some sort of logical answer.

"Why? Why would she make something like that up, Devon? She was obviously terrified and that's why she didn't say anything until now, now that Marcus is dead. She finally felt she was safe enough to tell someone what happened. I don't know, maybe she is lying. For what reason, I don't know, but I certainly don't want to believe it. But right now, nobody has told me anything else, so I'm torn. I'm lost. I'm not sure what the hell I'm supposed to believe anymore." Sophia began to get visibly upset.

"Hey, hey, it's okay, Soph. Don't worry about it, not now. The truth will all come out, I promise it will. You just need to trust that, and know that the investigators know what they're doing and trust that the answers will come. Honey, I am so sorry you have to go through this." Sam reached for her hand, trying to calm her.

Just then, Sophia's cell phone started ringing from her purse. She rifled through her bag until she finally found it, and as she pulled it out she glanced down at the display, checking who it was before answering. Her heart skipped a quick beat when she saw Detective Keller's name displayed on the screen. She quickly wiped her eyes, cleared her throat, and then put up her index finger, indicating to Sam and Devon that she had to take the call.

"Hello?"

"Mrs. Donovan. This is Detective Keller calling. I'm sorry to bother you, but I'm going to need to ask you to please come down to the station, as soon as you can," Keller asked, in her matter-of-fact tone.

"Um, yes. Um, is everything okay?" Sophia asked nervously.

"We can discuss it when you get here, Mrs. Donovan. If you can please just come down today, as soon you can, we would appreciate it. There are a few things we need to discuss with you."

Sophia could feel the familiar tremble returning to her knees, and a sense of panic crept into her chest. She wasn't certain what was going on, or why they wanted her to come down, but she knew she could now hear her own heartbeat in her head. She tried her best to remain calm as she replied to Keller, "Yes, of course. I will be there as soon as I can. Thank you, detective."

She pulled the phone away from her ear and hung it up. Sam and Devon had both listened quietly to her conversation and were waiting for her to share with them what was going on. She put her phone back in her purse and caught them both staring at her.

"I'm so sorry you guys, but I have to go. They want me at the station. She said there are some things they need to discuss with me." Both men could hear the shakiness in Sophia's voice. They both reached across the table, each taking one of Sophia's hands in their own.

"It's going to be okay, do you hear me? Everything is going to be okay. They're going to find out what happened, and we're both here for you whenever you need us. Please, Soph, please try and stay strong," Sam pleaded with Sophia as he squeezed her hand tightly.

She gently pulled her hands back and stood up, throwing her purse over her shoulder. Both men stood and gave her a tight hug, again reassuring her that it was all going to be okay. Sophia turned and walked to her car, and she couldn't help but think that maybe they were wrong. Maybe she wasn't going to be okay after all.

October 18, 2013 – Jealousy

Marcus laid on his back, staring up at the ceiling as he waited to catch his breath. The sweat gleamed off his chest in the soft glow of the candles that lit the room. Beside him, Cat lay panting, and she could feel her heart beating through her chest. The intensity of their lovemaking was unlike anything she had every experienced before. He was rough and aggressive and demanding, but she loved it. Every time he pulled her hair or smacked her ass, she felt powerful, even in control. She knew very well that Sophia was not like this in bed, especially lately from what Marcus had shared with her. She turned to watch Marcus sit himself up so he was leaning against the leather headboard of Cat's bed.

"That was amazing, baby. God, I love how you fuck me," Cat purred as she turned on her side to face him.

Marcus ignored her compliment as he turned on the bedside lamp and took a small vial off of the night stand. He pulled a small scoop of white powder out of the container, held it up to his nose and inhaled deeply. He laid his head back and closed his eyes as he allowed the sensations to engulf his body. He slowly opened his eyes and turned to acknowledge Cat.

"You want some?"

Cat took the vial from Marcus's hand, took a generous scoop, and quickly put it up to her nose. She screwed the cap back on and set it on the nightstand on her side of the bed. She could instantly feel that familiar sensation running down the back of her throat as she pulled the sheets up over her breasts and relaxed against the headboard.

"So what happened tonight?" Cat asked curiously.

Marcus rolled his head to look at Cat. "The same fucking shit. She's accusing me of screwing around and questions my every move. She thinks I have something going on with Natalie Mason."

"Oh? Well, I wonder why she would think that?" Cat accused.

Marcus shot her a look of contempt before he replied, "Christ, Cat, what the hell is that supposed to mean?"

Cat was beginning to know Marcus well enough that she could tell when he was getting defensive, and right now he was getting very defensive, but she pressed him anyway. "Well, Marcus, I mean, are you? Hell, you've been spending a shit-ton of time at the studio lately, and you're screwing around on Sophia with me, so what the hell is to stop you from screwing anybody else?" Cat argued.

"Really? I don't have to put up with enough of this shit from Soph, now I have to sit here and listen to this garbage from you? You're not my wife, remember? I don't have to answer to you," Marcus spat back.

Cat wasn't at all shocked by his response. She knew he was right – she wasn't his wife, Sophia was, so she had no say in what he did or who he fucked, no matter how much it hurt her.

"Look, I'm Sorry, baby, but this is hard on me, you know? You keep telling me that you love me and want to be with me, but you keep putting up with Sophia's shit. You know how difficult it is for us to be friends. All I think about every time we hang out now is how much I would rather be with you. When are you going to leave her, Marcus? We can figure out what we're going to tell her afterwards." Cat began to pout.

Marcus's frustration with Cat was abundantly clear as he banged his head gently against the headboard. He ran his fingers through his hair and sighed deeply. "Cat, Sophia is my wife. This isn't just as easy as me up and leaving. I have to be careful here. I have a damn good reputation to protect, do you understand that? Besides, I won't have her just walk away from this marriage with half of my fortune. If I leave her now, she can fuck me over. She will take me to the Goddamn cleaners, and I am not about to have that happen. I have worked way too hard to get to be who I am and no woman, not you, not her, not anyone, is going to take that away from me. I love you, Cat, and yes, I want to be with you, but I need you to understand that."

Cat felt like Marcus had punched her in the stomach. He had told her for months that he was going to leave Sophia, so that they could be together. She had been trying her best to be patient and understanding, but now it sounded like he may never follow through.

"I understand that you have worked hard for everything that you have, Marcus, and you have to know that I would never try to take that away from you, but you also have to know that I can't do this forever. I love you, and I want to be with you, but I can't sit back and watch you with her. It's too hard. I love her, she's still my friend, but I can't keep doing this."

"Cat, look, we'll figure something out. We can't tell her, though. Not yet, not now. Just, please, trust me, okay?" Marcus's voice turned soft as he tried his best to keep her calm. The last thing he needed was Cat to exploit them and ruin everything.

"And what about this stupid Halloween party that Sophia's planning? I suppose you expect me to go and, yet again, just stand by and watch as you two pretend to be the perfect little couple," Cat sulked.

Marcus's annoyance resurfaced as he listened to Cat's complaining. He understood where she was coming from, but backing him into a corner certainly wasn't making it any easier. Still, he had to do his best to appease her. "You better be there, missy," he teased, suddenly flirtatious. "And you had better be dressed up as something sexy, because you know you have to give me something to get excited about."

"Oh, baby, if sexy is what you want, then sexy is what you are going to get. I will make you wish your wife didn't exist, because you're going to want to screw me the second I enter the room."

Cat smiled seductively up at Marcus as she moved closer to him. She had an extremely hard time staying mad at him. She knew he had her wrapped around his little finger, but she loved him, and she knew that she was never going to give up on him.

August 14, 2015- The Sweet Release

Sophia walked cautiously up to the counter where a uniformed police officer sat at a computer. She cleared her throat to get his attention when he didn't acknowledge her presence. He finished typing whatever it was he was working on, and glanced up at Sophia.

"May I help you?" he asked.

"Yes, um, I'm here to see Detective Keller, please. She called me earlier asking me to come in," Sophia replied, somewhat intimidated by the Officer.

"Name, please?"

Just as she was about to respond, she was interrupted.

"It's okay, Officer Elmwood, I called her here." Keller stood in the hallway, motioning for Sophia to follow her.

Sophia gave Officer Elmwood a shy smile as she walked past him, and followed Detective Keller down the hall into the familiar room where she was originally questioned the day it all happened. As Detective Keller opened the door, Sophia saw Detective Stone already sitting at the table with a small pile of files in front of him. He stood to greet her when they entered the room.

"Sophia." Detective Stone reached for her hand. "How are you?" he asked, concerned.

"I'm doing alright, Detective Stone. I'll be better when I know why I'm here, though," Sophia replied as she squeezed his hand.

"Why don't you have a seat? Can we get you anything? A water, or a coffee? Stone offered.

Sophia recalled how horrible the coffee was the last time she was here, but water would be a saving grace. Dryness was beginning to overwhelm her mouth.

"Yes, a water, please. That would be great, thank you." Detective Stone walked out into the hall and filled a plastic cup with water. Sophia accepted the glass with another thank-you, and took a sip. . After setting the glass down, she tried adjusting herself in the uncomfortable chair.

"Mrs. Donovan, we have spent the last several days going through a lot of information pertaining to yourself and your husband, as well as Ms. Warner. I told you before this can get very difficult, and you may discover a lot of things about people you thought you trusted, things that may be very shocking to you. We received a visit from a Mrs. Gabriella Preston. Are you familiar with her?"

Sophia nodded. "Of course, yes. Gabriella is Alex Preston's wife. Marcus and Alex were very close friends," Sophia explained.

Keller jotted something down on her notepad before continuing. "Well, Gabriella came to us with some interesting information, and she claims it's information that she has been keeping to herself for some time now. She informed us that she hadn't even told her husband about it."

Sophia, of course, knew what the information was already, but she knew she needed to act shocked and upset, so she prepared herself accordingly.

"What information is that, Detective Keller?" she asked.

Keller pulled out Gabriella's written statement and quickly scanned it before replying.

"Mrs. Preston states that on the night of April 11, 2015, at a party which was being held at her and her husband's home, she discovered Mr. Donovan and Ms. Warner together," Detective Keller replied.

"Together? Of course, they were together. They went to the party together as I was out of town that weekend. Cat and Marcus were friends. So what if they came to the party together? I hardly think that is a cause for concern," Sophia said, trying her best to sound naïve.

Detective Stone stepped in, hoping he could ease her into this conversation a little bit better than his partner was doing. "Sophia, she means that Gabriella claims that she discovered your husband and Ms. Warner being intimate. They were having sex when she found them," Caleb stated matter-of-factly, all the while trying to remain sympathetic.

Sophia laughed softly to herself and shook her head. "That's ridiculous. I don't know why Gabby would say such a thing. I told you before: Marcus was faithful to me, and Cat was my best friend. There's just no way that happened. I think maybe Gabby had too much to drink that night, and she must have mistaken them for someone else." Sophia shook her head in denial.

"I understand this isn't easy to hear, and you're still grieving the loss of two people very close to you, but, Sophia, we're inclined to tell you everything, and to inform you of the results of this investigation." Caleb then pulled out a signed copy of a release form that they had retrieved from the Planned Family Centre in Santa Barbara. He pushed it across the table to Sophia.

"Sophia, Marcus signed a consent of release form for Ms. Warner from this clinic on June 12. Were you aware that he did this for her?" Detective Stone asked.

Even though she had already been privy to this information, every time she was reminded about it, she felt sick to her stomach. "Planned Family Centre?" she asked, confused. "What? She was pregnant when she died? Are you telling me that she was pregnant?" A look of devastation swept across Sophia's face.

Detective Keller pointed to the initialed section of the release. "Ms. Warner was there for an abortion. Mr. Donovan consented for her to be released into his care after the procedure. Now, I am assuming, Mrs. Donovan, that since you and Cat were such near and dear friends that if she had an abortion you would have been the first person she went to about it. Does it make sense to you? Why was your husband the one who took her, and signed for her to be left in his care?"

Sophia sat with her arms folded and tears found their way to her cheeks. Her jaw was tight, and a wave of nausea swept over her. She recalled how she felt when she first found out that not only was her best friend having an affair with her husband, but also that she had willingly chosen to abort the pregnancy. Even knowing how desperately Sophia had been trying for a family of her own, she still chose to abort that baby, all so she and Marcus could keep this betrayal a secret. She swallowed heavily and searched for the appropriate reaction.

"That doesn't mean anything, Detective Keller. Maybe she was ashamed to tell me. Maybe Marcus found out she was pregnant somehow, and she didn't want me to know. He was a good man. He would have tried to help her if he knew she was in trouble. No, I'm sorry but that doesn't prove anything." Sophia reached for her cup and took another sip of water.

Detective Keller pulled a stack of papers out of a legal-size envelope and handed them to Sophia. Sophia realized that it was the emails. All the emails. She read them over quietly, as if it was the first time she had seen them. As she flipped through them, her hands began to tremble.

"What is all this?" she asked Detective Keller.

"Those are deleted emails we pulled off of Ms. Warner's laptop. They date back to January of 2012, Mrs. Donovan. This is proof that your husband and best friend were having an affair for three years. For three years, they were sleeping around behind your back, and she gets pregnant and has an abortion, and you're still going to sit here and tell us that you knew nothing about this?" Detective Keller's accusation was loud and clear, and Sophia fidgeted in her seat. "I find it hard to believe that you are that self-absorbed, that you didn't realize what in the hell was going on, Mrs. Donovan."

"Detective Keller?" Caleb snapped loudly. "A word, outside," he demanded. As he stood up from the table and headed to the door, he noticed that Keller continued to sit, staring intimidatingly at Sophia. He could feel his patience with her running thin as he shouted at her again, "Keller, in my office, now."

October 31, 2013 – Masquerade

The Donovan home was decorated heavily, both on the outside and the inside. Fake grave sites, ghosts, and decrepit crosses were scattered over the front lawn, as fog machines pushed out heavy smoke and eerie music played in the background. If she didn't know any better, Sophia would have thought they were smack-dab in the middle of a horror movie. The music was also playing inside the dimly-lit house, where the guests would soon feast on a wide array of horrifying-looking drinks, and snacks that resembled mutilated limbs and other body parts. The whole main floor of Sophia and Marcus's home depicted death and terror. Around every corner, there was something to scare the unsuspecting to their very core.

As she walked around her home, observing the party planners' work, Sophia couldn't seem to escape an intense feeling of trepidation, and it had nothing to do with all of the decorations either. She had barely spoken to Marcus in the last two weeks, after another night when he didn't come home. He claimed he had slept at the studio, but she felt that excuse wearing thin with her. Marcus had been so hot and cold over the last couple weeks – one minute he was trying to get her to speak to him, so he could apologize, and the next she could feel anger and resentment in his icy stares across the dining room table. She loathed that her marriage was in this position, and it was becoming more and more difficult to depict a loving couple when there stood between them so much anger and animosity. Still, she went upstairs to put on her costume and prepare for the charade, because their guests would be arriving soon, and they were expecting happy hosts.

In her room, Sophia turned to look at her reflection in the full-length mirror and was quite pleased with how it all came together. She knew she wanted to look sexy, but not overly revealing, and she was confident she did just that. She wore a black patch over her left eye, and a silk scarf around her head with a mass of dark hair hanging out from underneath. Her corset, which hugged her stomach tightly, made her waist look as small as she could ever remember it being, and pushed her breasts up just enough to display a perfect amount of enticing cleavage. Her ragged skirt hung just past her knees and underneath she wore a pair of fishnet stockings and a pair of thigh-high boots. A pirate was a perfect choice.

As she was admiring her costume, Marcus came into the room. They gazed at each other in the mirror's reflection, and even though the tension was as thick as the smog downstairs, the sight of him in his fedora made her heart skip a beat. Even though he was dressed simply, as an Italian mobster, he still looked incredibly handsome, but she couldn't show her intrigue to him, so she covered it with a serious frown.

"Wow," Marcus exclaimed. "You look amazing."

Sophia allowed a soft smile. "It's all I could pull together. Thank you, though," she replied coolly as she headed for the door. As she passed Marcus, he grabbed her softly by the arm.

"Sophia, please, come on, don't be like this," he pleaded softly.

The look Sophia shot him was loud enough that she almost didn't even need to reply. "Me? Don't be like this? Like what exactly? Upset that my husband doesn't come home at night, upset that every time I try to broach the topic you turn the tables on me and accuse me of being a jealous bitch? Not to mention the shadiness with your phone calls, and how you've suddenly begun locking your office. Marcus, I don't know what you want from me. I want to know what the hell is going on here, and you just don't seem to give a fuck."

Marcus could feel his frustration creeping up as he looked down at her. Jesus, what right did she have to put him on the spot like this, to accuse him of all this with absolutely no proof? And what did she need to be going into his office for anyhow, to snoop around and see shit that she didn't need to see? He sighed heavily and forced his feelings down, and searched for the right answer.

"I don't know what you want me to tell you, Sophia. I have told you nothing is going on, there are no shady phone calls, there are no other women. Christ, Sophia what in the hell do you want me to say to make you feel better?"

"The truth, Marcus. How about trying the Goddamn truth once in a while? Why is it that you've been locking your office? What exactly is in there?" she asked again.

"Jesus, I told you: I'm working on some new projects I can't share with anyone, not now. Why can't you just believe me when I tell you that?" he replied, now obviously irritated.

Sophia could feel her own anger surfacing and knew she had better walk away before she said something that she would regret. She recalled one of their fights, not long ago, when she wouldn't drop the accusations, recalled the venom in his eyes and the seriousness of his voice when he told her that if she didn't shut up she was going to wish she were dead. It was then that she truly began struggling with the reality of her marriage. She turned away from him and headed down the stairs, trying not to disrupt the spider webs draped over the railings.

"Bitch," Marcus said under his breath, as he stood alone in the room where she left him. "Why can't she just fucking drop it?"

He unwillingly followed her down the stairs and found her in the kitchen, rearranging the food and drinks, making sure everything was perfect.

"What are you doing, Sophia? Everything is ready. It looks fine," he commented, trying his best to smooth the tension of the moment.

"Fine. Well, we need to make sure it looks perfect, now don't we, Marcus? I mean, what kind of wife would I be if I didn't make sure that everything was absolutely perfect, right?"

Marcus rubbed his hand across his cheek and took a deep breath before he walked over to Sophia and grabbed her lightly by her shoulders.

"Listen, I'm sorry you're mad at me, I am. But, baby, please, come on. I don't want to fight with you. I'm sorry I can be such an asshole, but, please, I don't mean it. You know that I love you. I just want you to trust me."

Sophia stood staring into her husband's eyes. She still, after all this time, and after all these apologies, could feel her heart weaken slightly when he looked at her like that, even though deep down she knew it wouldn't be long until something else happened. Right now, though, she knew she had to soften. She looked down at the floor for a moment, then answered her husband. "Marcus, I don't know what's going on. I just want you to be honest with me, and I don't think that you are. I do love you, I do, but I feel like maybe I'm fighting this battle alone sometimes."

"You're not. I'm here fighting with you, but, please, you need to just let go a bit. Let go of some of the suspicions and accusations. I can't take it, because I'm telling you the truth about everything. You can trust me, Sophia, I swear." Sophia could see a glisten in the corner of his eye.

"Look, I'm sorry I've been such an over-bearing bitch, but, Marcus, I need to know you're being honest with me about everything, because if you're not, I don't know. Maybe it's just best that we are honest with ourselves, and we should just go our separate ways."

"You mean a divorce?" Marcus questioned her angrily.

"No. Listen, let's just talk about this all later, okay? We can get through this. Forget I said anything. I'm just so tired of the fights. You're right, I do need to ease up on you." She hugged him before giving him a gentle kiss on the lips. Just then, the doorbell rang, and she left to answer the door.

Marcus watched her walk out of the kitchen, seething at her comment. If she thought she could just walk away from him, and take everything that he had worked so hard for, she was insane. He would make sure that would never happen, no matter what he had to do.

Within a couple of hours, Sophia and Marcus's home was filled with nearly a hundred guests. The costumes were impressive, so much so that, at first glance, it was difficult to tell who some people actually were. Sam and Devon were there, dressed adorably as salt and pepper shakers. Alex was Jason from Friday the Thirteenth, and Gabby portrayed the big breasted-bimbo with a fake knife sticking out of her stomach. Hailey, once Sophia's overly-energized Intern, was now an excessively bubbly Editorial Assistant and Sophia's good friend, and had come dressed as a cloud. Sophia couldn't help but laugh to herself, as she often told Hailey to get her head out of the clouds. Nate Weston was also there, with his wife Kate, as Danny and Sandy from the movie *Grease*. Nate's hair was heavily greased back and he sported tight jeans, rolled up at the bottoms, a tight white t-shirt, and, of course, a cigarette in his ear. Kate was dressed in skin-tight leather pants and a leather jacket, with her hair done in curls and her lips as red as blood.

Sophia stood at the bar and absorbed the love she felt as all of her friends gathered in her home. She noticed Marcus sitting on the couch, deep in conversation with one of the Production Assistants from his crew, who was barely recognizable with loose chunks of skin, horrible teeth, and deep, sunken eyes. He had obviously used the talents of the makeup crew to transform into a realistic-looking zombie. The one person Sophia had not yet seen was Cat. She glanced quickly at her watch, thinking to herself that she was sure Cat would have arrived by now. Just as the thought had crossed her mind, Cat appeared in front of her.

"Hey, there you are. I thought maybe you'd changed your mind," Sophia remarked, only half-kidding. She couldn't put her finger on it, but she felt something was different between her and Cat lately. Although they spoke frequently, Cat seemed distant, and no longer had time to hang out. Something always came up when they made plans. Sophia wondered if she was being over-sensitive. She had definitely developed insecurity over the year, and Cat was always telling her it was all in her head. Still, she was relieved to see her friend.

"Sorry, it took me forever to get into this fucking costume," Cat replied as she wiggled around in her tight, black patent-leather outfit.

Cat was dressed as a provocative Cat Woman, her breasts barely contained within the confines of the shiny black material. A perfectly perky pair of cat ears sat on her head, and a long, black tail protruded from her backside. Her smoky eyes and bright red lips stood out from her pale skin, and Sophia wondered to herself how Cat was managing to walk in the stiletto boots that shot up her thighs.

Sophia examined her friend from head to toe before responding. "Wow, Cat, you look amazing. Are you sure you can breathe, though?" she teased.

Cat laughed in response and ordered herself a gin-and-tonic from the bartender before she turned back to Sophia. "You look great, too. Everyone looks great." She looked around the house, impressed. "What a turnout. So, where is Marcus?" she asked, as nonchalantly as she could.

"Oh, I think he's over there talking to Ethan, that young Production Assistant from his movie," Sophia answered as she waved in their direction.

Cat took a sip of her drink, feeling awkward and hoping Sophia hadn't picked up on it. She figured it was best to go mingle, and, of course, go say hello to Marcus, before it became too obvious. Knowing she had to do her best to act herself, she said to Sophia, "Hey, I'll be back. I'm going to take a quick stroll around the place and check out the costumes, and see who I can get my claws into." Cat winked and kissed Sophia on the cheek quickly before turning to head through the crowd.

Marcus was having an intriguing conversation with Ethan about some of his ideas for the new movie when Cat walked up behind him and tapped him on the shoulder. He turned to see her in her seductive Cat Woman costume and was instantly caught off-guard. He politely excused himself from his conversation and turned to Cat, giving her a friendly hug and kiss on the cheek.

"Hey, you. Wow, look at you," he exclaimed.

Cat licked her lips inconspicuously and replied, "Thanks. Hey, you look pretty awesome yourself. You guys did a great job. This place looks amazing." Cat tried her best to maintain the friendly vibe.

"Hey, you know I had nothing to do with this. Sophia did this all herself, with the help of the prop team. She knows how to throw a party. What can I say? That's my wife." He raised his voice a little bit now.

Cat could feel jealously coursing through her veins. She knew they had to maintain an act, to avoid any suspicion, but this was the hardest part for her, having to deny what they had in public, then sit back and watch Marcus and Sophia pretend they were madly in love. She knew the truth. She knew Marcus didn't love Sophia anymore. He loved her now.

"Can I get you anything? A drink? App? Eyeball punch?" He tried teasing her, as he could sense the shift in her emotions.

"No, I'm fine, thank you," she said curtly.

Marcus suddenly felt awkward, and decided it best to continue on with his guests. It was strange: before all of this happened, he wouldn't have even questioned sitting here and talking with her all night, but now he felt like he had to be cautious of his every action around her.

"Well, help yourself, you know where everything is. Hey, there are a lot of single guys here." He kissed her on the cheek before turning his attention back to his prior conversation. Cat felt the blood rush to her cheeks. She'd expected more than that, a reaction of some sort at what she was wearing, but he'd barely acknowledged her, and the anger she began to feel at that was unfamiliar. She took the straw out of her drink, downed the remains of her glass, and headed back to the bar to get another drink.

After finishing up his conversation, Marcus headed up the stairs to the master bedroom, trying to clear his head. Cat looked hot, she always did, but he couldn't react to that. He would love to drag her into the bathroom and tear that plastic off her breasts and take her hard, but he couldn't, not here. He entered his room, only to see his wife standing at the window. Still trying to shake off the heat that was flowing through his body, he closed the door, then walked up to Sophia.

"What are you doing in here?" he asked her. "The party is downstairs."

She turned to him and he could still sense some anger from her. He couldn't understand why she couldn't just drop it, but he reached out and held his hand to her face. For a brief second, Sophia allowed his hand to remain on her cheek before she pulled it away and went into the bathroom.

"I just needed to get away for a moment," she responded as she examined herself in the vanity mirror. Marcus followed her in, and stood behind her.

"I'm sorry, baby," he whispered in her ear as he pushed her hair out of the way. The heat of his breath on her skin nearly made her forget everything, and when he began kissing her neck, her knees got weak. She knew she had to remain firm, though, and stand up for herself. She pulled her hair back into its place.

"Marcus, please, not now. I'm sorry, I just...."

Marcus didn't let her finish her sentence. "Just what? Sophia, Christ, what do I have to do to show you I'm sorry? Why can't you just let it go?" he demanded, watching her reaction in the mirror. He pulled her into him and began kissing her neck again. He could feel her tension release and his passion rise. His kisses turned into soft bites, and he could feel himself stiffen against her.

Sophia was torn. Part of her wanted to stop, and the other wanted him to take her right here, and before she decided what she would do, she felt Marcus's breath deepen as he pulled roughly at her cleavage. She felt his hands all over her, as his fingers explored her fishnets, and suddenly he pushed his fingers deep inside her, making her whimper. As he explored her with his fingers, his other hand tore her stockings off and unzipped his pants to free himself. Sophia realized that this wasn't right, this wasn't what she wanted, not in the bathroom as guests were downstairs, but the moment she felt Marcus's hands on her, she knew she was going to have a difficult time saying no. Her desire for him never faltered, but she tried to resist.

"Marcus, we have to stop. We have guests downstairs. This isn't the time," she panted through short breaths.

Marcus ignored his wife. He was angry, frustrated and horny, and, honestly, Sophia owed him this, so he tore the last of her stockings off to allow himself access to her. He pushed her forward, bringing her ass toward him, and she began to struggle.

"Sophia, I want you. You have no idea how bad I want you," he panted.

Sophia tried to stand up, but he pushed her back down aggressively.

"Marcus, please stop, I can't do this, not like this."

He plunged into her with a force she had never felt before. As desperately as she wanted to tell him to stop, she could feel herself open up to him. As he drove himself into her, she braced herself on the bathroom counter, watching him in the mirror. He had his eyes closed, like he was somewhere else, and that wasn't something she had seen him do before. As he continued pushing himself deeper and deeper, she could feel herself starting to lose control. She was tightening and throbbing, and at that moment she didn't care who he was thinking about.

Out in the hallway, Cat knocked on the door. When she got no response, she gently twisted the knob and poked her head in, but she didn't see anyone and thought to herself that maybe he didn't come up after all. Just as she was about to turn and head back downstairs, she heard the muffled moans, and she walked softly over the plush carpet until she caught the image in the mirror. She stood, glued to Marcus and Sophia, and she felt her throat tighten and her heart begin to race. She watched him forcefully take his wife, and wished desperately it was her instead.

It was at that moment that Cat realized that Marcus was truly never going to leave Sophia, no matter what he told her. And it was at that moment that Cat realized if she wanted to be with Marcus, then she was going to have to find another way.

August 14, 2015 – Letting go

Caleb followed Jill into his office and slammed the door behind them. She marched over to one of the chairs in front of his desk and took a seat as Caleb walked around and sat in the big leather chair across from her.

"What in the hell is your problem Keller?" Caleb demanded.

"I told you, Cal, I just feel like something is off here. I don't think Sophia is telling us everything, and I can't shake it. What do you want me do, just ignore my instincts?"

Caleb propped his head in his hands and shook his head in frustration. He knew that Keller was a damn good detective, but he also knew that she was stubborn, and sometimes her personal feelings were a major hindrance in the investigations. He couldn't figure out what her deal with Sophia Donovan was, but her suspicions were irritating Caleb to no end, because he knew where this case stood.

"Jill, what more evidence do you want? We have everything we could possibly need to close this case. We have emails, deleted emails, from three years ago that portray Cat's obsession with Marcus. We have texts and voicemail records from both of their phones, which clearly indicate that a very torrid love affair had been taking place. We have her medical records and financials. For God's sake, Jill, he was paying her $10,000 a month. Don't you think that it was blackmail? She wanted him, and she wanted that baby, but Marcus couldn't risk Sophia finding any of it out, so he agreed to pay her to keep her mouth shut." Caleb stood from his desk, clearly frustrated.

"Her alibi is tight, Jill. She was at the Malibu Resort the whole weekend. The room service attendant says that Sophia ordered, and signed for, room service during the hours of the murder. Listen, Jill, I know you sometimes want to chase the complicated, high-profile cases, and the fact that this is pretty much an open-and-closed case drives you nuts, but you need to drop this shit. Stop trying to intimidate her into giving you answers that don't exist." Caleb's tone was gentle but firm.

Keller sighed heavily and sunk back in her chair. She knew Cal was right, about most of it. She did thrive for high-intensity, complicated cases. This one just seemed too cut-and-dry, and she couldn't escape the nagging voices that were telling her that something was not what it seemed. She knew if she continued to push it, though, she was going to end up working on the shit cases that nobody wanted.

"Shit, Cal, you know I am a damn good detective, you know that's why I haven't let this go. If this case gets reopened, you better be damn sure I am on it."

Caleb's shoulders softened as he took a seat across from her again. Keller knew there was something on his mind, and she grew concerned as he searched for the words to tell her what he needed.

"Keller," he slowly began, "I want you to be the first to know this."

"What is it, Cal?"

"Keller, you know I love my job. I've been at it for a long time, but it seems too long. I'm done, I'm ready to let this part of my life go and continue on to the next phase of my life. I just think it's time. I have been through and seen enough negative shit in my career that I just want to move on and focus on a more positive future, an easy, relaxed future. You know, I've always wanted to buy a house by the beach and open a bar. Well, I think maybe it's my time."

Jill looked at him in astonishment, and grasped for the right words to respond. "You're going to retire? But you're only forty-five years old. What the hell are you going to do with next forty years of your life? Sit on some beach, serving booze to a bunch of beach bums? Cal, you can't. You know you would miss this life."

"It's already done. I spoke with Police Commissioner Hoffman a couple months ago and started all the paperwork. This is my last case. This is it, the end of my journey. So please, Keller, don't go fucking this up for me, alright? Just drop it. Drop the suspicions about Sophia Donovan, and just let me retire already." Caleb was half-teasing Jill, trying to ease the blow.

Keller smirked back at Caleb before answering. "Jesus, and here I thought you just wanted to get in her pants the whole time. All you really wanted to do was just wrap this shit up so you can fuck off to who-knows-where and leave me alone with the rest of these animals."

Caleb laughed at Jill's response and grew serious for one more moment. "I'm going to miss your stubborn ass you know that? But you're going to go far in this career. You'll be Lieutenant in no time flat, ordering all these sad sacks of shit around all day."

"I sure the fuck hope so," Jill replied confidently, with a smirk.

Caleb stood from his desk and walked over to Keller to give her a quick hug. He knew she wasn't the hugging type, but he was, and he was going to miss her in some small weird way. When he pulled away from her, he headed back to the door. "Come on, Jill, let's go. Let's go tell Sophia the truth about what happened to her husband."

When they walked back into the room, Sophia was sitting, pale-faced, sifting through all the emails, texts, and photographs that were strewn across the table. All of the images and the words that she read, from Marcus to Cat and Cat to Marcus, were still desperately hard to understand. In a way, it was as if she were reliving the whole nightmare in her mind as she studied all the evidence. She looked up at Detectives Stone and Keller as they sat back down at the table.

Keller cleared her throat, almost unable to force the words she knew she needed to say out of her mouth.

"Mrs. Donovan, I'm sorry that you have to find this all out this way. I can't imagine what you must be feeling right now. I would like to apologize for my behavior. I just want you to understand that this is my job, and I take it very seriously." Keller shifted in her seat. Apologies were definitely not one of her stronger suits.

Sophia was taken aback, and she glanced over at Detective Stone, who sat quietly, listening to his partner speak. Sophia could feel tears in her eyes as the realization of what was happening became clear in her mind. She pressed her lips together and swiped at her cheek, where she felt a tear falling down her face.

"I understand you're doing your job. I know that. I'm unable to process this information right now. I just can't understand or make sense of any of this. How did they do this, right under my nose, for that long? How stupid could I have possibly been this whole time, to think they both loved me? God, she had an abortion. They could have had a baby. Marcus and I tried for so long to have a baby." She cupped her hand over her mouth, trying to stifle the sobs that were beginning to escape.

"Sophia, we are informing you that the investigation has concluded that Catarina Warner murdered Marcus, and then turned the gun on herself. The emails, the texts, and the voicemails, and the money, all determine that this was beyond an affair for her. She was obsessed, in love with him to the point that, well, if she couldn't have him as her own, then she was going to do whatever it took to ensure you couldn't have him either," Caleb explained.

"We will be holding a press conference this afternoon to release the final details of this investigation to the public. I hope, as hard as all this information is to hear and to comprehend, I hope it allows you some sort of closure, and provides you the ability to heal from this, so you can move on and start a new future with someone who values you and loves you. You're young, Sophia. Take the time to heal and grieve, but please don't allow this to destroy your life." Keller sounded sympathetic for the first time since Sophia met her.

Sophia closed her eyes for a moment, letting Keller's words ring in her ears, then opened her eyes and glanced up to see Detective Stone looking at her with soft eyes, eyes that held a deep concern for her, but at the same time a sense of relief. She smiled back at Keller as she thought silently to herself that Keller was absolutely right. Sophia was not going to allow this to ruin her future or her life, because now that this was almost over, her life was just about to begin.

February 16, 2015 – The Visitor

Charlotte Benedict was the Marketing Manager for LA Today, and she thrived on Charity and being able to help out any way she could. Tonight she was hosting a gala at the Beverly Hilton, the proceeds from which were for a local charity dedicated to eradicating the pollution that was overwhelming the bays of the Pacific's West Coast.

The magazine had always offered as much help as they could to draw the largest crowds for Charlotte, as she had remained a long and faithful team member. Sophia and Sam had agreed to help her tie up some loose ends that evening, and as they entered the boardroom, Charlotte was hard at work, finishing up the seating charts for the dinner.

"You know you take on way too much every year, don't you?" Sam half-teased as he walked over to examine her progress.

Charlotte smiled widely at Sam as she took a moment and propped her black-framed glasses on top of her auburn hair. Charlotte was a modestly beautiful woman. She always cared more for others than about her appearance, but one look at her deep green eyes, porcelain skin, and supple lips was enough for anyone to notice that underneath it all she possessed a raw beauty.

"I know, Sam. Geez, I do this to myself every year, but you know what? Every year is a success, so with every success I must keep on going, right?" she asked rhetorically.

Sophia walked around the table and studied everything that Charlotte had so neatly organized. The menu, seating charts, and entertainment were all laid out in front of them, in perfect order. Sophia looked forward to these events every year. The charities were always near-and-dear to Charlotte's heart, and the evenings almost always turned out spectacular, with huge profits going towards the organizations.

"Well, it looks like you have everything pretty organized here. What can I do to help?" Sophia asked.

After taking a moment to observe everything on the table, and quickly referring back to her to-do list, Charlotte stood up, and propped her hands on her hips and pressed her lips together.

"Well, it would be great if you could just help me with this seating chart. I want to make sure I don't put anyone together that could cause any issues. Remember three years ago at the art studio?" Charlotte laughed out loud. She was referring to a little debacle between Cassidy Ryan and Desiree Hardy, the wife and ex-wife, respectively, of Blake Ryan, who owned the SoHo studio. Poor Charlotte didn't realize the massive mistake she made when she unknowingly placed all three at the same table. Looking back now, it was comical, but she hadn't thought so at the time. Two grown women, in excessively expensive dresses, with way too much excessively expensive champagne in their systems…. Well, it was a mistake she never cared to make again.

Sophia laughed at the memory and agreed with Charlotte that they needed to make sure it didn't happen again. She read over the names remaining on Charlotte's list. Sophia knew most of them well, and was familiar with the rest, so she was able to confidently fill in the seating chart.

She noticed while finishing up that Charlotte had placed her at the table with Devon and Samuel, Nate and Katie, and Charlotte and her husband, Ethan. There was one seat remaining, and Charlotte informed Sophia that the spot was taken, and not to worry about trying to fill it. This would be one of the first events that Sophia attended alone. Marcus had to be in New York to do some scouting for scenes in his newest project, and Cat, who would normally attend these with her, had been whisked away to Santa Barbara to spend the Valentine's weekend at the Four Seasons with a new and mysterious man in her life.

"Well, I think it looks good." Sophia stood back and observed the chart.

"I think we can assume we're going to be catfight free this evening," Sam chimed in as he studied it over Sophia's shoulder.

As the three of them laughed, Hailey poked her head in the conference room. "Hey, Soph, you have someone here to see you."

"Oh?" Sophia looked surprised. She wasn't expecting anyone. "Did they say who?" she asked Hailey.

Hailey shook her head and shrugged her shoulders. "Sorry, love, she didn't say, she just asked if you were here. You want me to tell her you're busy?" Hailey asked.

Shaking her head, and putting down the notes she held in her hand, Sophia answered, "No, no, that's fine. I'll be right out. Just have her wait in the lobby, please."

Hailey popped her gum and gave Sophia a wink. "Sure thing," she replied as she bounced out to relay the message.

"I'm sorry, Char, I'll be right back to help you get this done," Sophia said as she headed out of the room.

At first, Sophia didn't recognize the woman, but as soon as it came to her, she felt shocked and bewildered. "Taylor?" Sophia exclaimed.

Taylor stood as Sophia approached. Sophia could instantly tell she was nervous about being here, and it made her uncomfortable, as well. "Hi, Sophia, I'm so sorry to bother you here. I just didn't want to bother you at home, and, well, I was hoping to catch you alone."

"Um, yeah," Sophia muttered as she scratched her head, then continued, "Okay, why don't we head into my office then? We can have some privacy in there." She motioned for Taylor to follow her. The two women walked into Sophia's office and Sophia gently closed the door behind them. She invited Taylor to take a seat on her couch, and sat down beside her. When Taylor didn't speak, Sophia decided to break the ice.

"How are you, Taylor? It has been a very long time."

Taylor gave Sophia a weak smile and shook her head before answering. "I'm good, I'm okay. God, Sophia I am so sorry to come to you like this," she started, as she fidgeted with her hands in her lap.

"What are you doing here, Taylor?" Sophia inquired bluntly, then continued, "I'm sorry, I don't mean to sound rude, but you have to excuse my shock. I haven't seen you since before Christmas several years ago. You know, before you took off on Alex and accused my husband of sleeping with you?"

Taylor sighed deeply and searched for the best way to start. She knew why she wanted to come here, but now that she was here, she couldn't seem to find any of the right words.

"Sophia, I came here today because I felt I owed you the truth, the truth about what happened, then and now. I mean, shit, Sophia, I could be over-stepping my boundaries here, I'm not even sure where you and Marcus stand at this point, so I could be here for nothing, really."

Sophia could feel her throat tighten and her palms began to sweat. She knew Taylor wasn't here for good news. She knew she was here to share something that Sophia probably didn't want to hear, and she struggled with the idea of just throwing her out of her office before giving her a chance to say what she had to say, but her curiosity got the better of her.

"What do you mean, Taylor? I know the truth of what happened. Alex told us all about it shortly after you left. He showed us the letter that you left, so there's nothing to tell me. I know what happened. What I don't get is why you chose to lie about my husband like that, and then leave Alex so suddenly. You just up and left him, just like that. Are you here after five years to apologize, or what? I don't understand why you're here." Taylor could hear the anger beginning to rise in Sophia's voice now.

"Sophia, I know what I did was horrible. I really didn't want to hurt Alex like that. We had no business getting married that fast, but I still feel bad about the way I just up and left him. It hurt me for a long time, and I just hope he can one day forgive me for it." She paused and closed her eyes for a moment, then started again. "I didn't lie."

Sophia looked at her blankly. "You did lie, Taylor. You told him everything in your letter, you said you lied about the whole thing just to hurt him. I don't know what kind of person does that, but, well, you succeeded. You did hurt him, you hurt Marcus, and you hurt me."

"I didn't lie, Sophia, not to Alex. Everything I told him was true. I slept with Marcus multiple times, and everything I told Alex that night was the truth. What I'm telling you right now is the truth. You can choose to believe me or not, but it is the truth, and I'm sorry Sophia, I am. It was a horrible thing for me to do, but I was selfish and naïve, and I never wanted anyone to know, but I had to be honest with him." Taylor looked back at Sophia, waiting for a response.

Sophia's heart dropped into her stomach, but she was still unclear as to why Taylor was coming to her now. "Taylor, why would you tell Alex all that bullshit in that letter? Why would you just up and leave him like that?"

"Marcus. He came to see me the day after Christmas and he gave me no choice. He told me exactly what to say in the letter and he told me that if I didn't leave town and disappear from Alex's life that I would regret it. He threatened me, that if I showed my face ever again or blurted out any more bullshit, he was going to make me regret that I ever met him. If I ever tried to contact Alex or you, ever, he told me he was going to make sure I never took another breath." Taylor answered Sophia with a deep fear in her voice.

Sophia felt like someone had just punched her in the stomach. She couldn't believe what she had just heard. As many doubts and questions she'd had about her husband in the past, she didn't think she could possibly believe what Taylor was telling her in this moment. She felt the color drain from her face, and she fought with herself over how she should respond. "Why?" Tears began to form in Sophia's eyes, and her voice shook. "Why, Taylor? Why would you come to me, five years later, and tell me this? What possessed you to come clean to me now?"

Taylor felt horrible. She knew Sophia didn't deserve this. Taylor would see them on the entertainment news and in magazines, and feel sick that Sophia was being blinded by this man, this man who was going to eventually hurt her. Everyone thought they were this perfect couple, and that Marcus was this amazing devoted husband, but she knew better. She knew who he was, and knew that he had never changed. She knew that when she saw him walk out of the Four Seasons elevator with his mouth pressed against some attractive, tall blonde. As Taylor sat and watched Sophia breaking down, she wanted to reach out and hug her, but she knew that wasn't her place. Instead, she reached into her pocket and took out her cell phone. She scrolled through the photos before handing Sophia the phone.

"That is why I came to you, Sophia," Taylor finally answered her, as Sophia's eyes locked on Taylor's phone.

The image that stared back at her instantly took her breath away, and as she gazed at the photo of the most perfect looking child she had ever seen, Sophia knew without a doubt whose child it was. He had all of Marcus's features. She didn't even feel the need to question Taylor on why she was showing her this picture.

"You have a child?" Sophia whispered, as she kept staring down at the phone.

"Yes, his name is Jackson, and he is the most amazing little boy you could ever know," Taylor beamed proudly.

The tears began to flow down Sophia's cheeks. It was now obvious that Taylor was telling her the truth.

"Does he know?" Sophia asked finally, looking up to meet Taylor's eyes.

"Yes, I reached out to him shortly after Jack was born to let him know. He told me I was a lying bitch. He said he never wanted to hear from me again. Two weeks later, I received a check in my mailbox, for $25,000, and a note saying he knows that I am lying, but to take this money and to keep my mouth shut anyways." Taylor's voice now also started to shake.

"Sophia, I live in Santa Barbara with my amazing husband and my beautiful child, and I love my life. My husband decided to take me to the Four Seasons for Valentine's Day, and I saw him, I saw Marcus getting out of the elevator with some tall blonde woman. I couldn't see her face, but it was clear they were together. As far as I knew, you guys were still together. I mean, I see it all the time on the news and magazines. I don't know what really made me come to you, other than my son, knowing how I will protect him from ever knowing the truth about his father and wanting to prevent this from happening to anyone else. Sophia, I just ask you please, please don't tell him I came to you. I have no idea what he would do, I honestly don't, but I just really felt like I needed you to know this. But please, please, don't tell him I came." Sophia could hear the desperation in Taylor's voice as tears escaped her eyes.

Sophia was tormented with every emotion she could possibly bear. She knew everything Taylor was saying to her was the truth. Jackson was a beautiful child, and she knew with every ounce of her soul this child was Marcus's. She turned to Taylor and reached for her hands.

"I won't tell him. I am so sorry, Taylor. I'm so sorry that he made you go through this alone, and pushed you out of your own life here. I'm thankful that you came here today to tell me this. I don't even know what to do with any of this information, but, regardless, thank you." Then, before she even knew what happened, Taylor embraced her in a warm hug before standing up.

"I'm so sorry, Sophia. I just I guess I just wanted to try to protect you somehow from getting hurt. He's a dangerous man, and I think he would do anything to protect himself. I just don't want anyone else to get hurt, that's all." Taylor headed for the door, and before she opened it, she turned one more time to Sophia. "Goodbye, Sophia." With her last words, she turned and walked out of the office, closing the door behind her.

Sophia fell back on her couch and allowed herself to feel every emotion coming to her. She slowly curled herself into a ball as the tears began to escape her in gasping sobs. The last ten years began to flash in her memory, the happiness, and the sadness, and she recalled all of the horrible memories, the fights, the yelling, the name-calling, the threats, and every time he put his hands on her. And as she sat, trying to put together all the pieces of the madness in front of her, one more thought suddenly came to her. The Four Seasons in Santa Barbara. Cat was going to the Four Seasons in Santa Barbara.

She tried to forget that the thought even came to her, but now that it was exposed, it was never going to leave her mind.

"No," she softly whispered to herself. "No, they wouldn't do that me. Please, tell me they wouldn't do that me."

August 14, 2015 – Closure

The media gathered in front of the steps of the police station, where the press conference was going to be held. Every local reporter was there, waiting to hear the conclusion of the investigation. The sidewalks were littered with paparazzi and fans, waiting to find out what happened. Sophia could hear the murmurs as everyone discussed their own personal opinions, and what conclusions they had come to in regards to the case. Camera flashes were going off in every direction, even though there was nothing to take pictures of yet. Sophia had made sure to call everyone that she knew would want to be there, as soon as she was released from Detectives Stone and Keller's meeting that morning. She stood off to one side, alone, observing the insanity before her, until her mother ran up to her.

Isabelle grabbed her daughter the moment she was in her reach and pulled her tight to her. "Oh, my God," Isabelle cried.

"Oh, Mom, it's over. I can't believe any of this. I don't want to believe any of this, but the evidence was just so overwhelming. Oh, Mom, how was I so blind?" Sophia sobbed as her mother rubbed her back gently before pulling away to look her in the eyes.

"You are not blind. This isn't your fault. Honey, you were betrayed by both of them, and I can't even imagine what you're going through, but we have the answers now. You can start to heal and move forward." Isabelle hugged her again.

Over her mother's shoulder, Sophia could see Bruce and Adele's car pulling up. When it came to a stop, Marcus's mother, father, and sister stepped out. Bruce walked around to his wife, and as Adele grabbed onto his arm, Olivia left them both behind and headed over to where Sophia and her mother stood.

"Sophia." Olivia addressed her sister-in-law rather gently as she approached the two women.

"Olivia. Hello," she replied, just as Bruce and Adele walked up to join their daughter. Without notice, Bruce Donovan pulled Sophia toward him and she could feel his body begin to tremble as they hugged.

"Sophia, I am so terribly sorry," he sobbed.

"Oh, Bruce, I'm sorry, too. I wish this wasn't true, any of it," she replied as she hugged him back.

When Bruce released her, Adele stepped up and hugged her as well. Sophia glanced over her shoulder to Olivia, but she couldn't determine the look on her face. She sensed anger and bitterness, but she also sensed relief, and regret. Sophia pulled away from Adele and faced everyone.

"The press conference should begin shortly. They would prefer if the family stood up together when they release the details. It's important that we stay strong and we stay united through this. From this point forward, we all have to begin to heal, we have to heal in whatever ways we know how, and know that we have one another to get through this."

"Sophia," Olivia chimed in.

Sophia turned to Olivia and she could see her eyes glistening as she tried to fight the tears coming to the surface.

"Yes, Olivia?"

"I'm sorry for all the nasty things I said to you during this. I just want my brother back. I hate that he did what he did to you, and I hate your friend for taking him away from us, but I had no right to attack you and make this worse on you."

Olivia's tears finally fell, and Sophia pulled her in tight as she whispered in her ear, "It's okay, I understand. Please know that I fully understand, and you have nothing to apologize for."

Just then, the commotion of the crowd intensified as they noticed that the detectives were heading out of the front doors of the building. Sophia ushered everyone up the stairs, and they took their places behind the podium. Sophia stood in between her mother and her mother-in-law, and she took both of their hands in hers as they waited for Detective Stone to begin the conference.

The cameras flashed like bolts of lightning as Caleb walked up to the microphone. He had to hush the crowd multiple times, like a teacher would have to hush their classroom, before he started to speak.

"Ladies and gentlemen, as you all know Marcus Donovan was found in his home, alongside the body of Ms. Catarina Warner, in the early morning hours of July 20, 2015, by his wife, Mrs. Sophia Donovan. Mrs. Donovan immediately contacted the authorities upon discovery of her husband and her friend's bodies, and upon the coroner's confirmation of death, an investigation immediately commenced.

"A wide array of individuals, such as family, friends, and colleagues of both the victims, were questioned regarding the victims' lives and the events surrounding this incident. Financial, medical, and personal records were pulled for Mr. Donovan and Ms. Warner, as well as Mrs. Donovan herself. It was discovered in our examination of this material, as well as several deleted email and text messages, that Ms. Warner and Mr. Donovan were in fact involved in a very heated love affair over the course of the last four years, which eventually led to the incident in the Donovan Home on July 20. The evidence supports our conclusion that the relationship between Mr. Donovan and Ms. Warner took a wrong turn, most likely due to the fact that Mr. Donovan was unwilling to leave his wife, and that Ms. Warner decided to take matters into her own hands.

"The affair between her husband and her best friend of eleven years was unknown to Mrs. Donovan until our team of highly skilled investigators discovered the long-kept secret and were forced to share our findings with her shortly before this press conference.

"In summary, with all of our written and verbal statements from family, friends and colleagues, along with the findings from heavily-researched personal records from both victims, as well as emails, text messages and voicemails retrieved from both victims' laptops and cellphones, it has been concluded by this division of the Los Angeles Police Department that this was, in fact, a murder-suicide, premeditated by Ms. Warner. If any further evidence shall present itself in the future, we may consider reopening the case, however, at this time our findings are conclusive." Caleb stopped to take a sip of his water and clear his throat before he continued.

"I would also like to acknowledge this brave family standing here beside me. Mrs. Donovan, her mother, Isabelle Vaughn, Bruce and Adele Donovan, who were the proud parents of Marcus, and Olivia, his younger sister. I want to offer you all our condolences in this matter and let you all know that if there is anything you need, please, not hesitate to come to us." Caleb's words were filled with sincerity as he looked at each person with sympathy in his eyes.

Sophia softly squeezed Isabelle and Adele's hands, to reassure them both that they were going to be okay, that they were going to get through this, but as she glanced around at the audience, she could see that some of the faces staring back at her were still not convinced. She was fully aware that she was going to be put on display, and that, no matter what the investigation led to, opinions would still be had about her innocence.

As she continued surveying the crowd, she caught the gaze of Paul Warner. He was standing alone in the back, where no one would notice him. As soon as he noticed that Sophia had seen him, he looked solemnly at her from across the crowd, then turned and walked away. Sophia could feel her heart break for him. Even though he was a shitty father and husband, she knew that she was always going to be partially responsible for taking away any chance of him building a relationship with his daughter.

Detective Stone had opened the press conference up to questions from the media, and reporters were yelling questions in his direction. Sophia blocked out the barrage of questions and turned her attention back to her family. They all headed off to the side to wait out the rest of the conference.

"I can't believe this is all still happening," Isabelle said as she reached for her daughter one more time.

"I know, Mom, me either. It still feels like a dream that I can't wake up from, but at least, we have answers now. As horrible as those answers are, we can still all try and move forward."

As the conference wound down, Bruce, Adele, and Olivia said their goodbyes. They were taking Olivia home to Riverside with them for a few days, so they could spend some time together before they had to resume their lives. They all hugged Sophia and Isabelle, and then headed across the street, back to their vehicle. Sophia watched until they had all gotten into the car and drove away. She felt such as a huge sense of relief that this was over, but she still couldn't help but struggle with the profound guilt she felt in causing them so much pain. If they only knew the truth. Sophia then turned back to face her mother.

"I can stay with you as long as you need, honey," Isabelle said.

"I know you will, Mom, but you know what? You have done so much for me, and you can't put your life on hold for me any longer. I am so thankful that you have been here, and I honestly don't know what I would have done without you, but I think I need to take some time for myself, Mom, and really focus on what I need to do next to move forward."

The two women glanced over to the quickly dispersing crowd, and Sophia watched Detective Keller walk back into the building. Caleb was discussing something with one of the other sheriffs, and as their conversation came to an end he glanced over at Sophia. Their eyes met for a long moment and Isabelle instantly noticed the look that fell between her daughter and Detective Stone. She wondered then if perhaps he had taken to Sophia over these last several weeks. She hoped Sophia allowed herself time before opening her heart up to another man.

"Come, sweetie, let's go. I have a lot of packing to do." Isabelle pulled her daughter away, breaking the gaze between her and Stone, and Sophia held her mother's arm as they headed down the street.

Caleb stood and watched as the two women walked away and he was overwhelmed with a sense of relief, relief for everyone that was involved in this nightmare, knowing that it was now over and how all of their lives were going to be forever changed.

February 16, 2015 – The Gala

Sophia sat in the back of the limousine on the way to the Beverly Hilton for Charlotte's gala. She wanted to cancel and stay home after the news she heard today, but she didn't want anyone to know what she had just found out, and she had to continue on as if things were normal, even though Sophia was beginning to lose her grasp on what normal even was anymore. The one thing she did know for certain now was that her marriage was going to soon be over. In her mind, it was already over. Obviously, all of her doubts about Marcus were true. Who was this man she was married to, she thought to herself as the limo continued down the road. She should have trusted her instincts before, she should have left a long time ago, but she didn't. She stayed loyal and devoted to her marriage.

And now there were her suspicions about Cat. Sophia wondered what she should do regarding her speculations about the two of them. The thought that she had put nearly eleven years into this marriage almost made Sophia sick to her stomach, even more-so when she thought that Cat could be having an affair with her husband after everything they had been through.

The limo slowly pulled up outside of the Beverley Hilton, and she waited for the driver to come around and open her door. She did her best to compose herself. She was going to try and enjoy the evening as much as possible, without giving any indication that she was, in fact, in utter dismay. The door to the limo propped open, and the driver offered her his hand to help her out.

"Thank you, Charles," she said graciously as she handed him a fifty dollar bill. She walked to the front doors, which were being attended by two young men in bellboy uniforms, and as Sophia approached the door both of the men smiled at her, obviously noticing her beauty. Her hair was swept up in loose curls, and the perfect frame of her body was outlined by a gorgeous black Vera Wang evening gown.

"Good evening, ma'am." The man on the left spoke as he opened the door for her.

"Thank you," she replied as she glided in past him.

She found the doors leading into the ballroom of the gala. As she pushed the doors open, she was greeted with a beautifully-decorated ballroom. The chandeliers hung high on the soaring ceilings and were giving off a beautiful glow. The tables were dressed perfectly in ivory tablecloths, and in the center of each table stood an elegant array of flowers. From the center of each bouquet stood a tall crystal candle-holder, which contained dimly-lit pillar candles. Banners were draped on either side of the ballroom, displaying the name of the charity that Charlotte was raising money for that evening, and Sophia knew already it would be a huge success. The room was already filled nearly to capacity.

When a waiter approached, Sophia accepted a flute of bubbly champagne and was instantly brought back to her days working for Fresh Catering, when she met both Cat and Marcus. She used to think she was lucky to have worked there. Because of that job she met Marcus and Cat. Today, she wished more than anything that she could go back and change it all.

"Sophia!" She heard her name being called and turned around to see Charlotte and Ethan heading towards her. She instantly noticed how gorgeous Charlotte looked, wearing a beautiful strapless teal gown, the whole top covered in shimmering rhinestones. Her auburn hair fell in massive waves around her shoulders, and on her arm was her equally-attractive husband in an impressive Gucci suit.

"Hey, Charlotte!" she exclaimed as she turned to greet them.

"Oh, I'm so glad you could make it tonight. I really think this is going to be a huge success. I wanted to thank you again for helping me out today." Charlotte touched her arm gently.

"Oh, no problem at all. Ethan, you look dashing, as always."

"Why, thank you, Sophia, as do you. Well, more stunning than dashing," he joked.

"Have you seen Sam and Devon? Are they here yet?" Sophia asked Charlotte as her eyes scanned the room.

Waving her hand in the direction of the bar, Charlotte answered, "Yes, they're here, and in the full swing of things already. Hey, listen, I hope you're okay with who I seated at the table with us tonight. He seems like a great guy, and has always been a very generous contributor to the charities every year. I actually don't know him too well, outside of that, but I think I'm probably safe to say that he shouldn't start a raging cat fight tonight."

"Of course, I'm sure it will be fine. I just hope this evening is a huge success for you," Sophia responded. Charlotte could tell something was off with Sophia this evening, and thought she was probably upset she had to spend Valentine's Day alone this year, and to top it off attend tonight's gala solo.

"It's really too bad that Marcus couldn't be here tonight. I do hope you still enjoy yourself this evening, though, Sophia, and I'm so glad you could make it." Charlotte gave her a quick kiss on the cheek before heading into the crowd with Ethan, to make sure everything was finalized for the evening.

Sophia walked through the crowd and was immediately caught off guard by a handsome man looking in her direction. He was not intimidating her with his gaze, but she could sense instantly that he was intrigued with her. It had been so long since she noticed men noticing her, but tonight, in her mind frame, knowing the state of her marriage, she seemed to be more aware of the attention that she could draw. She was unexpectedly drawn to his striking features, and she became aware, upon studying his face for a moment, how attractive he actually was. The last time a man caught her off-guard like this was the day she first laid eyes on Marcus. Back then, the intensity of Marcus's gaze, the penetration of his stare, was overwhelming. Now, she felt at ease and comfortable as they stood looking at each other. Sophia smiled softly in his direction and he nodded his head slightly, raising his glass to her before bringing the glass to his mouth. She hesitated a moment before unlocking her gaze from his, but she knew it was time to go find Sam and Devon. She turned to walk away but couldn't resist peeking over her shoulder, happy to find that he was still gazing after her.

"Sophia, oh, there you are, honey!" Devon shouted when he saw her approaching.

"Hey, guys." She gave Devon a quick hug before reaching for Sam.

"You look stunning, girl, that dress is amazing. Can we say hello boobs?" Devon joked. Sophia blushed as she slapped him softly on the arm.

"Devon!" she exclaimed, slightly embarrassed.

"No kidding, Devon, way to make a girl feel awkward," Sam said. "But he isn't kidding Soph. You look amazing, and so do the girls," Sam teased.

"Thanks, guys, I tried. Wow, there really are a lot of people here tonight. At a thousand dollars a plate, Char is going to do pretty well this evening, and that's just the dinner, not even counting the donations," Sophia remarked as she looked around the crowded room.

Sam nodded his head while swallowing a mouthful of champagne. "Yup, every year it seems to become a bigger and better event. I am so proud of that woman. She puts so much work into it every year, and she helps these organizations more than she will probably ever know."

"Well, it does suck that Marcus could not be here tonight, so it looks like you're stuck with us two handsome devils." Devon chuckled while throwing his arm around Sophia's shoulders. "And I couldn't be happier. How often do we get to steal you all to ourselves?" he continued as the three of them went to search out their table.

After they walked around the ballroom for a few moments, they eventually came to a round table where they found all of their names calligraphed onto perfectly-folded place cards. Samuel pulled Sophia's chair out for her and she adjusted herself to a comfortable position as Sam took his spot next to her.

"I'm starving, I can't wait for dinner to start. And, you know, I limited myself to only three martinis so far this evening, just so I could actually remember the meal. How dedicated am I?" Devon joked.

"I'm starving, too, I've barely eaten all day," replied Sophia, trying her best to keep her voice from betraying her true feelings from her meeting with Taylor earlier.

Sam could sense something in her voice, as much as she tried to hide it. He had known her long enough to know when she wasn't herself. He could tell she was trying to act like she was fine, so he didn't want to question her too much, certain she would share her feelings with him and Devon if it was anything big. In the meantime, he, at least, wanted to make sure she was okay.

"Is everything all right, Sophia? You seem, I don't know, just a little off tonight."

Sophia was shocked by his question. She'd thought she was doing a great job of hiding her emotions. She took a deep breath and smiled back at Sam before responding, "Of course. I'm perfectly fine. I might just be a little bit tired. I've had a few late nights, that's all, but other than that I am perfectly fine." She smiled again at both men.

Sam felt she wasn't being honest with him, but he knew it was probably best to leave it for now. Charlotte and Ethan were joining them at the table, and Charlotte began a conversation with Devon, while Ethan decided he should go get a couple more drinks before dinner started. Sophia listened as Charlotte shared more information with Devon about the charity that was being sponsored. She felt someone step up beside her, and looked up over her shoulder, happily surprised to see the man from earlier in the evening.

"Excuse me, I believe this is where I am supposed to be sitting for dinner. I don't mean to interrupt," he apologized politely, before he pulled his chair out from the table.

"Oh, please, there's no need to apologize. Please, have a seat and join us," Sophia responded, almost eagerly, which caught her off-guard.

"Thank you," he said as he sat down. His hazel eyes held Sophia's attention, and she thought to herself that he was, even more, attractive up close. His strong jawline, his dirty blond hair combed back off his face, and a smile that she was sure could melt ice. She wasn't sure if it was the events of earlier today and realizing the reality of her marriage, or if she was sincerely being drawn to this man, but right now she didn't care. She just knew that she was going to try and enjoy this evening.

"Well, I would like to apologize that you had the unfortunate luck to get seated with us. Well, with them," she joked happily as she pointed to Sam and Devon, who were laughing along with her.

"Oh, I don't think it's unfortunate at all," he replied, with that ice-melting smile.

Sophia laughed coyly as she reached out her hand to introduce herself.

"I'm sorry, how rude of me. My name is Sophia, Sophia Donovan."

He reached for her hand and softly held it in his, and even though he was aware of who she was – everyone knew who she was – he couldn't believe how taken aback he was by her sheer beauty, and how just being in her presence made him feel, without even knowing her. He tried his best to maintain a friendly composure as he gripped her hand a little bit tighter, shaking it softly and smiling widely back at her.

"It is great to meet you, Sophia. My name is Caleb, Caleb Stone."

August 16, 2015 – Revelations

As Sophia walked into room 103 of the Palm Heights Hotel, she noticed that the room was simple, yet comfortable, small, but cozy, and, most importantly, it was in a remote location, yet not overly secluded. The queen-size bed, which was placed almost perfectly in the middle of the room, was covered in a floral bedspread with two matching pillows propped up against the wooden headboard. The furniture definitely seemed dated, but a fairly modern flat-screen TV was hanging on the wall above the oak dresser directly across from the bed. She continued to walk through the room, opening and closing the drawers of the nightstands and dresser, a habit she'd developed as a young girl after finding an abandoned Barbie doll on one of their family vacations to Florida. Quickly realizing that she had no such luck today, she continued on through to the quaint little bathroom, just big enough for the bathtub, toilet, and vanity.

As she turned to head out of the bathroom, she caught her reflection in the mirror and was surprised to find that she was beginning to recognize the person staring back at her. After everything that had transpired over the last month, she was finally beginning to feel like herself, and after being lost for so long, it was a sense of relief that she couldn't even begin to describe. She turned off the light, sat on the edge of the bed, reached for the remote control on the nightstand, and pointed it at the TV.

"...The affair that went horribly wrong. What led this young woman to commit such a ghastly crime in the name of love? Up next on the LA Insider," reported a well-dressed man, standing beside a petite brunette in six-inch heels.

It was still all over the news. Now that the investigation had broken, every major entertainment and news magazine was trying to unravel the mystery behind Marcus Donovan's shocking affair. Fans were still trying to make sense out of how this man, who they'd never even known, could do such a thing. How could he be cheating on his loving wife of eleven years? That was not the man they thought they knew.

Sophia knew that soon the piranhas would be trying to reach her to get her story, her side of it all, and they would pay handsomely for it, but that wasn't why she had done this. She had plenty of money and fame, but that was the last thing that she'd wanted. Pointing the remote back up to the TV, she flipped through the channels, stopping on an old black–and–white movie starring Clark Gable and Lana Turner.

"This is better," Sophia mumbled to herself, even though she had never even seen a black-and-white movie before. Still, she was happy with anything that would help her escape the constant reminders around her. As she watched the classic love scene unfold, she couldn't help but let her memory drift back to the beginning of all this, a time when things were not unlike the love in this movie. For a moment, Sophia could feel her heart breaking when she thought of how drastically their lives had changed over the course of these years. Every time she allowed the memory of them to creep back into her mind, she did her best to push it aside. It was still much too painful to acknowledge the lengths they were willing to go to, to be together without her in the picture. Realizing the movie was not helping to distract her, she shut off the TV and stood up, only to begin pacing back and forth at the foot of the bed.

She had waited so patiently for this moment for so long, but now that it was here, so close to her, she could barely manage to keep still as she waited. Over the last several months, she often found herself wondering, what if she had never found out the truth, and what if Taylor had decided not to come to her and tell her about any of this? What would have happened then? There were so many unanswered questions, questions that would never have an answer. As she continued to pace, she heard a car pull up outside and she knew it was finally time. After all the pain, the heartache, and this huge risk she took to save her life, it was time. She heard the car door slam shut, and after a few seconds, there was a soft knock on the door.

Her stomach began to do flips, and her heart beat rapidly in her chest. She was filled with excitement and fear all at the same time, but it felt good. She took in a deep breath and checked herself quickly in the mirror before she walked to the door and opened it. As she caught her first glance of him, she could feel her heart melting in her chest.

"Hi," She spoke while sighing deeply with relief.

"Hi," he replied.

"Come in," she said as she stepped to the side. As he walked past her, she felt a shiver of electricity race over her body. As soon as he was in the room, she closed the door and turned to face him. Within seconds, he had grabbed her in the tightest embrace he could possibly manage without hurting her. She clung desperately to him, with her arms draped around his neck, and as the mixture of desire, relief and fear all came to the surface, she couldn't help but break down in tears.

They stood holding each other for several moments, and when Sophia finally pulled herself out of his embrace she found his gaze with her tear-soaked eyes. He gently laid a soft kiss on her forehead before he whispered in her ear, "You're free now, baby."

With the realization of the truth behind his words, Sophia began to sob into his chest again. When she was finally able to catch her breath, she reached up and placed her hands on either side of his face and replied, "I'm free because of you, my Love. Caleb, you saved my life."

June 3, 2015 – And the Story Unfolds

Cat stood quickly from the couch as Marcus stormed through the front door, slamming it behind him, causing the walls to vibrate with the intensity. The look of raw anger across his face had Cat feeling extremely nervous, wondering what could have happened to cause him to become so enraged, unsure if she should go to him or step back and give him space. She decided it best to just give him space. He paced furiously across her living room floor as he dug his fingers through his hair, and Cat could see a look in his eyes that she had never seen before. She knew something was horribly wrong, but was too apprehensive to approach him to find out what it was. She thought it best to just sit back down and wait until he calmed down enough to speak.

After several moments, he finally turned to look down at her, sitting on the couch, and angrily shouted, "That fucking bitch!"

Cat continued to sit, staring up at Marcus. She knew who he must be talking about, but she couldn't figure out just what Sophia must have done to outrage him to this point. However, now that he opened up to her, she felt more comfortable to inquire further.

"Marcus, baby, what is? What in the hell did she do?"

"She's having an affair. I've been having her followed, and just found out today. That little whore is cheating," Marcus spat.

The news was shocking to Cat. She never figured Sophia would have an affair. She knew she wasn't happy and wanted out of the marriage, but to have an affair, that was a surprise to her. What was also somewhat surprising to her was Marcus's reaction. She couldn't comprehend why he was so angry to find this out. In her eyes, this was good news. It hit her, then, that he was never intending to leave Sophia, because, if he was, this would be the perfect out for him.

"Marcus, it's okay. Why do you care if she's having an affair? We've been sleeping together for years now. Don't you get it? Don't you see what this means for us? Marcus, she wants out of this marriage, and so do you, so why can't we just tell her now and move past this? Why do you care so much?" Cat asked him, almost fearing his answer.

Marcus could feel his temper rising as he stared down at Cat. He was furious that she didn't understand why this made him so angry. He did his best to stay calm as he replied to her coldly, "Cat, what the hell have I been telling you for the last couple years? She's my bloody wife, and we have been together for nearly eleven fucking years. If she leaves me, she will walk away with a huge chunk of my fortune, and I will not have that, especially now, knowing that she's out there spreading her legs for some other fucking man."

Cat could feel her own frustration begin to surface. She was so tired of hearing the same excuse, and she unexpectedly felt the impulse to put her foot down and tell Marcus how she felt.

"Jesus Christ, Marcus!" she shouted at him as she stood up from the couch.

Her sudden outburst caught Marcus completely off-guard, and his attention was immediately focused on what Cat was going to say.

"I am so fucking sick of this. I am sick of hearing about Sophia, and how she is still your wife. Marcus, what in the hell do you want? Because I don't give a shit anymore about your excuses. I am sick of being your fucking mistress, and I am sick of having to listen to her Goddamn sob stories about trying to save her marriage. This isn't fair to me, Marcus, and I understand that you don't want to lose so much of what you worked for, but tell me what the hell do we have to do to be together? What is it going to take for you to walk away from this and just fucking be with me, huh? Does she need to be dead before you'll actually walk away, is that it?" Cat could feel her heart beating heavily in her chest as the frustration and anger came out with a vengeance.

Marcus heard every word she said and stood in silence as he let it all sink in. She was right, this wasn't fair to her. And he did want to be with her, but after discovering what he had today, he wouldn't allow that cheating whore to get a penny from him. Maybe that was it. Maybe the only way he could truly walk away from this, with everything intact, was if she was no longer here.

Cat stood staring at Marcus, waiting for him to respond in some way. She didn't expect him to stand in silence after what she'd just said. She was sure he was going to fire back, like he had in the past, that he didn't need the added pressure from her to do what he needed to do. She began to get slightly nervous that perhaps she went too far and pushed him past his breaking point. She was half-expecting at any moment for him to tell her to go to hell, and to leave her alone with nowhere to turn. Finally, after what felt like an eternity of silence, he sighed heavily and fell into the chair behind him.

"You're right, Cat, I won't ever leave her," he replied bluntly.

Cat's throat tightened at his response. She was certain this was it, he was going to end it, and he was going to go back to her, even though he just found out that she was having an affair. After all this time together, and all the promises, and all the pain of having to watch him live a fake existence with Sophia, and having to sit and listen to Sophia cry about her marriage, after all of it, he was going to sit here and tell her it was all over, and that thought enraged her to the core.

"You're a bastard, do you know that? After everything, you're going to sit here and tell me that you aren't going to leave her, even now, after finding out what you just did? Fuck, Marcus, what the hell is wrong..." Her words were cut off as Marcus raised his finger to her, signaling her to stop talking.

Marcus understood, now, that if he wanted to be with Cat then he was going to have to do something about it, something drastic. But this wouldn't be the first time he took drastic measures to make sure he was going to get what he wanted. His mind briefly went back to the night after finding Adam with Sophia. It was an incident that he'd managed to push out of his mind until now, but it reminded him how easy it was to take matters into your own hands when people get in the way of what you want.

"Cat, I didn't mean that the way it sounded, but it's true: I probably won't ever leave her. I couldn't stand myself if I let that cheating whore walk away from this and take my money with her."

Still not understanding what Marcus was trying to say, she responded, "I don't understand, Marcus. Do you want to be with me, or not? Because it sounds like you're telling me that, it isn't going to happen."

"No, Cat, I'm not saying that, but I want you to listen to me, and I want you to hear what I am saying. If you really want us to be together, and you really love me and want me to be happy, then I need you to listen to me." Marcus's gaze penetrated into Cat's.

"I do love you, Marcus, and I would give anything for us to be together without her, without having to lie to her, and without having to sit by and watch her destroy your happiness. Whatever we need to do, Marcus, to be together, we can do it. Just tell me what it is so we can just move on and be happy."

Marcus resisted the idea for a fleeting moment, and then, upon concluding that it was the only way, he prepared himself for what he was about to say next.

"She has to die, Cat. That's the only way we can truly be together. She has to die."

Cat felt her stomach turn, and her chest felt as if a weight had been dropped on her. She was desperate to be with Marcus, and thought she would do nearly anything to make that happen, but as she sat paralyzed in her seat, she questioned whether she could bring herself to do this.

August 16, 2015 – Longing

The relief that Sophia felt as Caleb's arms wrapped tightly around her was overwhelming. She knew in this moment that every choice she made had been the right one.

Standing with her head resting on his shoulder, she knew that she was no longer in harm's way, and that he would always be there to protect her. He let his hands glide gently over her back, coming to rest on her hips, and when she lifted her head up from his shoulder to meet his gaze their eyes locked in an intense stare. Sophia knew that Caleb had been waiting for this moment, when they could finally be together, because she, too, had counted the minutes until she could feel his breath on her skin again.

He reached one hand up and placed it on her neck, rubbing the line of her jaw with his thumb, and as her head fell softly to one side and she smiled up at him, Caleb knew he could no longer wait. He pressed his lips firmly, but gently, onto her lips and Sophia opened her mouth, allowing his tongue to meet hers. As the kiss between them deepened, Caleb heard a low moan escape from Sophia's throat, and with that, he let his other hand trace its way up her stomach to find the top button of her cardigan. As he cautiously unbuttoned each button, making sure not to rip her shirt, she thought about how different he was from Marcus. He was slow and soft and not aggressive in any way, and every time he touched her she could feel the love coming through his fingers.

"It's all over, baby, I'm here for you now," he whispered in her ear as he kissed his way to her collarbone.

Finally releasing the last button, he let the sweater fall open, exposing Sophia's red lace bra. She shrugged her arms free, tossing it to the floor. Caleb reached behind her, finding her lips again as he did so, and unclasped her bra and pulled it off her in one motion. He traced his fingers down her spine, causing her hairs to rise and a shiver to run through her body. Sophia pulled at his suit jacket and tie, and within minutes both lay on the floor near her sweater. The urge to pull at his shirt till the buttons flew off passed over her, but Sophia wanted to savor every single one of these moments with Caleb. This was the beginning of a new life for both of them, and she wanted to drink in every morsel of its pleasure, so she gently began unbuttoning his white dress shirt, taking the same caution he did with hers.

Soon they both stood topless, and he reached up to cup her breast in his hand, fondling her erect nipple as he did so. He could instantly sense her arousal beneath his hand, which made him reach for the front of her jeans. He got down on his knees in front of her, kissing her stomach as he helped her step out of her pants. He remained in front of her and she could feel the warmth of his breath on her stomach as he slid his hands up the back of her legs, cupping her ass in his palms, pulling her closer.

"Caleb, please, I need you," she begged as she pulled him up from the ground.

She reached for his belt and yanked it out from the belt loops that held it in place. As soon as he was fully undressed, he picked Sophia up and carried her to the bed, laying her down gently as he leaned over her with his muscular arms. He kissed her stomach and used his tongue to form a trail from her navel to her panty line, and seductively pulled her panties away from her skin with his teeth. Looking down at him, watching him tease her, was driving Sophia crazy, and she knew she wouldn't be able to wait much longer to have him inside her. Finally removing the last article of her clothing, Caleb kneeled above Sophia, admiring the beauty of this woman he'd fallen so madly in love with, this woman Caleb knew he would protect until his last breath.

Sophia reached for him and he lowered himself on top of her, bending forward to find her lips again. He could hear her breath growing deeper and she arched herself towards him, her body almost pleading for him to take her. He slid easily into her and he could feel her nails on his back as he pushed himself deeper. Their bodies fell into an easy rhythm and their hearts almost seemed to begin to beat as one. The intensity of the moment was almost too much for Sophia to bear, and she couldn't help the tears that began to fall down her cheeks. Noticing this, Caleb reached his thumb to her face, wiping the wetness away.

"I told you I would do anything for you, Sophia. I love you so much."

Sophia began to feel the intensity deepen with every kiss of his mouth and every touch of his hand. She could soon no longer fight off the overwhelming quiver that began to take over her body. As it drew closer and closer, she arched her back off the bed and gripped the blankets tightly, every muscle in her body tightened, and Caleb knew she had released herself to him. As her body arched and she began to tighten around him, he pushed himself deeply into her one last time before collapsing beside her. As he fell beside her, the sheer emotion of it all became too much for Sophia to comprehend, and she couldn't help but let her body become overwhelmed with tears.

"Baby, it's okay. What's wrong?" He pulled her into him as soon as he realized what was happening.

"I am so sorry, Caleb. I am so sorry you had to have anything to do with this. I put your life in danger, I put your career in danger, and I am so sorry. I had no right to drag you into this mess of mine, but, Caleb, I love you so much and don't know where I would be right now if you hadn't walked into my life when you did." Sophia cried heavily as Caleb held her in his arms. Hearing her words, he pulled away from her and brought her chin up to look him in the eye.

"You have nothing to be sorry for. The only thing there is to be sorry for is that we didn't meet sooner. I did everything I did to protect you, and I would do it all over again. Sophia, when you told me that you wanted to be the one to take care of this, there was just no way I was going to allow you to do that. I didn't want to risk losing you because of that man, but when you came to me, and begged to do this your way, I knew it was the only thing that could be done. It was the only way you would be free from his chains. That was my choice, Sophia. I chose to step into your life and help you do this, and I am just so God damn grateful I came into your life when I did, because had it been any longer I may have never gotten the chance to meet you at all.

"God, Sophia, when I started having him tracked, I knew his every move before he even knew he was going to make it. And, you know, maybe I shouldn't have asked you to hold off after finding out about her abortion, but then, when I found out that he knew about you having an affair, I just knew he was going to do something stupid. That piece of shit, Sophia. That piece of shit was going to have you killed, and as badly as I wanted to destroy him myself, I couldn't say no to you when you told me you wanted to end this. I could not deny you that. I would risk my life and my career all over again just to know that you got to end both of their miserable lives."

"I just shudder when I think about what would have happened if something went wrong. I would have never been able to live with myself, Caleb, if anyone found out the truth of what I did. Oh, my God." Panic began to rise in Sophia's voice, and Caleb looked at her reassuringly before answering.

"I did it all to protect you, Sophia. I had the best PI and computer genius in my back pocket, and I knew what evidence to leave and which to get rid of. The fact that we had proof that they were planning to have you killed while you were at the resort, that didn't need to be known. The abuse, the affair, I knew it was important that you claimed to be unaware of any of it. Sophia, I knew what I was doing. I've been doing this a long time, and that's why I agreed to this, because I knew we could get away with it. And I knew it was going to be difficult for us, but I also knew that you were strong enough to get through it and I was right. You are the strongest and bravest woman I know, and I can't wait to get out of this God-forsaken city and start my life with you, do you hear me? It's over now and you never have to apologize to me again for it, because I would do it over and over again if it meant that it was going to save your life."

"I love you, Caleb. I am so sorry." Sophia smiled up at him as she wiped that last of her tears away.

Caleb kissed her on the forehead and Sophia could see a glisten in his eyes as he responded, "Sophia, you will never have to be sorry for anything ever again, I promise."

June 23, 2015 – Playing Games

As she slid the key into the lock of her front door, Sophia could feel the familiar feeling of her stomach twisting into knots and her skin crawling. It was a sensation that she quickly became aware of every time she knew was going to have to face him. How desperately she wished she could just tell him everything she knew about him, and all of the horrible things he had done, but it was not yet time. She had to be patient, otherwise, he would make sure that she would be walking away with nothing. Sophia was well aware that he was already trying to make that happen, and that was why it was so important that she remain patient and let it unfold the way it was supposed to. No matter how difficult it was right now, soon she would be able to walk away from him and Cat for good. Knowing that Caleb had come into her life at just the right time, and knowing he was going to be there for her at the end of this, made her more able to tolerate the sickening feeling of having to pretend that everything was okay and that she was still a loving, devoted wife trying to salvage her marriage.

The door clicked open and she made her way quietly into the entrance. Right away, she noticed how quiet it was, and thought to herself that Marcus must be locked away in his office, like he frequently was lately. Placing her purse down on the table in the middle of the large foyer, she prepared herself to go speak to her husband. She walked down the short hallway and found his office doors sitting open. She glanced inside, but found the room empty, so she made her way into the kitchen. Upon entering, she discovered he wasn't sitting at the island with a drink in his hand, as she'd suspected he would be. A small sense of peace settled over her, thinking that perhaps he wasn't home. But that wouldn't explain his SUV in the driveway, so she walked to the wine rack and pulled herself out an expensive merlot. She placed the corkscrew into the cork, and as she pulled it out of the bottle she was startled by the sound it made. Laughing at her own uneasiness, she reached for a wine glass and poured herself a healthy drink. As she leaned against the counter, she brought the glass to her lips, and just as she was about to take the first taste, she heard Marcus moving around upstairs.

"Here we go," she mumbled to herself as she headed for the staircase, to meet him in their bedroom. She opened the doors and was astonished at what lay before her.

Marcus turned to his wife as she walked into the room and a broad smile found its way across his face. "Hi, sweetheart," he said as she came into the room.

Sophia studied the glow of each and every candle, their tiny flames lighting up the dimness of the room. A bouquet of flowers sat beautifully on her nightstand, and Enya played softly over the speakers of the stereo. She walked into the bathroom and was welcomed by the same beautiful glow of the candles, and her claw-foot tub was full nearly to the rim, a sprinkling of rose petals floating on the water. She struggled to find any words. This had caught her completely off guard. She turned around to find Marcus standing in the doorway.

"What is all this Marcus?" Sophia asked nervously.

Marcus examined his wife's reaction carefully before he answered. "This is for you. This is all for you. You deserve all of this, honey, and I guess it's my way of saying I'm sorry for things, the way I have been acting and, well, just everything in general. I just want you to know that this is all for you. Let's just put everything behind us and move forward, let's just forget everything that has happened in the past. Regardless of what either one of us has done or not done, let's just put it to rest and move on with our own marriage."

Not sure what to make of it all, and feeling a lack of sincerity from Marcus, she responded, "Everything that either one of us has done? Marcus, is there something that you're not telling me?"

"Of course not, Sophia, I just mean everything that we have gone through. I haven't been perfect, but I don't keep things from you, you should know that. I trust that you haven't kept anything from me, as well. I know you would never do anything stupid or careless, would you?" Sophia could hear the accusation behind his voice, yet decided it best to ignore it.

"This is lovely, Marcus, thank you." She walked up to him and gave him a kiss on the cheek, and he surprised her by turning to put his lips to hers, kissing her without warning. Sophia was suddenly aware of the spine-chilling shudder that passed through her body. She pulled away from him slowly, so as not to draw attention to her unease, and she smiled cautiously up at him.

"And, Sophia, I also did something else for you," He spoke kindly.

"You didn't have to do anything else for me, Marcus, it's really not necessary."

"Yes, it is necessary, Sophia. In fact, it is completely necessary. Look, our anniversary is next month, so I booked you a relaxing weekend away at your favourite resort in Malibu. You can just enjoy the weekend and some alone time and get pampered, and then when I get back from New York, I will take my beautifully-refreshed and relaxed wife out for an amazing anniversary dinner. It is the least I can do, and I want you to just go and enjoy some time alone."

Sophia had to admit that it sounded amazing. Some time on her own, to relax and forget everything that had transpired over the last several months, was something she definitely needed. There was wariness behind Marcus's eyes that caused her to feel concerned, but she felt it best to accept his offer graciously.

"Oh, that sounds lovely, Marcus. I could really use some alone time, and dinner would be wonderful. However, maybe I could take Cat with me. You know, make it a girl's weekend?"

She watched his reaction, a small part of her hoping he wouldn't reject her idea. Maybe, just maybe, if that was the case, he really was softening and realizing the huge mistakes he was making, but as she figured, he immediately insisted, "No, no, Sophia, this weekend is for you. I want you to spend some time alone, relaxing and getting rejuvenated and refreshed. If Cat goes with you, it's just going to be a crazy girls' weekend of drinks and dancing, and who knows what else you girls do, but, please, just let me do this for you. Just you."

Satisfied now with her suspicion, that Marcus was just trying to get her out of town to share a weekend with Cat, she quietly acknowledged him as he stood waiting. "Of course, Marcus. It'll be great. And thank you." She looked towards the tub and continued, "Well, I better get in before the water cools down. Are you going to join me?" she asked, praying to herself that he was going to decline.

"I am going to start our dinner. You enjoy your bath. I drew it just for you." Marcus turned to head out of the room, then stopped and turned back to face Sophia. "Sophia, it's all going to be fine. Everyone will be happy again soon."

Sophia watched him leave, and she couldn't help but detect deviousness behind his comment. She felt the sudden urge to close the door as she began to undress. She slid into the warm water, allowing it to embrace her body, and she closed her eyes, hoping to block out all of the tension that surrounded her. She wanted nothing more than Marcus's actions tonight to be sincere, and for him to be remorseful for everything he had done, but as she lay in the warmth of the water and recalled the last words he said to her, she knew in her gut that he would never be remorseful. Whatever reason he had for making this attempt to save their marriage, Sophia knew that their marriage was already over.

August 16, 2015 – A Daughter's Goodbye

The anticipation of the upcoming conversation with her mother was weighing heavily on Sophia's mind, but she knew it had to be done. Sophia was so thankful for her mother, and she knew without her through this whole ordeal, she would have crumbled. Although her mother was unaware of the truths that Sophia held tightly to her heart, Isabelle knew her daughter was crumbling, and she made damn sure she was there to help pick up all the pieces. And as Sophia cruised down the 101 towards San Diego, she tried her best to foresee how her mother was going to take the news that Sophia was about to tell her. This was a drive she had taken so often in her life, and now it suddenly hit her that this may be one of the last times she would take it. She felt the overwhelming need to study and absorb every detail that she could possibly retain. She still hadn't fully accepted the reality of it all, that she was finally free of the lies that had hung so heavily over her head for so many years. But she was at peace now, a feeling she hadn't experienced in a long time.

Sophia pulled off at the exit ramp and crossed into the city limits of the small little surfer community where she was raised. Imperial Beach was just south of San Diego, and Sophia couldn't have asked for a better community to grow up in. The people were friendly and welcoming, and it always felt so calm and relaxing. There was never the hustle-and-bustle that you would find in larger cities. She recalled how she and Adam used to love to walk down to the pier to get a Coke and sit watching all the surfers as they danced gracefully, the waves cascading around them. They loved to sit and watch all the fishermen cast their lines out into the water, and waited with anticipation to see what kind of cool fish would take their bait. Tears formed in her eyes at the memory of Adam. Although she had never found out for sure, she knew in her heart that Marcus had everything to do with his untimely death. It was for the best, though, that her suspicions had never been proven true. She couldn't imagine the amount of pain and tragedy it would have caused for everyone involved if anyone were to ever know the secret behind Adam's death.

Sophia pulled onto the street where she had lived for so many years and found her mother's house. Not wanting her mother to notice how upset she was at Adam's memory, she sat in the driveway and she wiped her eyes, regaining as much composure as she could muster. This was going to be a difficult conversation to have, but Sophia knew there was absolutely no way she could leave without explaining it all to her. Just then, the front door of her mother's modest bungalow swung open and Isabelle came racing across the lawn. Sophia stepped out of her vehicle and gently closed the door behind her, then met her mother with extended arms.

"Oh, honey, I'm so happy to see you." Isabelle pulled her daughter in as tightly as she possibly could, not wanting to release her. "How are you doing, sweetheart?" she asked before she finally pulled away and held Sophia at arm's length.

"I'm okay, Mom. I'm happy to be home, though. After everything that's happened, it truly feels so good to be home." Sophia smiled at her mother and drew her closer to hug her one more time.

"Come, let's go inside. I just made a fresh pitcher of lemonade, nice and sweet, just like you love it." Sophia's mother draped her arm over her daughter's shoulders and Sophia put her arm snugly around Isabelle's waist as they walked together into the house.

The moment Sophia entered her childhood home, she stood and inhaled the comforting scents that were so familiar to her. It was funny how a smell could be so comforting to a person. Every time she came home, she was welcomed by the same aromas that filled the air of her mother's house. For as long as she could remember, the fragrant smells of the salty ocean air mixed with freshly-picked flowers would linger in the house. It was as if a garden were planted within the walls of the home, and it was also paired with the tantalizing aroma of something being freshly baked in the oven, whether it be bread, cookies, or pies. Today, she immediately knew it was her favorite: chocolate chunk cookies. She knew her mother wouldn't fail to have her favorite treat ready for when she arrived.

The two women walked into the living room and as Sophia settled herself comfortably on the couch, Isabelle went into the kitchen to retrieve them each a glass of the sweet lemonade. Sophia sat and took in her surroundings, and as she looked at all of the photographs displayed proudly on her mother's walls, she couldn't help but feel an overwhelming sadness. Seeing the pictures of her father and mother so happy and in love broke her heart, not because of their remarkable love and dedication to each other for nearly thirty years, but at how different her own marriage ended. Knowing that she was robbed of that kind of love and devotion, and knowing that it took her eleven years to discover it. Most of all, knowing that, with the exception of Caleb, she would never be able to talk about it with anyone close to her, especially her mother, made her heart ache.

"Here we go," Isabelle sang as she walked back into the room and placed a tray down on the table. She picked up the pitcher of lemonade and poured them each a glass, then handed Sophia hers. Sophia took a sip and was immediately comforted by the sweetness of the juice.

"Mmm, mom that is delicious. And I could be wrong, but is that double chunk chocolate chip cookies I smell baking in the oven?" Sophia inhaled deeply as her mother laughed at her.

"Of course, how could I not have your favorite cookies baking for you? It's been awhile since you have been home, I just wanted to make sure you felt nothing but welcomed back here. I have missed you so much, and although the circumstances were nothing short of tragic, I am thankful that I, at least, got to spend that much time with you, taking care of you." Isabelle tried to fight back the tears that were making their way to her eyes and took a sip of her lemonade. "I just need to know that my baby girl is okay. Are you okay?"

"Mom, I'm okay. I mean, this has been extraordinarily difficult on me, and, well, on everyone. I never thought this was going to be how my life ended up, and that my marriage was going to lead to this. It's still too much to comprehend, but I'm just glad we finally got the answers we needed, as horrible and earth shattering as those answers were, well, it gave us closure, and now it's time to move forward the best we can." Sophia paused for a moment and gently cocked her head to one side as she studied her mother's expression before continuing. "And that's why I came here today, Mom. It's time for me to move on, the best that I can."

Isabelle began to feel nervous, as she knew this conversation wasn't going to go in the best of directions, but she also knew that she would support her daughter in whatever she needed to do to get through this. Isabelle reached for Sophia's hand, holding it in hers as she replied, "Sophia, I can't imagine what it was like to go through what you went through. I try to picture it, but I just can't empathize, because to even try and imagine it is too much to take. When your father died, it was an unimaginable amount of pain to lose the man I loved so dearly. To have him taken away from me was undeniably heart-wrenching, but I know that he left this world loving me more than I could even have possibly known. He left me with nothing but the most cherished of memories that I will always hold tight to my heart. Sweetheart, that was who your father was, and when I think of the pain that Marcus has caused you, my heart breaks, because you deserve nothing less than being loved like I was loved."

It took all of Sophia's strength not to break down, but when she heard her mother speak of her father, it melted her heart, and it broke her heart knowing that such an amazing woman had to lose such an amazing love. Knowing that soon she wasn't going to have her so close stung, and she started to second-guess herself, that perhaps she was making the wrong decision after all, and as she struggled with herself, her mother shocked her by saying, "Don't you dare let me stand in the way of that kind of love. You go, honey. Do you hear me? Don't let it slip away."

Sophia's astonishment was written all over her face, so clearly that Isabelle knew exactly what she was thinking, and without even having to ask the question, Isabelle answered her. "Oh, Sophia, I saw the way you two looked at each other from the very beginning. I know what love looks like. Not once did I see that from Marcus, and don't get me wrong, I know he loved you, but not the way you deserve to be loved. Honey, Caleb did everything he could to protect you every single step of the way, and maybe it wasn't obvious to others, but I saw it, and I saw it in your eyes every time you spoke his name. It's okay, sweetheart, you don't have to explain anything to me."

Trying to find the appropriate words to respond was nearly impossible. Sophia was so sure that she'd kept her feelings buried, but she knew there was no point in lying to her mother. "Mom, I'm sorry, but you're right. He does love me, and I love him, and I don't know if what I'm doing is okay, or stupid, or I don't know, but I do know that he loves me and protects me in a way I have never experienced, and I so badly wanted to talk to you about it, but I didn't know what you would think or say, and I just, well, I just knew that I needed to be with him, especially after all of this, and we couldn't say anything to anyone, you know that right?" Sophia waited for her mother's response, but Isabelle just pulled her tightly into a loving embrace and held her in silence for several moments. Isabelle wanted nothing but her daughter's happiness, and with every suspicion that crossed her mind as this case unraveled, she knew it just didn't matter as long as her daughter was safe and happy.

"I don't know the details, and I don't need to know the details, but what I do know is your strength and your courage, and you don't ever have to feel obligated to tell me anything, but I want you to know that if I were ever in your shoes, and if I were faced with life-shattering obstacles, that without a doubt I would have done the exact same thing as you."

Sophia suddenly pulled away from her mother, and Isabelle could see the paleness wash over her face. She never wanted to confront or interrogate her daughter about her suspicions, that wasn't her place. She wanted to let Sophia know that she was there for her, no matter what she needed to tell her, and as she reached up and wiped a falling tear from Sophia's cheek, she said, "You are so much a part of me, I know you more than you even know yourself, and I love you more than you could possibly know, so, baby, please, I want you to promise two very important things before you leave. Promise me that you will go. Please don't worry about me, I am fine, and trust me, I will have no problems coming to visit you as often as you will have me. Secondly, honey, please promise me that if the truths you live with everyday become too much to take, know that I will always be here to listen. You have nothing to hide from me, you have nothing to be ashamed of. So, please, promise me that you understand I will always be here."

The amount of love she felt for her mother in this moment was unlike anything she had felt before, and as both women sat together crying on the couch, she knew that she was never going to have to hide anything from her ever again.

June 26, 2015 – Betrayal

Caleb drew back the curtains of the little cabin that was nestled comfortably near Lake Arrowhead. It was private, beautiful, and serene, and he thought it would be perfect for a getaway for him and Sophia. As he peered out the window and saw her pull up, his heart skipped a bit, just like a school boy's when his crush enters the room. Caleb was beyond ecstatic to spend the weekend with Sophia, although he regretted the news that he would be sharing with her tonight. This information that was monumentally important, and would quickly make her realize the severity of the situation she was in. The one thing that Caleb did know for certain was that he would never allow anything to happen to her, and it weighed heavily on his shoulders as he struggled with the news he was about to share with her. The uncertainty remained, though, as to whether he should tell her everything, or just what was necessary at this time. The last thing he ever wanted to do was to scare her, or make her question his loyalty to her. She had definitely been through enough over the last several months, and he knew it was now his job to protect her from any more harm. A soft knock interrupted his thoughts, and he rushed to open the door. As soon as she was in front of him, he picked her up in a tight embrace and closed the door behind them.

"Oh, my God, I missed you so much, baby," Caleb mumbled to her in between passionate kisses.

"Oh, you have no idea how much I missed you, Caleb. I couldn't wait to get up here and feel your arms around me. It feels so good to hold you and kiss you, please tell me I never have to let you go," she groaned quietly into his ear.

They held each other tightly, hungrily kissing as their hands freely explored each other's bodies, and as Caleb felt the intensity of his desire increasing, he suddenly pulled away, knowing that, as badly as he wanted her, it was important that he talk to her first and get it out of the way.

"I'm so sorry, baby, you're driving me crazy, and I'm not going to be able to resist you much longer," Caleb apologized sincerely as he looked down at Sophia's confused expression.

"Well, then, don't resist me. Trust me, you have my permission to do with me as you will," she teased him, making it much more difficult to keep his hands off of her, but Sophia quickly realized that something serious was on his mind.

"What is it? Is everything okay?" she asked him as she took his hand and led him to the bed so they could sit down.

"Listen, baby, I don't want you to panic or get scared or anything, okay, because you're safe. We have it taken care of, and nobody is going to hurt you, but I want you to know something, okay?"

Sophia could feel her palms begin to sweat and an alarming panic began to find its way over her. She tried her best to remain calm, but she was sure that whatever he had to share with her was probably not something she wanted to hear. She tried to summon her strength and prepared herself to find out what was wrong.

"You have what taken care of? Caleb, what in the hell is going on? You're scaring me."

Caleb instinctively reached out and gently brushed his knuckles across her cheek, and then grabbed her hand before he continued. "Marcus knows about us, Sophia. He knows that you're having an affair. He has been following you, probably for months. Who knows, maybe even longer, but he knows. That is why I was adamant about you coming up this weekend, because with him gone to New York again, I had to let you know this."

"That bastard!" she exclaimed. "That lying son of a bitch. I knew it. It didn't feel right to me, any of it." She paused, then looked up at Caleb as she continued. "The candles, the bath, the roses, I knew something was wrong. He was screwing with me, wasn't he?" Sophia asked Caleb, hoping he could give her the right answer. Caleb was unaware to this point of the little date night Marcus had set up for her, as Sophia hadn't had the chance to share with him yet, but Caleb knew well why he did it.

"Shit, Sophia, I am sorry that he is doing this to you, but, yes, it's all a ploy. But that's not all I have to tell you."

Sophia wasn't sure she could take any more. What else was there to share? Her husband was trying to ruin her life. He was toying with her, like a cat chasing a string. She couldn't possibly think of anything else that he was up to.

"What else is there, Caleb? What else did you find out about that lying sack of shit? Oh wait, does he have more bastard children? Has he threatened other women into leaving town? Or, wait, has he killed any more of my friends?" Sophia exclaimed angrily and as she glanced up at Caleb, she realized he looked shocked.

"What do you mean, kill your friends?" he asked.

Sophia realized she hadn't shared that with him yet. Really, what was there to share? It was all speculation for her. She was sure that the truth would never come out about Adam, but she knew her instincts were right, so she felt comfortable in sharing it with him now.

"I believe that Marcus had something to do with the death of a very dear friend of mine. I don't know for sure, but I just know that my gut is right on it. I just have a very hard time comprehending how, days after Marcus sees me talking to him on the street, he winds up dead while jogging in Runyon Park. I could be crazy, but after learning about Marcus's secrets, I really believe that he would have been capable of it."

Caleb's stomach turned inside out as he realized the actual severity of the situation. He felt guilt unlike he had ever felt before, as he knew he was about to validate her every inclination. It was also at this moment that he knew she wouldn't be able to handle the full truth of the entire situation. He knew it was up to him to carry this through, and in order to do that, he needed to remain calm for her.

"You're right, he is capable of it. Babe, do you know anything about a weekend in Malibu? Did Marcus say anything to you about that?" Caleb was sure he already knew the answer, but waited for her response.

"Yes, the other day, with all the flowers and candles and shit. He was determined to make our marriage work and swore he was sorry and all the same shit I have heard time and time again. He told me he booked a reservation for me for a weekend of 'me time' before our anniversary, while he's in New York. I told you, I didn't feel good about it. My gut was telling me that something just didn't feel right. Why? I mean, obviously, I'm not going to accept it. I'm not going to go," Sophia said adamantly.

Caleb's nerves began to vibrate as he prepared to tell her. He was apprehensive about what her reaction would be, but he knew she needed the truth. At least, he could give her that.

"Sophia, listen to me very carefully, please. There is a reason he booked that and asked you to go."

"Yeah, I know. So he could have the weekend with Cat, to plot and scheme on how they are going to try and fuck me over. That is why he was so insistent I go alone," Sophia interrupted.

Caleb reached for her hand again, hoping it would ease the blow. "Soph, he is planning to have you killed. We have tracked him diligently, and I'm sorry to tell you this, but Marcus and Cat have hired someone to have you killed while you are in Malibu that weekend."

Caleb paused for a second to let her react. Sophia sat, stone-cold silent, as the words floated around in her head. She desperately tried to make sense of what she was just told, but it wouldn't happen.

"Sophia, we have him. I can nail him to the wall. Both of them. We have proof they are conspiring to commit murder. You don't have to worry about anything, okay? I promise, when I get that son of a bitch into my custody, I will make him pay for this. He will never touch you again, and he will never hurt you again. I will do anything and everything in my power to make sure of that. I will do whatever it takes to protect you. Do you understand me, Sophia? I will do anything." Caleb's eyes were locked on hers, and he suddenly became aware of an unfamiliar darkness in her eyes as she sat staring at him.

Sophia was wracked with rage at the thought of this ultimate betrayal. She couldn't believe that she was being faced with this life-altering decision. She wondered how either one of them could possibly do this to her, and struggled with what she was to do with the information. Should she just step aside and allow Caleb to take them away? Would that make her feel any better, and help her sleep peacefully at night, knowing they would both be rotting in prison? The two closest people in her life had betrayed her in the most unimaginable ways possible, and she knew there was truly only one way she wanted to make this right, but was she capable of such a thing? Would she be able to live with herself?

Sophia's mind was running in every direction, and she knew she was probably thinking completely irrationally. She should take some time to think it through, but something so over-powering kept insisting that she had to do whatever it took to protect herself, and seek the revenge she desperately wanted.

"Sophia." Caleb interrupted her, as he was becoming more worried. Sophia snapped out of her silent battle as she jerked her head up to look at him. "Sophia, talk to me, Baby. What do you want me to do? I'll do whatever you need me to do." Sophia sat with her eyes fixed on the floor and pressed her lips tightly together. Caleb could see the anguish she was in, and just wanted to help her feel better in any way he could, but he was completely astonished at what she said next.

"Caleb, I need you to help," she replied with coldness to her voice. "I need you to help me kill that sick son of a bitch."

And as her words slowly sank in, Caleb Stone knew in that moment that he was going to do whatever it took to help Sophia Donovan get away with a perfect murder.

September 15, 2015 – A Truth Untold

The warmth of the sun beat down heavily, reflecting its rays off of the turquoise water of the Caribbean, and the flour-white sand that graced the shores of the impeccably beautiful beach of Shoal Bay, Anguilla. Everything about this island was amazing. It was the most breathtaking place Caleb had ever seen in his life, and he couldn't wait to share it all with Sophia. The last month had been nothing short of torture for Caleb as he waited for her to make the journey so she could finally join him, and they could finally begin their lives together, something that they had both been waiting for, for so long. He sat sipping a cold beer on his deck, overlooking the ocean, and basked in the heat of the sun as he looked out over the serenity that stood only steps away from the modest, perfect little condo he was renting. The anticipation of her arrival was more than he could handle, and he couldn't wait to hold Sophia in his arms and kiss her. He thought to himself that he never wanted to stop kissing her.

Even with the immense excitement of knowing it was soon time to be with her again, he couldn't seem to escape the insistent torment of the guilt he felt, now being completely honest about himself and the part he truly played in Marcus and Cat's murder. He only wanted to protect her from Marcus and, as utterly shocked as he was when Sophia told him what she wanted to do, and how she wanted to take care of it herself, Caleb knew he owed that to her. As risky as it was, he knew he needed to help her murder both of them. No part of him ever wanted to deceive Sophia, but the decisions he made were in order to protect her. But, still, the nagging feeling he felt every day was overwhelming, and he wasn't sure he could begin a future with her, living with that guilt.

He brought his wrist up and checked the time on his watch. Realizing it was nearly four o'clock, his heart skipped a beat. She would soon be here. Caleb had a car waiting at the small airport to bring her here. He wanted to make sure everything was perfect for her arrival. He did his best to ignore the guilt and focus on what their lives were going to be like. As he took another sip of beer, his thoughts were suddenly interrupted.

"Caleb."

He instantly recognized her beautiful voice, and turned to see Sophia standing in the doorway, her dark hair blowing softly in the ocean breeze. He stood up quickly, knocking his chair down behind him and leapt towards her, pulling her into him as he lifted her right off her feet.

"Sophia, oh, my God, baby, I've missed you so much. I can't believe you're finally here," he softly murmured in her ear as he spun her around.

The intensity of the relief and happiness that Sophia felt as Caleb held her was astounding, and she began to sob heavily into his shoulder. When she knew she could finally speak in between sobs, she replied, "Caleb, I love you so much. That was the longest, most excruciating month of my entire life. I don't know if I could have made it another day. Please, make sure we never have to be apart again, please, Caleb." Sophia continued to cry as Caleb cradled her in his arms.

He slowly pulled away from her and wiped her tears softly off her cheeks, and replied, "Never again will we be apart, Sophia. We have been through so much together, and now that it's all over, I promise you I will never let you go."

He leaned in and kissed her softly on the mouth, and she reciprocated easily. They could both instantly feel the surge of passion as it coursed through their bodies. The feel of her soft skin beneath his hands, and seeing the perfect curve of her breasts beneath her clingy sundress, made Caleb's hunger for her intensify feverishly, and as he felt her hands slide underneath his t-shirt, his knees began to feel weak. He pulled the flimsy straps of her dress off her shoulders and leaned down to trace the curve of her neck and collarbone with his lips. Sophia quickly pulled his shirt up over his head, revealing his muscular and tanned chest. She placed her mouth around his nipple and ran her tongue gently down his stomach. A part of Caleb thought that perhaps they should go inside, but he knew they were fairly secluded, and at this moment he truly didn't care if anyone were to see them.

Sophia knelt down in front of Caleb and he could feel her hands gliding over the front of his shorts as she began to undo his button and zipper, slowly pulling them down around Caleb's feet.

He could feel her warm breath as her kisses made their way up his inner thighs and then finally he felt her mouth wrap seductively around him. He could feel every movement of her tongue as it explored every inch of him, and as she slowly slid her mouth back and forth, his breath began to grow deeper. Bracing himself by holding on to the side of the door, he knew he was not going to be able to have her continue on much longer. Caleb gently pulled her up from the ground and found her lips again, and as their kiss deepened, Sophia exclaimed with a raspy voice, "Oh, Caleb, make love to me. Right here, right now."

Caleb pulled the closest chair underneath him and seated himself as Sophia placed her legs on either side of him and carefully guided herself over him. When she could feel him reaching to meet her, she allowed him to enter her easily, and as she straddled him on the chair, she could feel him hardening between her legs. Caleb's hands reached up and released her breasts from the top of her sundress and he pulled himself towards her so he could taste the saltiness of the beads of sweat that had formed on her skin. He ran his tongue gently around her nipples, feeling them swell and harden as he explored them hungrily.

He then stood up, making sure not to break the bond that was holding them together, and walked into the house, directly to the bedroom. He laid her down on the bed and, as he leaned himself gently over her, he carefully pushed her knees up towards her head. Sophia gasped at the sensation of being able to feel him enter her so deeply. As Caleb watched himself sliding into her, he began to feel the familiar heat creeping towards his groin, so he began to push himself deeper and deeper into her. Sophia could no longer hold back the urge to scream, and she could feel Caleb begin to throb as she met him in the most intense climax she had ever felt. As their bodies united as one, she could feel the warmth release into her, and with that Caleb could feel his legs wanting to betray him. He fell on top of Sophia and kissed her lovingly on the mouth.

"I will never want to stop doing that," he teased.

Sophia's breath was rapid, and she giggled coyly at Caleb. "You better not, because I'm going to want you to do that every single day for the rest of our lives," Sophia teased back.

They sat on the deck, cuddled into the loveseat, watching the sun as it began to make its descent into the horizon, and Sophia was in awe of the beauty that stood before her. She couldn't believe that this was where her life had taken her. She thought back to the beginning of the year, and how different her life was, and how devastated she was to learn the secrets that Marcus had been holding onto so tightly. Never would she have thought this is where it would lead her, but she couldn't be more thankful that it did. She still, to this day, didn't understand how it all went so smoothly and effortlessly, and wondered if that was just fate leading them both through to fulfill the destiny they were meant to share. Or was Caleb that good at his job, and eliminating any evidence that may have hindered their dangerous plan? She knew she was safe with him through the whole journey, but she was interested to find out now that it was over just exactly how he was able to stay so seamlessly ahead of Marcus every step of the way.

She took a sip of her wine and turned to look at Caleb. She was still captivated by his handsomeness, and felt that perhaps soon she would wake up to realize it was all just a dream. Caleb could feel her looking at him and he turned away from the sunset and smiled at her. "What are you looking at?" he asked her happily.

"You, baby. I'm looking at you. You are so amazing. Everything about you is so breathtaking, and I cannot believe we are here right now, in this moment, together." Sophia shook her head in disbelief. "God, how did this happen? How did we manage to pull this off?"

"Easy, Sophia: we did what we needed to do to protect you, and so we could be together. I am just so thankful I was there for you. As much as I didn't want you to risk anything, I'm thankful that I was there to help you," Caleb answered honestly.

Sophia wondered if she should just ask him some of the things that were weighing on her mind. She didn't want to pry into his business, and she was sure it wasn't a big deal, but now that this whole nightmare was over, she was curious about it all, curious about how he managed to execute this so perfectly. Caleb instantly noticed Sophia was distracted.

"What is it, babe? What is going on in that pretty little head of yours?"

Sophia decided to just go ahead and bring it up. She was sure it wasn't going to be a big deal for him to share it all with her now. She was sure that there had been many things he didn't want her knowing to keep her safe.

"Oh, nothing, I'm fine. I've just been thinking so much about everything, and how perfectly it all went, and, Caleb, I'm so thankful you were with me every step of the way. I'm just curious, though, about something, and I'm sure there is a simple explanation, but, who was it? Who was the person that Marcus hired to kill me?"

Her question caught him off guard. Even though he had been tormented with guilt about it all, he truly didn't think that she would ever bring this up. But as her words hung heavy in the air, he desperately tried to figure out what he should say. He was terrified of telling her the whole truth, he feared she just wouldn't understand, and that he would lose her. But he also knew that he loved her more than anything in this world, and if he wanted a solid future with her, maybe it was just best he was honest. Maybe it was time to tell her the truth. He turned his gaze back to the sunset and, as it slowly dipped below the horizon, he was just praying he was about to do the right thing.

"Caleb? Are you okay? Listen, baby, I didn't mean to upset you. You don't have to tell me anything. I know, I was probably kept out of the loop on a lot of things to protect me. I just I couldn't seem to figure out who he could have hired, and I didn't know how you managed to stop it from happening, that's all. But, baby, if you don't want to tell me anything, I'm sure it's for a good reason. I'm sorry." Sophia felt horrible that she put him on the spot and she reached for his hand, and Caleb grabbed her hand and prepared himself for what he was about to say next.

"Sophia, there's something I have to tell you, and, baby, please, know it's not going to be easy to hear. Just know that I would never hurt you, nor will I ever hurt you, and I'm telling you this because you deserve to know the truth. You deserve to know everything that happened. I will tell you absolutely everything you want to know, but I'm begging you to hear me out, and let me tell you everything. Please, understand why I wanted to protect you from this. There is something about me that you don't know, and I'm telling you because I know you love me, and I love you, but in order for you to truly love all of me you need to know all of me, all the good parts, and all the not so good parts."

Sophia could feel his palm sweating in her hand, and she felt a sudden panic rise in her throat. She trusted Caleb more than anything, but she knew he was hiding something serious to keep her safe. As she studied his expression carefully, it became abundantly clear that it was something she wasn't sure she wanted to hear.

"Caleb, you're scaring me. You know that you can always tell me anything. Whatever it is, please, I want to know. It's all over now, so you can tell me. Baby, does this have anything to do with who they hired to kill me? Oh, God, do you think I'm still in danger? Do you know who it was?" Sophia begged, as the panic began to deepen. "Caleb, who was it?" She now raised her voice. "Please, tell me. I want to know."

His throat felt restricted, and his mouth had lost all moisture. He hated to see her so scared and panicked, and he knew she was no longer in danger, but the fear of losing her nearly paralyzed him. Still, he knew she needed to know everything about him, everything that would eventually lead him directly into her life. There was no turning back now, and he turned to face the woman he so desperately loved, and released the truth that had been burdening him since the moment she was brought into his life.

"It was me, Sophia. I was the one they hired to kill you."

Debbra Lynn

Beyond The Red Carpet

Part one of the series
"Hollywood Lies"

Be sure to watch for the next riveting novel of the series.

Coming in June of 2016

"Heart of Stone"

Debbra Lynn will continue to share the gripping tale, of all the secrets that lie, Beyond the Red Carpet.

Beyond The Red Carpet

Thank you for reading my book, I hope you enjoyed it. Please take the time to leave me a review on Amazon.com.

You can follow me:

Facebook.com/debbralynnredcarpet

@debbralynn21 on Twitter

You can go to my website www.debbralynn.com and go to the contact me link. Send me an email with your email address and I will add you to my email list so you can keep up to date on the release of my future novels.

57418598R10124

Made in the USA
Charleston, SC
12 June 2016